MW01227384

AN ALIEN'S GUIDE TO WORLD DOMINATION

To Barbara:

"My mother gets credit for this book, all my worldly success, the fact that I am a nice person, and, well, anything else she wants credit for, really."

Is that about right?

With love, & gratitude,

[signature]

What Readers Are Saying About
AN ALIEN'S GUIDE TO WORLD DOMINATION

I inhaled this book with glee and you will too.—*Jo M, reader review*

This is a fast-paced, humorous, and exciting look at our world from a very different point of view. I can recommend it to any lovers of science fiction.—*Long And Short Reviews*

If you are looking for something different, something fun, something with heart, this is the book to read. Vivid characters, aliens that resemble snot, and a world in peril, what more could you ask for?—*Square Peg reader review*

This book is really entertaining, a story well-told, with elements of both suspense and humor. A great read for the summer.—*Lois H, reader review*

...a fun read with plenty of action and humor.—*Mary M, reader review*

Louie remembered seeing this sort of thing happen in movies and reading it in books. None of it prepared her for what took place before her eyes. Jones' head split in two, starting behind one ear and moving across the top of his scalp. The back of his head and face peeled away as if they were being unzipped, making a horrible, ripping-Velcro sound. Then she saw an actual zipper running down Jones' head, neck, and chest—she couldn't look any lower. His skin and clothing peeled next and what emerged from them was almost too hideous to bear, but Louie couldn't tear her gaze away.

Something like a head appeared. Formed from a misshapen oval the color of snot, yellow-green snot ejected from a deeply infected sinus, with things that seemed to be eyes, but twelve of them—little beads of purple light set into the infected snot mass. Below the head, his hulking body seemed far wider and lumpier than Jones appeared, like lime Jell-O gone terribly, terribly wrong. Louie heard a high-pitched noise over the growl and gradually realized she was screaming.

"Hush." Even though the head was no longer Jones, somehow the voice was still his. "Stop screaming for Spryxl's sake."

Louie stopped screaming. Hearing Jones's voice come out of that green lump brought her back to herself at least for a moment. *I'm dreaming again. I'm still in bed with Buddy and I hit snooze one too many times and I'm dreaming.* She grabbed a hunk of the skin on her arm between her thumb and forefinger and gave it a sharp twist.

"Ow!"

"What in Spryxl's Name are you doing?" asked the Jones lump.

"Pinching myself." Louie winced.

"Why?"

"That's what you do to wake yourself up from a dream. I've seen it in movies."

"Well, stop it. It's very disconcerting to watch a human inflict pain on itself. We prefer to do that ourselves."

One more sharp twist that hurt like hell. *Crap. Not only is my boss some kind of alien, but I'm going to have a wicked bruise on my arm from pinching myself so hard.*

BURST Presents

An Alien's Guide To World Domination

By

Elizabeth Fountain

This is a work of fiction. The characters, incidents and dialogues in this book are of the author's imagination and are not to be construed as real. Any resemblance to actual events or persons, living or dead, is completely coincidental.

No part of this book may be reproduced or transmitted in any form or by any means, electronic or mechanical, including photocopying, recording, or by any information storage and retrieval system, without permission in writing from the publisher.

BURST
www.burstbooks.ca
A Division of Champagne Books
Copyright 2013 by Elizabeth Fountain
ISBN 978-1-77155-135-9
April 2013
Cover Art by Petra K.
Produced in Canada

Champagne Book Group
#2 19-3 Avenue SE
High River, AB T1V 1G3
Canada

Dedication

To all my chosen family, and my very own long-lost brother, with deepest gratitude.

Prologue

"Have you brought me what I seek?" The continuous sonic boom of the alien lord's voice came from somewhere near the middle of his giant black bulk, poised on his throne in a shape that recalled a comma. Sergio, in his wiry short human form, felt his knees tremble but tried to show confidence.

"Yes, my lord. You will have the largest cyborg army in the galaxy."

In his luxurious chamber on the spaceship Kryha, the lord of the planet Kleptofargh roared with pleasure. Sergio began to shake despite himself.

"And where is this army?"

"Well, it doesn't actually exist yet, my lord."

The lord roared again, this time with displeasure. Sergio felt his trousers turn warm and wet. *It's a good thing the lord has no eyes, so he can't see I've peed myself.*

"What?" roared the lord. "You told me you brought me what I seek. And I can smell the piss in your pants, peon."

Damn. I can't win with this lord. "You will have your army, my lord. But I need a little more time."

"What happened to the plan?"

"My lord, we had to reconsider it, adjust it a bit, in order to adapt it to the, um, contextual realities 'on the ground,' so to speak..."

"Yes, yes, yes." The lord always hated Sergio's way of taking ten words to say what could be expressed in one. "And?"

"My lord, the Grythylwecs are bit less...stupid, shall we say, than we initially thought. And a bit more brutal." Sergio shuddered, remembering watching his boss tormented by the Grythylwecs. Still, his boss's death resulted in his own promotion to this post, which came with a big title and a modest but meaningful raise in salary. He supposed he owed the Grythylwecs something.

"And, my lord, the Earth humans are a bit more...fragile than we anticipated. The first one broke completely during the 'migration.' We were attracting the interest of the authorities in America. So we shifted the migration operation to another part of the planet, where there appears to be less concern, shall we say, about individual humans."

The planet Sergio referred to was so small compared to the lord's, this meant virtually nothing to him. "And the Grythylwecs?"

"My lord, the Grythylwecs still do not know that the army will ultimately be yours. They tasked me with constructing the plan for using the army after General Rogers perished so unfortunately in their care, and I took his place."

The lord laughed, a sickening, gagging, somehow crunchy sound that almost made Sergio wet himself again. "I thought they were not so stupid! And yet they think you will produce a plan?"

Sergio stiffened his shoulders and made as if to hike up his damp trousers. Then he remembered who he was talking to. "Yes, my lord." Sergio swallowed what little was left of his pride in one big gulp. "They do believe it, for now."

"Of course you will give them no such plan, even if you could come up with one," chuckled the lord.

"No, my lord, but they are getting a bit anxious…"

"Well, that's why you have a fancy title and a modest, but meaningful, raise in salary. I pay you to handle their anxiety, and deliver the army to me as promised."

Sergio nodded and squirmed. He tried to recall a time in his life when he actually delivered what he promised, and his mind went disconcertingly blank. Still, he'd always pulled his ass out of the fire at the last minute or—more accurately—someone or something else always had. Like the Grythylwec believing that it was Sergio's boss, General Rogers, who messed up the first migration, when in fact Sergio simply forgot to plug the 0356 cable into the XLGF port. *Poof!* There went the first foot soldier in the galaxy's largest cyborg army, not to mention about seven hundred billion Grthylwec dollars invested in the now-fried equipment. Once he'd realized what he'd done, Sergio slipped out the back door, and went straight to the Grythylwec CEO, practicing his story along the way. By the time he got there, he was able, ever so reluctantly, to divulge the error his boss, the "careless General Rogers," made. The CEO—going by the name of Jones—had been both enraged and relieved to have a scapegoat, and immediately ordered Sergio's boss into the chambers of torment. *Well, who knows? My luck hasn't deserted me yet.*

"Yes, my lord. I promise you will have your army."

"What, are you still here, peon?" roared the lord. "I thought you'd left seconds ago." Sergio knew his slow mind and pissy trousers tried the lord's patience. Still, he hoped the lord would assume he really could deliver the cyborg army, and let him stay alive for a little while longer. The lord boomed again: "I am done with you. Begone."

Sergio left the lord's chambers and went straight to his ship, without stopping to change his now clammy pants. As far as he was concerned, he couldn't get off of Kleptofargh fast enough. Earth might be small, and humans pitifully easy to manipulate, but at least it was the kind of place that allowed someone like him to strut about and feel important. He'd even picked his name there, after seeing the greatest Western movie of all time, *The Good, the Bad, and the Ugly.* He'd combined the name of the genius director with the outrageously tough and handsome star. *Sergio Leone Eastwood.* Yes, Sergio was happy—as much as anyone exiled from DKLD-64 could be happy— to be heading back to such a place as Earth.

One

On the boy's planet, orphaned, disabled, or otherwise different or unwanted children entered a lottery to be sent away. The powers-that-be knew they were destroying their home world, and were well past the time when they could reverse the destruction. They needed to find another planet—or two or three—to colonize. But they didn't know whether they would survive in these other places. So they instituted a kind of draft, in which unwanted children were put in a lottery. Those whose numbers were drawn were sent randomly to other points in the galaxy. Outfitted with a tracking device that allowed researchers to monitor the state of their health, the exiled children provided data to help determine which other planets would be the best candidates for colonization. Useless old people accompanied them, thereby solving problems related to maintaining orphanages and nursing homes at the same time.

When the boy turned twelve, his ID number was entered into the lottery, and it was drawn right away. The boy's parents both died in an accident, and he and his twin sister were put into the care of the authorities. She hadn't spoken since their arrival at the orphanage, and while the adults thought it was because she couldn't—they thought she was retarded—the boy always thought it was because she just didn't want to.

The day the boy's number was drawn he faced his worst fear. Separated from his sister, he knew she would have no one to look out for her. He wanted to take her with him, so even if they didn't survive on this other, random planet, they would be together. He knew the authorities would not approve such a radical departure from standard operating procedure. Still, there were a couple of weeks between the drawing and the actual departure, and he schemed about a way to take her with him.

The boy learned as much as he could about how the children were sent away. Each was first fitted with the tracking device, and then monitored for ten days to make sure it worked correctly. Scientists figured out how to adjust for any disabilities of the children, so the readings would accurately tell them if people of their species could survive in the places they were being sent. The old people sent with them did not receive implants—the authorities did not really care if they survived, as their job was only to serve the children and help them through their first few days on the other planets. After the ten days of monitoring, the child would be randomly assigned to coordinates somewhere in the galaxy. It was rare these days but, on occasion, those coordinates would wind up depositing the child and elderly escort into the void of space. After three days to prepare a space pod for transport, the child and elder were loaded aboard and sent to the pre-determined coordinates.

The children would also receive a little electronic device about the size of a paperback book, designed to download information about their new world, its inhabitants, their cultures, and history, so it could be read by the child. This, the scientists hoped, would allow the children, if they survived physically, to also find a way to fit in and live. But it depended on the host planet having some kind of technology system that surrounded it with information bits in its atmosphere. Very primitive civilizations would have no such systems, and the children who landed there were completely at a loss as to what to do. Sometimes the old people were able to help in these cases, serving as kind of surrogate parents while the children grew. Other times, hostile inhabitants killed both child and elder as soon as they came into contact. Often, the elders felt little or no responsibility for their small charges, blaming them for their own exile, and abandoned them to meet their separate fates.

The little book-like devices held many pages of electronically sensitive plastic between two hard covers. The plastic pages would find the information in the atmosphere, download it, and display it in a language the child would recognize. Over time, that language would change to one native to the planet where the child landed. In order to disguise their true purpose, these devices would transform themselves into ordinary objects on their new home planets, like little books with innocuous titles. The boy's device was small, brown, and its title, when it eventually resolved itself into English, became *The House at Pooh Corner*.

The space pods provided everything the children and elders needed for a voyage of up to one thousand light years. They were also designed to completely self-destruct five minutes after impact, so there would be nothing for any inhabitants of the planet to find. The children and elders emerged from the pods, ran as far as they could get in five minutes, and turned to watch the spectacular yet silent *poof!* as the pod disappeared.

The boy got his implant and knew he needed to figure out something about his sister quickly. He was assigned a companion, a man about seventy years old. It was the custom of the authorities to encourage the children to view their elderly escorts as kindly relatives, so they introduced him to the boy as Uncle. Uncle seemed nice enough, and soon he and the boy developed a kind of friendship. He accompanied the boy to his implant monitoring sessions, and began to tell him stories of the old days on the planet, before the current political regime, and before the planet's resources were being irreversibly depleted. Neither wanted to become too close, knowing that in mere days they would be sent into an uncertain future, and loss was likely. But they were easy together, and one day when they were taking a walk around the compound, Uncle mentioned his wife.

"What is a wife, Uncle?"

"A woman who I love more than anything," Uncle responded.

"Where is she?"

"She is near, but when I was assigned to you, we were forced to separate. I don't think I'll ever see her again." Uncle's voice carried the weight of his sadness. The boy thought for a moment. He decided to take a risk.

"I have a wife, too."

Uncle stared at him. "That's absurd. What are you talking about?"

"There is a woman—well, a girl, really—who I love more than anything." The boy blushed as he spoke.

Uncle laughed. "Oh, a sweetheart, eh?" The boy nodded. He didn't know what the word sweetheart meant, but it sounded nice, like his sister.

"I want to take her with me. I don't want to be separated from her, just like you don't want to be separated from your wife."

Uncle stopped walking. "Boy, you know that is impossible. The authorities will never allow it."

"Yes, Uncle, I know that. But I think there might be a way to do it anyway. Maybe we could both bring our wives with us."

"Even if we could, we might be bringing them to their deaths, you know."

The boy was too young to really understand what death meant. He only knew that he didn't want to be alone, without his sister. "I know. But at least we would be together."

"How could we do this, boy?"

"The pod. I've watched them get it ready. There is a storage area they load up with food and water. If we could sneak in and unload the supplies, there is room for someone to hide there. How big is your wife? Mine is very small. If yours is small, too, I think they could both fit." The boy made this last statement with such earnestness that Uncle felt a surge of feeling for his young companion.

"How would we get in to unload the supplies?"

"At night, there is only one guard on the pods. I've seen him—he falls asleep about an hour after the other guard leaves. Our pod is the farthest from where he sleeps."

"And wouldn't they notice a pile of food and water the next morning, boy?"

"Not if we put it in the garbage hole. Every morning they push another load of garbage in—the food and water would be buried before anyone saw it there."

"How would we sneak our—wives—in?" Uncle started to appreciate how much thought the boy had given this plan, but he was only twelve years old, after all. Surely he'd forgotten something.

"After we dump the food and water, they would have to hide in the storage cabinet. We'd have to do it the very night before we leave, so they would only be in there for a few hours before launch."

Uncle walked again, faster than usual, so the boy trotted to keep up with him.

"You've really thought this out, boy, I'm impressed. But you've forgotten one small detail."

The boy wracked his brain. "I don't think so. As long as we time everything right—"

"And what would we do on the journey without food and water, boy? How would we survive until we land wherever we're going? We don't know how long it is going to take to get there. We might die of thirst or starvation before we even land."

It was the boy's turn to stop. How could he not have thought of this? All his thinking about how to get his sister on the pod with him, and he hadn't thought about anything past the launch. It was impossible. They would not be able to stay together after all. He really was a stupid child. He could not hope to win against the system. Why even try?

Uncle walked back to where the boy stopped. He spoke gently. "Boy, you did an amazing thing. You thought and thought, and you came up with a plan based on the love in your heart for your sweetheart. You cannot blame yourself for not thinking of everything. You are just a child, after all. It is absurd to expect a child to think of everything. But, you tried anyway. And I know one thing you don't. I know that sometimes, the absurd and impossible can actually happen. While it is very likely that we will not survive the journey, it is certain our hearts will not continue to beat without our wives. Isn't it?"

The boy nodded. Uncle went on. "I think it is worth the risk. There are four days left until we leave. You must start eating and eating. Eat as much as you can, so you will have nourishment to last a while. Tell your sweetheart the same. Eat and eat and eat. Meanwhile, I will contact my wife."

"How?" the boy wondered.

"I don't know yet, but I will find a way. And we'll figure out how to bring some water—not a lot, but enough for the four of us to wet our lips now and then. I have some ideas...." Uncle squeezed the boy's shoulder and gave him a gentle shove in the direction of his quarters before walking off the other direction. When the boy got back to his room, he told his sister about the plan. She stared at him with her green eyes. The boy did not need her to speak to know that she understood.

"We are going together," he told her. "It is absurd and impossible, but we are going together."

Over the next three days, the boy ate, and made sure his sister did, too. The scientists monitoring his implant noticed he was gaining weight. They thought it was funny. "Fattening up for the trip, eh, boy?" they chuckled. Meanwhile, he did not see much of Uncle. They caught glimpses of each other now and then, and would give no sign of acknowledgment. The boy wondered if he had been able to contact his wife, able to figure out how to bring water.

At the end of the third day, Uncle came up to the boy and spoke quietly. "Meet me at the gate to the pod section at three in the morning, and bring your wife," he whispered, and walked on without looking back. The boy stared after him. It was happening. He felt terrified and exhilarated. He did not worry about waking up in time, as he knew he would not sleep at all. At two forty-five am he woke his sister. They dressed in silence and left their bunks.

They tiptoed across the compound to the pod area. The system had been in place for so long, with no escape attempts in so many years, that the guards became lax. The last thing they would expect in any case was a child trying to get into a pod instead of away from one. At the gate the boy looked around. He did not see Uncle. His heart began to skip. What if he didn't make it? Just as the boy decided he would go ahead with his sister anyway, he heard a kind of hiss. He looked around and saw Uncle on the other side of the gate. Next to him was a tiny woman, about his same age, with the kindest face the boy could remember seeing.

The boy and his sister slipped through the gate and went to them. Uncle looked grave. "Boy, this is my wife."

"Pleased to meet you. This is my wife, too." His sister stared at them, one at a time.

"Pleased to meet you," whispered Uncle's wife.

"Let's get going," urged Uncle. The four of them were able to unload the supplies and get them to the garbage pit in about an hour. They went back to look at the storage area. Uncle kept a small pile next to the pod. "I think there is enough room for both of them in there, just like you said. And we can put this pile in front of them, so they will be hidden."

"Uncle, what about the water?"

"Honey, show the boy." Uncle's wife opened her jacket. Two plastic bladders filled with water were taped to her sides. "We took them from the garbage pit last night," whispered Uncle. "The scientists use them to store chemicals, and throw them in the pit when they're empty. I've seen them do it many times. We filled them with water. There's enough for the four of us for about, oh, one hundred light years, at average pod speed."

The boy nodded. The first rays of light were showing in the sky. It was time to get the wives stowed away. They crawled into the storage closet and snuggled into each other's arms. Uncle's wife whispered, "Oh, my dear, we are going to be together for a while. I think we'll be great friends." The boy's sister just looked at her with her big green eyes. Then she turned her face to the boy and smiled. The boy smiled back. "See you in a few hours."

The boy and Uncle left the wives and went back to their respective dormitories. The boy felt like he had just tucked himself back in when the lights came on and he heard his number called.

"Time to go, son." The man in the white coat touched the boy's shoulder. "Make sure you bring your book."

The boy grabbed his book and followed the man. "Do I get breakfast, sir?"

"Breakfast? No, it's best to launch on an empty stomach, trust me. Besides, there is plenty of food on board the pod. Don't worry."

Two

The boy and Uncle loaded on board, the doors to the pod sealed, and the launch began. It was rough enough that the boy was indeed glad he'd skipped his last meal. As soon as they cleared the planet's gravity, about thirty minutes later, Uncle opened the storage area and pulled out the small pile of supplies. Uncle's wife and the boy's sister crawled out.

"We're a little stiff, but fine," Uncle's wife declared. "I learned all about this girl during the last few hours."

The boy stared. "How? She doesn't talk."

"Well, she talked non-stop to me. Child, your sister has a fine mind."

"Sister?" asked Uncle. "I thought she was your sweetheart!"

The boy was confused. "What's the difference?"

His sister smiled. "Silly boy. Your sweetheart becomes your wife, the woman you love more than anything."

"But I love you more than anything!" the boy protested, a bit hurt that she'd talked to the old woman before she talked to him.

"You do now, but when you meet your sweetheart, you will love her more—or differently, anyway. Like Uncle and his wife love each other. You'll want to make more boys and girls together."

The boy stared. Where and when did his sister learn about all this? Certainly not just in the few hours in the storage closet with Uncle's wife.

"I've been reading for years, silly." His sister spoke as if she was reading his mind right that second. "I know a lot more than you think."

"Why didn't you ever say anything?"

"It was safer for us both if I didn't. No one really noticed me, and that left you free to watch and learn, and look what you did—you got us both out of there. My job was to read and learn, and that's what I did—I know where we are going, and I know what we are getting away from."

"Where are we going?"

"A planet called Earth, third from the Sun, in the Terra system. I looked up the coordinates in a book."

"What are we getting away from?" The boy thought he knew this already—they were leaving a dying planet and its corrupt leaders—so his sister's response surprised him.

"Do you remember the night our parents were killed?"

"The accident? I remember being told they were dead."

"It was no accident. I snuck out and followed them. They were part of a group trying to stop this practice of sending children and old people away. They discovered the planet isn't on the verge of destruction, and the authorities know all about it, but they don't want to stop sending unwanted people away."

"Why?" Uncle and his wife appeared equally curious.

"I never figured that out. I only know they don't need to send people out to other planets. They don't need to colonize anything. I heard our parents talking to the others about it."

"What happened?"

"One of the group members—oh, it was terrible—he was a spy. He was another child, a boy with black eyes. As the group meeting was breaking up, he pulled out a gun and began shooting. Everyone, he killed everyone. Then he saw me where I was hiding. He looked me right in the eye. I'll never forget those black eyes, staring at me. He shot at me, but he missed. I pretended he'd hit me, and played dead. After he'd left, I ran all the way home, got into bed, and never spoke another word."

Everything he thought he knew about his parents was a lie? The boy's mind threatened to spin out of control, so he kept asking questions. "Did you ever see that boy again?"

"Yes, I did. He was at the orphanage." His sister trembled.

Her brother grasped her hand. "Why?"

"One of the group he killed—it was his own father. He made himself an orphan. Then they sent him away," she answered.

"Where did he go?"

"I don't know. I don't want to. There was something about him…I think he'd planned to kill his father all along."

Her brother struggled to absorb all this. But he was, by nature, a practical boy, and he thought his sister might know something else important. "You said we are going to a planet called Earth."

"Yes?"

"How far is it? How long will it take us to get there? Will we have enough supplies?" Even though the boy accepted that his scheme might result in their perishing in the pod before they landed anywhere, he now discovered in himself a strong hope to survive, if he could. The idea of meeting someone he loved even more—or at least differently—than his sister, and of making more boys and girls, and of living in a place where they didn't send children and old people away—he wanted to see what this possible future would be like.

His sister laughed. "We should be there in about ten hours, if I've understood the speed calculation correctly. It's only one hundred light years away."

Uncle and his wife hugged each other and giggled like schoolchildren. The boy was annoyed. "You couldn't have spoken up about this sooner, when we were all afraid we'd die?"

"Would you have believed me?" his sister countered.

"Would you have told us if we were going too far, if you knew that we were going to die along the way?"

It was his sister's turn to stare. "I don't—I never thought about—" She looked so confused that the boy felt his heart soften. He took her into his arms and hugged her.

"It's okay. We're going to make it, that's the main thing. Still, you're an idiot, you know."

Uncle's wife took the children by the hands. "It looks like we are family now. And I'm hungry. Let's have something to eat and get ready for landing."

Three

When they landed—the boy, his sister, Uncle, and Aunt—they knew they had about five minutes to get as far away from the pod as they could before it self-destructed. What they couldn't have anticipated, not with all of the boy's curiosity and his sister's reading, not with all of Aunt and Uncle's experience, was landing in Madison County, Idaho on June fifth, nineteen-seventy-six.

On the Snake River.

As the Teton Dam was filling for the first time.

Their curiosity, reading, and experience, however, would have made it easy for them to understand the consequences of an alien landing pod blowing itself up on a dam as millions of gallons of water created astounding pressure behind it. The small hole it made wasn't small for long. The collapse of the dam and the resulting wind blew them far apart. Their alien forms, substantial on their home planet, were almost weightless on Earth. Uncle hung on to the boy, and Aunt held onto his sister, but they could not hang on to each other.

The boy and Uncle landed in a small town in eastern Washington called Selah.

On the main street, around the corner from the tavern, a young human boy ate a cluster of mushrooms he'd found in the dirt under an oak tree. He was sure they were safe. As their poison worked on him, he stumbled toward the road, and collided with the alien boy just as his human heart ceased beating. The alien boy found himself inside the human boy's body and realized it helped him navigate the terrain fairly well. He told Uncle, who gaped at the spot where his young companion used to be.

"We should find one for you." Uncle only shook himself and

walked on, looking to any humans who might catch a glimpse like a kind of heat mirage shimmer on the sidewalk.

The poor little town featured almost as many uninhabited houses as full ones. They found an empty one in relatively good condition, with some abandoned furniture inside, and set about making themselves a shelter while they considered what to do.

The boy considered, anyway. Uncle slumped on the battered sofa in defeat, submerged in grief from the loss of his wife. The boy wasn't ready to admit he'd lost anything yet—after all, his sister and Uncle's wife could walk in any minute, couldn't they? The boy tried consulting his book, in his pocket when the dam exploded, but it wasn't working very well, or maybe this planet didn't have much of a system to feed it the information it needed. He could be patient. But time was slippery on this planet, much different than what he was used to, and it slipped away even faster when he turned on what looked like a large wooden box with some kind of screen. The boy knew screens usually meant information transmission, so he pushed buttons on the box until an image slowly formed.

As he watched, he realized the television was like a large version of the books they'd been sent away with. Turn it on, and the screen filled with images and information pulled out of the air. Maybe that's why Uncle and the boy found themselves drawn to it, turning it on earlier and leaving it on later each day, until soon it was the first thing they turned on every morning and the last thing they turned off every night. This was true for Uncle and the boy, and for many of the others who'd found their way to Earth over the years. Most of them took their Earth names from this magic box. Many chose names too soon, before they really knew enough about customs and habits on Earth to make sense.

As the Earth weeks and months wore on, the boy became fascinated by what he saw on the box. The body he'd slipped into was fascinated, too, especially one particular "show," as they called the little stories on the box here. There were three beautiful women, and they did amazing things. Smart and brave, they listened to a voice called "Uncle Charlie" from another kind of box, and solved mysteries to get rid of bad guys. The boy wanted to be just like them. The body he borrowed wanted to be like them too, he judged by the way it responded while he watched them.

Especially when they wore less on their bodies.

And most especially when they seemed to dance in something he learned to call a "swimming pool," wearing very little and getting quite wet. His new body got warm all over, and its belly felt very, very soft, and the thing between its legs got harder and harder.

For some reason he liked the dark-haired, serious one, even though the other brunette was funny and the blonde made his body react more. The dark one was quieter, more mysterious, and seemed to harbor a secret, like he did. So he decided to take her name. But he already knew enough not to take her character's name. That would be too obvious. No, he chose the name at the end of every episode, Jacklyn Smith.

"Jacklyn Smith." He tried saying it out loud. It sounded good. "Uncle, my name is Jacklyn Smith."

At that point, days had passed since the last time the old man spoke. He withdrew into himself more and more, and the boy worried soon he would be on his own. But, for some reason, the old man roused himself from his grief to hear the boy this time and responded.

"Jacklyn Smith? That's the name you want?"

"Yes, Uncle."

"Why?"

The boy pointed at the television. "Because she is like me."

Uncle chuckled. "In many ways, perhaps, but not all. She is a girl, for one thing. You're a boy."

"What does that mean? Why does it make a difference?"

"In some worlds, it wouldn't." Uncle learned a great deal from watching this world depicted on the box in their living room. "But in this one, it makes a big difference. You go around with a girl's name, you scare people. The ones on this planet, they don't like people to be too different or unpredictable. They like conformity. A boy taking a girl's name, in this world, it's absurd."

The boy didn't understand most of what Uncle was saying. But he was stubborn. "I want to be Jacklyn Smith, Uncle. That is my name."

The old man looked at him. "Well, at least go by Jack, for heaven's sake. Jack Smith."

Jack Smith. The boy thought about it. "That will work. I'm Jack Smith."

"And I'm your Uncle Charlie, then, Jack Smith."

"Uncle Charlie." The boy smiled. "Sounds good."

Four

Jack tried to find his sister. He figured if he and Uncle landed somewhere, she and Aunt had, too, and all he needed to do was find out where.

Because he was young, because he already survived so much, this did not seem at all impossible. He did not know how long it would take—a long time, probably, maybe even more than an Earth year—but he never doubted that he would find her. He read everything he could about the Grand Teton dam collapse, once he realized the catastrophe blew them apart. He checked meteorology books out of the library and marked up maps to show where the winds might have blown them. He scoured newspapers, magazines, television shows for any hints to lead him to her.

Somewhere in the zone he calculated, two people showed up who'd never been there before. Or, if they'd taken human bodies the same way he did, two people who were supposed to die were still alive. Somewhere there would be a trace of this.

Besides, she would be looking for him, too. He was sure of it. She'd feel the same thing—they couldn't lose each other again. She'd read and learned so much in the orphanage, he could picture her doing the same things he did now. They would search for each other and they would eventually collide. That's just how it would happen. He wouldn't let himself consider the alternative. When the thought of never seeing her again snuck into his mind, he just wanted to leave his human body and disintegrate into a million shimmering points of light, never to think or act or feel again.

But Earth years went by faster than Jack expected. It seemed, all of a sudden, he was the human version of grown up. It was time to leave the town he'd come to know and set out on his own.

Humans did, when they turned eighteen years old. He'd seen it in movies, television shows, read it in books. Real books, not like the book his planet's scientists sent him off with, but ones made of paper, written by people with magical imaginations, who described whole worlds related to this one, but still somehow different.

Jack realized he'd fallen in love with this world, and he didn't want to leave it. He knew the scientists from his planet would follow him with his tracking device, they would know he was still alive and relatively healthy. Who knew what else they already learned about this planet? If it was accurate, they'd schedule it for colonization, and soon.

What was the story his sister told, during that all-too-brief time they were together, and she began speaking? About their parents being part of a group who discovered their home planet could be saved. They didn't need to send the orphans and elderly away, but the powers that be did not want anyone to know it. *Why?* Wouldn't it make people happy to know they could stay on their own planet? That orphans, elderly, and other weak or different people could be placed with real families, and live their lives out happily?

Jack didn't understand it. None of it made sense to him, but he was developing a sense of what the beings on his new planet would call *right* and *wrong*, and he knew it was wrong.

In fact, he read a book he found in the house he and Uncle lived in. It was a big, thick, black book with writing that was very difficult to understand. It seemed like poetry but it didn't rhyme, and it went on and on. A lot of the book seemed to be about how this world came into being and whoever wrote that part showed a super great imagination. He read enough science books and knew enough about geology, physics, and other sciences from his education on his own planet to know it couldn't have happened the way the book described, but what a story! Only six days to create a whole world, with creatures, plants, and everything. But some of the creatures—ones like the body he borrowed—didn't follow the rules of the creator and they were made to leave the beautiful place he'd created for them.

That part of the story made Jack think about his own breaking of the rules to bring his sister—and Uncle's wife—along with them on their trip. *Maybe that's why we were separated so quickly when we got here. I broke the rules and needed to be punished, like Adam and Eve in this Earth story.*

But that didn't really make sense either. If he—and Uncle—broke the rules, why did their punishment include Aunt and his sister? They sort of broke the rules by coming along, but it wasn't their idea. And what about all the other people hurt by the dam collapse that blew them apart? No, a creator who went to so much time and trouble to make things wouldn't tear them down and hurt so many innocent people just to punish one or two.

So, Jack started to wonder if there was another creator, one who only created bad things. There were stories in the big black book about that, too. About destruction, violence, and hatred.

Jack realized he needed to learn more about this world in order to search for his sister intelligently. Like his days at the orphanage, when he learned everything he could about the pods and the process for sending the children away. Eventually he'd come up with a plan that worked, with Uncle's help and a little luck, and there was no reason for him to believe he didn't still have some luck. He'd already seen and done more absurd and impossible things.

The first time he ventured out on his own to look for his sister was about six Earth years after his arrival and the dam collapse. He decided there was no better place to start than the next town over. He didn't really have any sense of the size of the planet he now lived on. His first plan was simply to visit one town at a time, assuming they were mostly like the one he'd been staying in, and talk to everyone he could find. He pictured it like a series of ever-expanding circles from the center point—the collapsed dam —and a cone-shaped section of territory where she was apt to have landed, given the prevailing winds that day. Once in a while it occurred to him that his sister might have gone on to another place for some reason, a place well outside the cone, but he'd shake such thoughts away. Denial, humans called it, but the boy didn't think of it that way. He was practical, and his sister moving to some random place he couldn't predict was impractical, and that was all.

He still sensed a kind of connection to her—he could feel her, often right behind his left ear—but she was fuzzy, indistinct, and growing more so all the time. Six Earth years seemed a long time to its native species, but it went by very quickly for the boy. Even so, he knew he needed to start visiting those towns soon or she might blur into oblivion. So he hitchhiked to the next town over, arriving in Zillah on a Friday night—high school football game night. The other kids his Earth-age all gathered at the school gym for the post-game dance.

When Jack arrived, he saw a fight about to break out, between a tall boy and a short one, with someone in between who he couldn't quite make out. The short boy seemed drunk. Jack's left ear tingled so much it hurt, like when his foot fell asleep and the blood finally started circulating again and the pain of that extremity reawakening grew nearly intolerable, made him want to die and he started to swear—*fuckfuckfuckfuckfuck*. He'd read that Earth scientists finally discovered that swearing actually does release physical pain, creating the sensation of relief, and since pain is a completely subjective phenomenon—there was virtually no way to measure it or even prove its existence except in the descriptions of the person who is experiencing it—well, that meant it was entirely up to each person to decide which curse words would release the pain. Like magic. Jack swore up a blue streak and hopped around on his left foot, trying to shake the pain out of his ear, and he did this as he entered the high school gym where the dance was well underway.

The pain wasn't only because his sister was close. She must also be in some kind of trouble.

The human chaperone looked concerned when the boy came up to him, shaking and hopping, and mumbled, "Ohshitfuckdamn, my sister, fuck shithellshit, sister, fuck, she's in fuckshitdamn trouble shitshitshitshit take her home shit uncle fuck my sister now she's in trouble."

Jack wasn't drunk, but the humans thought he was. He sounded a lot like a drunk kid saying he was going to take his pregnant sister home to his uncle who might be the one who made her pregnant and no adult human worth chaperoning a high school dance would let that happen. Since most of the local kids left the dance by the time he showed up, the chaperones shut it down and took Jack to the police station to explain, which took some time.

After Jack got the adults to believe he was sober and let him go, he returned to the high school gym, but no one remained.

Or so it seemed. Jack didn't see another boy, about his age by the looks of him, skinny with black eyes. The black-eyed boy began to follow Jack, to watch him, and to wait.

Five

His first attempt to find his sister failed, and Jack redoubled his efforts to learn about the world he'd landed on. He quickly realized he needed something called money to get by. The way to get money was to have something else, called a job. Jack would need a lot of money, or at least what seemed to him like a lot, to keep searching for his sister.

Traveling around this world wasn't easy without a pod. It was a big world, and it required a different kind of vehicle, one that was bigger, heavier, and slower, just like these human bodies. Humans called these vehicles cars, when they were meant to carry just a few of them, or buses, when they carried lots of humans. Cars, despite their limited capacity, cost more than buses, which were far more efficient. This was a lesson in the strange economies of his new home.

To get enough money to continue his search, Jack realized he needed what humans called a "good job." In all the books he read and television shows he watched, the key to a good job was a college degree. To get one, he would need to spend time in large rooms in large brick buildings, listening to older humans talk endlessly about all kinds of things, then writing down what they talked about in small blank books bound with blue paper. If he did this enough times, Jack discovered, the older humans would get tired of him and give him a diploma so that he would go away.

And if he did it for a really long time, and added one really long paper the older humans called a "thesis," they would give him something called a "master's degree." This piece of paper didn't seem to give anyone mastery over anything, really, but if he chose the topic of his paper well, he could spend all his time surrounded by books. Some of the books were really boring, but Jack chose a subject called "literature," which seemed to have fewer boring books than, say, "philosophy."

Jack became relatively content until he could collect enough money to search for his sister in earnest. He gave himself a graduation present of a trip to Seattle— the largest city in the cone he'd drawn on that map so many Earth years before—the geographical area where his sister and Aunt were most likely to have landed. His plan of searching each town in the cone finally brought him here, and he wandered the area downtown near where the big Greyhound bus dropped him off just a few before.

Jack walked up to a box office window. The sound of music told him it hid some kind of concert. "Any tickets left?"

"Sorry. The show is sold out."

A jolt of electricity shocked Jack as a group jostled past him. A woman in the group caught his eye. He noticed her set shoulders, as if she was determined, or angry, or in pain, or all of the above. "Fine. Don't say anything. Happy birthday to me, I guess," Jack heard the man with her say.

She is definitely not having a good night. Seeing her made him even more determined to get into the concert.

I bought my woman a Chevrolet, and she said I want a Cadillac. The lines from a song rose up from his memory. In the time Uncle stayed with Jack, they discovered the music of this world, especially the blues. Jack recalled the words from a tune his Uncle played over and over again, echoed in the music coming from inside the concert hall.

"Are you sure there's nothing?" Jack turned on his charm. He learned, from watching the way women reacted to him, he could often get what he wanted by acting more like a young boy. Especially certain women, like the one behind the ticket counter— over fifty, frosted hair, false fingernails, blouse buttons strained to conceal deep cleavage, strong perfume. He guessed he brought out the mother in them.

"I was supposed to meet my sister here. We haven't seen each other in years. I was stupid and forgot to get a ticket and, well, if I don't get in to meet her she might think I lied to her or something." He wasn't sure where the lie came from, exactly, but the expression on the woman's face indicated it might work. He dropped his voice to almost a whisper. "She's sick, you know."

"Cancer?" The woman's voice sounded thick. Jack knew

cancer was a bad thing.

"Yes," he sniffed, "cancer."

"Oh no, honey, that's terrible. Is she older than you? You look awfully young."

"We're twins, actually." That wasn't a lie, at least.

The woman in the box office clucked her tongue. "There's a lot they can do these days, sweetie. Maybe she'll have a miracle."

"Maybe." Jack tried to squeeze a tear or two out. Thinking about his sister made it pretty easy.

"I'll tell you what. I'm not supposed to do this, but we do hold some press tickets until the last minute. If no one claims them when the opening act is done, I'll give one to you."

Jack wanted to get in right away, to find the couple again, but he decided not to push it. "Thank you ma'am. How long will that be, about?"

The woman glanced at the little clock on the counter. "Oh, it's already started."

Jack noticed that almost all the people had drifted inside.

"Never takes more than an hour, so maybe forty five minutes from now?" Time regularly fooled Jack, but forty-five minutes didn't seem too long. "Why don't you go across the street and get a coffee, honey, and then come back?" The woman gestured toward a small, brightly lit coffee shop with a green sign.

"You'll be here when I do?" Jack only meant to make sure he wouldn't have to start over with someone else, but he saw the woman's cheeks redden under her thick makeup.

"Of course, honey, I'm stuck here until half an hour past the headliner." Jack wasn't sure what that meant, exactly, but he was reassured enough to walk across the street to the coffee shop.

Coffee was a treat this planet offered for which Jack was eternally grateful. Tonight he chose a dry cappuccino, extra hot, and looked forward to the first warm, slightly bitter sip sliding down his throat, bringing a blush of the caffeine high to come. On hot days he loved coffee over ice, mixed with chocolate, an experience that engendered a deep appreciation for the ways the beings of this world played with the chemical compositions of their bodies to create pleasures unthinkable in his previous form. *They must be the best at it in the whole universe.*

When that thought occupied Jack's mind, the opening act swung into its last couple of tunes in the theatre across the street. But Jack lost track of time, swirling the foam on his third cappuccino. When the headliner had been on stage for thirty minutes, the woman in the box office sighed and pulled the metal shade down on the window.

Coffee did something to Jack, and any other beings from his planet, though he didn't know it at the time. Coffee disabled the tracking device implanted in him before he left. Because of the differences in the way time moved between their world and Earth, the scientists on his home planet followed him for about ten of their days, then *poof!* He was gone from their scans.

Six

Standing outside the concert hall, alone and lost, Jack grasped the hand of friendship extended to him by a man who introduced himself as Gil Munroe. At least it seemed like it could be friendship, and Jack decided to take it. The phrase "running away" wouldn't necessarily have come to his mind then. At that moment, he understood despair, and he wanted it to stop. It seemed the way to make it stop would be to move himself from that spot in front of the concert hall, the spot that had been, until that moment, the last step in his plan. It seemed as though the terrible feeling rooted to the spot, like an organic mass, grown there from seed in the time it took Jack to realize the concert was over—he missed it, missed her, like he missed her every other time he thought he was close. It grew from a seed to be a towering oak tree in an instant, and if he stayed there it would turn him into wood, too. So when Gil-what's-his-name offered the hand of what stood a reasonable chance of being friendship along with escape, Jack took it gratefully and without much question.

"Hey. You look like you just lost your best friend," Gil appeared in front of the concert hall out of nowhere, invited Jack for a beer, and explained his situation. Gil was leaving for Eastern Europe in three days, for a job with an English-language newspaper in Prague. Gil's about-to-be boss, another American ex-pat named Mrs. Booth, mentioned an American company, PP-something, recently opened a factory in a town nearby. Mrs. Booth's brother-in-law was being hired by this PP-whatever company to manage it, and the company demanded the employees learn at least some English. Mrs. Booth asked Gil if he knew anyone who might be able to teach language classes to the factory employees. Gil told her he did, sure, because he knew it would make him more valuable to Mrs. Booth. In fact, he hadn't known any such potential English instructors until he met Jack that night, or so he claimed. But he never doubted he'd find someone by the time he needed to leave.

They made an unlikely pair of friends, Gil with his height, easy good looks, and easier charm, especially with women. Gil showed outstanding patience, as far as Jack could tell, and a tendency to disappear whenever a situation got dicey. Jack, in his despair, developed a tendency to dive headlong into dicey situations as if being blown by a wind out of his control. This gave Gil plenty of chances to show the cowardly side of himself.

Jack learned a few things about women, too. He learned women could fall in love with him easily. They sensed something different about him, something decidedly non-prick-like. He learned they fell out of love with him with equal alacrity, often for the same reason—not that they wanted to date pricks, but they found his easy friendship so comforting, and they wanted to keep it that way. Jack didn't know for a long time that "let's just be friends" was an Earth cliché. He thought it was his own specific fate.

He wasn't a virgin in his Earth body, though. He experienced sex twice. The first time was on his eighteenth Earth birthday, at an event his fellow high school students called a "kegger," held far out in the valley near Selah. Beer played a role, but not as big as that of a fragrant "weed" cigarette passed from kid to kid. Jack wasn't usually invited to these big group parties—he didn't make a lot of friends among the boys, and most of the girls wanted to be with their boyfriends. But one girl fell for him, at least temporarily, and she made sure he got word of the time and location of the party. Unfortunately, between the small amount of beer and the large number of puffs on the weed cigarette, Jack remembered almost nothing of the encounter, except a warm feeling in the pit of his stomach, the sensation of lips and skin in contact with other lips and skin, and the sound of the girl's "real" boyfriend yelling, waking them up from a deep post-coital sleep. Jack ran away from the boyfriend's shouted threats, and never saw the girl again.

The second time Jack had sex was fifteen Earth years later, when he followed Gil to Eastern Europe to the little factory town. Gil was determined to get Jack a date. "It's important for your physical and mental health to get, you know, polished up every once in a while," Gil said with utter sincerity. By then, Jack worked hard to convince himself his sister was dead or entirely lost, so he could accept the fact he'd abandoned his failed search. The more time he spent on this planet with its odd, maddening, endearing inhabitants, the more he loved it. But he hated it, too, this place with its huge dams and small holes and strong, determined winds, for blowing his sister away from him. This inner conflict kept him apart from other Earthlings more, in many ways, than the fact that he came from another planet.

Jack and Gil arrived a couple of weeks earlier to the factory town. Gil wanted to find a date and Jack was bored, too, ready for a beer, anyway. The crowded pub served good beer, better than any Jack could remember having stateside, not that he drank much beer in America, since it just wasn't that good. Because Jack came from America, he drew attention from the locals. Because he wasn't attached to America, not connected enough to act like a typical American—walk with a swagger, carry dollars, and an expensive camera, or engage in earnest political discussions about the dark side of American democracy—the locals liked him even more.

Some of the local old men gravitated to Jack and told him stories of the place and their lives in it, funny raunchy stories, most of them, stories Jack loved. The women flocked around Gil, all ages of them, and he was in heaven entertaining them with a few stories of his own, or so it seemed. Jack saw something in Gil's eyes now and then that might mean Gil wasn't as comfortable or happy as he appeared, but Jack wouldn't pry, and Gil didn't volunteer to explain.

So the evening wore on and Gil whittled his way down to three of the prettiest women, and Jack to three of the crustiest old men, and the beer kept flowing.

Among the ways the beings of this planet mixed up their own chemistry for fun, beer affected Jack much differently than coffee. Coffee charged through his system and made him feel alert, ready, warm, and eager. Beer was far gentler, though equally enjoyable. It made him relaxed, silly, and open—open with his own stories, open to whatever might happen next.

If, that night, Jack stuck to coffee, or if Gil chose the woman he wanted to take home a bit sooner, or if one of the old men talking to Jack, the crustiest one, as it turned out, had been anyone other than who he was—the ex-mayor of the next town over—maybe they all would've gone home happy. Sometimes the chanciest things make all the difference.

It would be predictable to say the woman Gil picked was the mayor's daughter, or worse, his beautiful young second wife, and that started the brouhaha. Actually, Jack triggered events that evening. After his third beer, the mayor launched into a story about the dark days of communism in the next town over—except they weren't so dark, according to him, since it was the communists who'd put him in power, and who kept the streets clean and the buses running on time. There was one dark spot though, a party functionary who came out of nowhere to challenge him for his job as mayor. Unheard of, since the party picked candidates well before balloting, making sure their chosen ones got the seats they were promised. But this functionary seemed to have something on the old guard, something that made them melt out of his way. Of course, by then the party was crumbling anyway, the apparatus was showing cracks, and that made it easier for this functionary to come to the fore. The thing was, according to the ex-mayor, the functionary, wouldn't show himself in public for months. When he did, he didn't even look Czech. He was a skinny small man, with black hair and black eyes, and a dreadful habit of speaking with more words than the average person even knew. He had the most ridiculous name. The ex-mayor wanted to get the name exactly right for Jack, because he wouldn't believe this name—*východný drevo*.

"Hey," the ex mayor shouted to his friend. "How would you say that in English? East what? East wood?"

"That's right, like the film star," the friend shouted back. "Eastwood."

Jack's beer-induced openness made him incautious and when he heard black eyes, the hair on the back of his neck stood up. He recalled his sister told him about the night their parents died. The boy who killed his own father, who made himself an orphan, too. Did he somehow come to Earth? "When was this? What year?"

"Eighty five, or was it eighty six?" the ex mayor replied. "My memory for dates isn't what it used to be."

"How old was he?" asked Jack.

"Oh, a young pup, early twenties. But the strangest thing about it was that this functionary kept claiming he made a deal for the post, he'd been promised it in exchange for finding an investor to build that little factory outside of town. None of us knew anything about such a promise, and it was a small town, so we would know, and of course it was the party who funded the factory, not an outside investor. I called him a liar but he just kept saying it, over and over. We had a deal, we had a deal."

"I wonder," murmured Jack. "I wonder if it could be him."

"Hajzl!" yelled the ex mayor. "Sonofabitch! You're a friend of his? You come here as a stranger, and American, and your friend tries to take over our elections?" The drunk ex-mayor forgot this particular election was twenty years ago. That the particular American sitting with him now could not have been involved. Gil looked over when the yelling started, mouthed something at Jack that looked like *what the fu—?*

Before Jack could respond, the old man took a swing at him—a full swing, with all the power and fury of an ex-communist cheated out of a free and fair election behind it—and Jack learned to defend himself, to fight physically. He ducked, and the blow landed on another crusty old man, the husband of the young and beautiful second wife with whom Gil was about to leave.

Jack escaped the resulting melee because a chair came out of nowhere and deflected a blow meant for his temple. He ran out of the pub into the square, mostly empty at that hour, and kept running until he reached home. One of the young women from the pub ran with him, and made love to him that night, an experience for which Jack was always grateful. He didn't see Gil again until nearly noon the next day, when Gil's explanation was simply that he'd seen big trouble brewing and slipped out the back of the pub and kept his distance until it seemed safe to come home.

That was Jack's official welcome to expatriate status as an American living in eastern Europe, and after that bar fight, he was accepted as one of their own, with the exception of the ex-mayor, who never really forgave him, and the old man married to Gil's would-be date, who never forgave Jack either, though Jack didn't cause that part of the evening's brawl.

Jack learned something else during his time in Europe. He learned how to make humans laugh. It made it much easier to get by. Without his sister to search for, that's all he wanted to do—just get by. Over time, any memory, any recollection of that old self reminded him of how much of a failure he'd been. Not able to help his parents when they needed him—his sister knew where they were, what they were doing, and followed them, not Jack. Not able to save his sister from the orphanage or exile. Not able to hold onto her when they landed far from home, never able to find her since—only close calls that brought his failure into high definition. Jack began a dedicated effort to forget his past, erase the memory of his failures, and focused on making everyone around him laugh.

Seven

This is killing me. The night everything changed for Louise Armstrong Holliday, that single overpowering thought filled her mind. Louie christened the thing killing her *The Archive Project*—capital letters, like The Andromeda Strain—because she believed it to be the source of her inevitable demise.

It started innocently enough, six months earlier, when Louie stumbled on a closet near her office filled with office party supplies. The paper plates and cases of soda didn't quite hide a stack of battered cardboard boxes stuffed with old documents. If Mac hadn't been with her, Louie wouldn't have given the stack of boxes a second thought. She would've just stolen a can of warm Coke for herself, like she took home office supplies with increasing frequency—rationalizing that it didn't cost the company much compared to all the hours over forty she donated to it each week—but Mac saw the cardboard boxes and looked inside one.

"Holy shit." Mac's bluntness was endearing.

Her full name was Macrina, and most people didn't call her that twice, after receiving her trademark raised eyebrow in return. "If you have time to use all those extra syllables," the eyebrow said, "you don't have enough work to do. And I can fix that." What saved her in the eyes of her colleagues was that Mac Delaney worked harder than any of them.

"This is where this stuff wound up? In here with the party supplies and..." Mac looked up at the ceiling. "Oh cripes. If that fire sprinkler ever goes off, we'll lose the company's history." Mac was about two inches taller than Louie in stocking feet and always wore heels. Mac could walk faster in those heels than Louie could run in sneakers. Jogging to keep up, Louie almost crashed into Mac when she finally stopped in front of an open door.

"I thought so. Here's an empty office. Bunselmeier used it before he got fired. No one wants it. They think it has the curse of the Bunselmeier on it. It's perfect. I'll have the boxes moved here."

Bunselmeier's nervous breakdown had been caused, most everyone at the company believed, by the close proximity of his office to the only working color copy machine in the whole place and the constant stream of employees using it to copy their resumes, lost cat posters, and garage sale flyers drove him mad. A few suggested it didn't have anything to do with his antipathy to misuse of the company's resources. They'd pointed out Bunselmeier was never seen in the office again after standing up at an all-staff meeting to ask about rumors of a huge and expensive data migration project. But Louie didn't believe simple curiosity would result in termination. She'd heard Bunselmeier's rants about unauthorized personal color copying, how much it cost the company, and yes, they were extreme.

"I'll give you Bea. She can get all those documents organized and scanned and into an electronic library," Mac stared at Bunselmeier's now empty office and, at first Louie didn't catch that Mac no longer referred to herself as the owner of this new little project.

Then it clicked. "Oh, no, Mac. Bea? Not Bea. And why me?"

"Because you're the Chief Strategy Officer and these are all strategic documents." Mac did not miss a beat.

"They are?"

"Sure. These are all the records of Paster's legal wranglings, fights with the board of directors, pleas to the IRS, foreign manufacturing set ups. Everything is in cardboard boxes waiting for the fire sprinkler to go off the next time Willa burns her toast in the kitchen."

PPP3, the Seattle company they worked for, started up about twenty years earlier, when Jerome Paster invented his first gadget, a plastic thing shaped like a giant cigarette, meant for *chopping. Anything! Carrots, celery, onions, potatoes, you name it, the Pasterizer™ can chop it!* Never mind that it died after the second onion, somehow Paster sold enough on late -night television to invest the slim profit into other inventions, until pretty soon every poorly-made household gadget hawked on the tube owed its success to him. Three years before Mac and Louie found the old boxes, Paster suddenly sold the company and left town. The new ownership regime gave everyone trendy titles in lieu of raises. Mac, previously Vice President for Customer Service, was now the Chief Experience Officer. Louie became the Chief Strategy Officer but couldn't see any difference in her job, plodding away on useless research and planning to make the company ready for the next crappy plastic late-night sales sensation.

"You know Bea is perfect for the job. You and me and everyone else in the company has a file crammed full of paper copies of every round of every email string Bea was involved in, courtesy of Bea's obsessive compulsive disorder." Mac fended off any objection. Louie'd nodded, nose wrinkled, remembering how her file also reeked with Bea's disdain for anyone less scrupulous about record-keeping than she was. "Tell her to go through all the papers and scan them, create an archive we can store on the server that backs up every night. And," Mac lowered her voice, "when Bea retires in six months, much to the relief of everyone who's ever worked with her, you can keep her salary line and hire that research assistant you've always wanted." This was vintage Mac. Offer a deal that can't be refused, backed by logic that couldn't be argued, then get an agreement before the other person realized Mac always walked away the winner. Louie loved watching Mac's brilliant mind at work. Intelligence unencumbered by emotion, unlike Louie, whose heart almost always out-maneuvered her head.

"Okay, but you owe me one."

Mac smiled. They both knew they'd each pulled each other's ass out of the fire many times over the eight years they worked together and would do so many times in the future, so neither bothered to keep count.

"Great. I'll tell Bea. Now I have to go meet with a customer who says the sales rep who called him used a racial slur." Mac made a face but Louie knew she loved this stuff—rushing from one crisis to another, fixing them all, working insane hours, but always, always being in the middle of everything. "Why do they do this to me?" Mac whined. "Are they trying to ruin my Monday?"

Six months later, Bea's broken hip had confined her at home on disability leave. Mac had left the company and the Archive Project was all Louie's. As soon as it turned six pm, with nothing to do but wait for traffic to ease before hitting the freeway, Louie grabbed her third or fourth cup of coffee of the day and went to sort through another box. Occasionally, she came across something interesting related to the legal squabbles, threats, posturing, all the drama of the company's checkered history.

But most of it was the dullest bureaucratese imaginable. She dutifully pulled out paper clips, removed staples, shredded duplicates, scanned originals, cross-referenced and organized files. She'd made it through about a third of the boxes so far, noting that, at this rate, the Archive Project would kill her for at least another half a year.

~ * ~

Louie walked down the hall to the Archive Project room. She flipped on the harsh florescent lights, sat down in the desk chair with the broken arm and pulled another musty-smelling box close.

For the millionth time, she wished they let her bring her dog to work. At least she'd have some company. Her dog, Buddy, was a blind mini-Schnauzer she'd rescued five years before. He was dear and loving with her, cranky and snappy with everyone else. Given the long hours she worked, it was a blessing she'd found a doggy daycare that could handle Buddy. They kept him in the "anxious dogs" area, with the owner's big black Lab, Arthur. Buddy loved Arthur. He spent his days panting at Arthur, playing with him, sleeping with him, sharing his doggy treats. Stuart, the daycare owner, also loved Buddy. Louie thought about Buddy now, probably napping with Arthur, waiting for her to come pick him up and take him for one long walk before bedtime. On their walks Louie shared all her frustrations and worries with Buddy, who ignored her while he sniffed every shrub, tree, fire hydrant, and stray leaf in their neighborhood. By the time they wound their way back home, both were exhausted and happy. Buddy would get a cookie and Louie would eat toast or cereal, and they curled in bed together to go to sleep. On her lucky nights, one or both of her cats would join them. Animal behavior made sense to Louie. Humans were the mystery.

No one called Louie by her full name because she never shared it with anyone. It embarrassed her, in some way she couldn't quite put her finger on, maybe because it sounded like the name of a little old lady or something. Even Louie's few close friends didn't know she was Louise Armstrong and, after first introductions, few people paid attention to her last name, Holliday. She was just Louie.

A lot of things about Louie were vague. On rare occasions, when people tried to describe her looks, they usually wound up saying things like, "You know, medium height, medium build, medium brown hair...you know, medium." Mostly they didn't bother, because it was like trying to describe one of those shimmery heat mirages you can't quite recall as soon as it disappears and they found it so much easier to describe her in other ways. *The reliable one. The thoughtful one. The quiet one. You know, Mac's pal.* They knew Mac wouldn't befriend an idiot, so they watched for, and quickly became aware of, Louie's intelligence, and the kindest of them also forgave her for how impulsive she could be when her emotions took control.

One colleague at PPP3, a Native American whose own deep wisdom took him off to other professional pursuits after less than a year at the company, told Louie if he were to give her an Indian name, it would be "Heart in the Right Place." Louie laughed, asking him if she couldn't please have something more aspirational, like "Kicks Some Ass." But, in truth, she never seemed to know where her heart was. Her center seemed shrouded in an inner fog, so she secretly cherished the name he might have given her, and the idea that her heart might be in the right place after all.

"Or Green Water Eyes," her colleague added. "No one forgets your eyes after they've met you, do they?" Louie blushed at that, and wondered if it were true. She'd thought it was more likely they never forgot her clumsiness, or her tendency to lose it once in a while and send long email rants.

She'd sent one earlier that day to her friend Jack, who helped run PPP3's Eastern European factory. Already, as she sat in the Archive Project room just a few hours later, she struggled to remember exactly which stupid thing her boss did that triggered her outburst.

From: *LouieA*
To: *JackS*
Re: *My theory about Real Middle-Aged White Men*

All Real Middle-Aged White Men are pricks. Pricks are men whose primary purpose in life is to seek privilege, keep privilege once they have it, and then get more privilege. They are not power seekers per se—the power seekers are an elite group of pricks, who have important jobs in industries where they will make a lot of money, use that money to bring them power, and then use that power to bring them more money. Most pricks need enough money to be privileged, but they don't want the discomfort that comes with real power. They don't want to work that hard or make the really tough decisions. Pricks always have women around to take care of them— their moms did their laundry, made their meals, smoothed their way, and their wives pick right up where their moms left off. Pricks want to continue the comfortable life they have—they want to travel, they like to think they like fine wine, they read all the right books, they listen to classical music, they wear tweeds and corduroys, leather jackets, suits when needed, but with Jerry Garcia ties. There is a spectrum of pricks—the less bad ones generally keep their first wives, know their kids' names, and even take them with them on their travels. The worse ones dump their first wives, alienate their first batch of kids, and travel to get away from them. But they are all pricks, and they seek privilege above all else. They expect others to bring them the world's riches, and they believe they deserve them. They might be nice to others in order to make this happen, or they might not. Their own behavior is incidental to the result. They want the goodies. They are pricks.

There are men who are between the ages of forty and sixty-five, who are Caucasian, and they are not Real Middle-Aged White Men. These are the guys who learned early on to take care of themselves. These guys grew up outsiders and never lost that sense. They seek connection, not privilege. They want someone to belong to, and someone to belong to them. They want to take care of the people they love, and spend time with them, and laugh with them, and cry with them. They know they have to work for stuff, and they don't mind. They just don't want to have to spend too much time dealing with the pricks. They are connectors. They are lovers. They don't expect other people to make the world easy for them, to pick over the world's riches and deliver them. They don't know what they would do with the world's riches anyway. The world's riches would take up too much of the room they need for their loved ones. They would throw the world's riches away to be with the people they love. And they just want the pricks to stay the hell out of their way. Like you, Jack. I have a feeling you're not one of the real pricks in this world, are you?

As soon as she'd hit "send," Louie wished she hadn't. She regularly sent Jack long personal messages and then wished them unsent. Distracting herself from embarrassment and avoiding his reply, if he'd sent one, was another reason she headed to the Archive Project room that evening.

The Archive Project room was a small spare office with no windows and buzzing fluorescent lights in the company's headquarters, located in a non-descript business park in a suburb of Seattle. *How on Earth did I wind up here?* Louie's life often puzzled her. After earning a master's degree in philosophy, of all things, Louie looked for a job to pay back her student loans and get out of her aunt's house. She'd been ready to take anything that came along, and the first thing that did so was a position as a part-time market research assistant at PPP3. Perfect, Louie thought—work as little as possible, use the rest of her time to write the book she carried around in the back of her mind. It became a little too perfect, with Louie proving to be just a tiny bit better at her job than necessary, and as the company's founder was wont to fire people higher up without provocation, pretty soon she got promoted and grew used to a full-time salary. She'd bought a little fixer-upper house in an older Seattle neighborhood, a place just big enough for her, her cats, and her dog.

Now forty loomed and she kept doing what was put in front of her, no matter how absurd, surviving the founder's purges until she became a fixture at the company. It was security, anyway, and the book could always come later.

Sitting in the Archive Project room, she fingered her key chain. Touching the little silver house charm hanging there helped calm her. One of the few things she kept, she had it with her for what seemed like forever. Louie didn't save much stuff. Stuff cost money and, sooner or later, she'd have to move it. There was nothing worse than having to move all your stuff.

Books were the exception, her one vice, her first addiction—caffeine was her second, and a coffee cup or Coke was never far from her side. She convinced herself she'd sell her books if, when, she moved again. Sometimes she wondered what a stranger would deduce about her from her bookshelves. Philosophy books from grad school. Sartre and Locke and Hobbes and Merleau-Ponty and Russell, her fun reads—Douglas Adams and Jasper Fforde and P.G. Wodehouse, her favorites. *A Confederacy of Dunces* and *To Kill a Mockingbird, Away, The Remains of the Day, Love and Garbage*; and one torn and ragged little brown book from her childhood, half a book, really, an old copy of *The House at Pooh Corner*.

Snapping out of her reverie, Louie realized the document she held was different than the any of the others she'd sorted. It bore a strange logo at the top and the made of a plastic like material—thick, pliable, slick and translucent. The logo changed every time she looked at it—first blue, then red, then yellow. First a fish, then a bird, then a—spaceship? Louie closed her eyes and shook her head. She was tired, this project whipped her ass, and she wanted to go home to walk Buddy. She was probably seeing things.

She opened her eyes and looked again at the purple logo in the shape of what looked like a UFO out of some nineteen-fifties movie. At least it seemed like it was going to stay that way for a while, now that it stopped changing color and shape. Under the UFO were the words, *United Federation of Outerspace: Our Vision is Your Future.*

She scanned down the page. At first, the rest of the writing, if that's what it was, were a series of unintelligible scribbles. As she stared, they slowly formed themselves into words she could recognize as words—but Chinese, then Spanish, then German, and finally English. *Almost like the words are trying to fix themselves into a language I can understand.* But of course that never happens in real life. In real life, documents don't change themselves before your eyes. So she must be really, really tired.

Then she read the English words for the first time.

"I'm not tired, I'm asleep. I fell asleep in the Archive Project room and I am dreaming," Louie mumbled. She read:

> *Owner, CEO, and Chief Executive Officer Jerome Paster does hereby agree to turn over all controlling rights and interests in Paster's Performance Products—hereafter referred to as PPP3—including all physical assets, all intellectual property, and all real and potential income, to the United Federation of Outerspace, hereafter known as the UFO—"Our Vision is Your Future"—for the total price of one billion US dollars.*

One billion dollars? Who in the whole wide universe would be stupid enough to pay one billion dollars for a little company that never made much money and was always in trouble with some regulatory authority or other? Louie blinked and kept reading.

> *The terms and conditions of this agreement are as follows:*
> *Jerome Paster will not disclose the fact or terms of this sale to anyone, human or otherwise.*
> *Jerome Paster will immediately retire to the planet Phnx along with his wife, children, and children's spouses.*
> *Jerome Paster and all family members will not seek to return to Earth for a period of no less than ten Phnx years, or one thousand Earth years, whichever is longer.*
> *The UFO's payment is considered payment in full, with no residual payments or share of revenues to revert to Jerome Paster for all eternity.*
> *The UFO agrees to operate PPP3 within all federal and state regulations, standards, and intergalactic laws, as it deems practicable.*
> *The UFO agrees to appoint 06733366691245, known on Earth as Thomas Lee Jones, as Owner, Chief Executive Officer, and Chairman of All Important Functions, of PPP3, for a period of at*

least ten Sprxlsgyzm years or one thousand Earth years, whichever is longer.

These terms and conditions, and the fact that Thomas Lee Jones—Louie's boss—was listed as a member of the UFO, as bizarre as they were, were not what disturbed her the most. It was the last line:

Executed for the UFO this fifth day of February, 2002, by the being known on Earth as Sergio Leone Eastwood.

Oh no, thought Louie. The Vice Chairman of Darkness really was.

Eight

Two days after she found the UFO agreement in the Archive Room, Louie's regular weekly meeting with her boss, Thomas Lee Jones, was coming to an end. Louie brought the odd document with her, stashing it in the back of her folder as she ran out the door of her office, late as usual. She wasn't sure she would show it to Jones. Probably she wouldn't, knowing it was most likely some kind of crazy joke. Still, she was curious as to his reaction, especially to Sergio's signature. It looked genuine enough, and Louie had a weakness for anything that might make the Vice Chairman of Darkness look foolish.

After she finished updating Jones about the latest competitor research, he asked if she had anything else to discuss. He seemed distracted, ready to end the meeting. This always irked Louie. Her work was only important to him when he needed something yesterday, otherwise he gave off an *I really can't be bothered* vibe. Out of sheer annoyance, she decided to show him the agreement.

"Tom, there is one other thing, just to make you laugh." She pulled the paper out of her folder. "I found this when I was going through the archive stuff—"

Louie stopped mid-sentence. Jones' face contorted in shock. "Tom, are you okay?" Then out of the corner of her eye, she saw the paper start again—the logo changing color and shape, the words shifting from English back into incomprehensible marks.

"Where did you find that?" Jones choked out.

"It was in the archive but I thought I was dreaming before. I read it and thought it must be a joke—Tom, do you need some water?" Louie heard a sound, like a low growl, coming from somewhere under the table. She looked at Jones. He was turning green. She began to feel a little dizzy herself. The sound got louder and she realized it came from him. Then the table shook.

Louie remembered seeing this sort of thing happen in movies and reading it in books. None of it prepared her for what took place before her eyes. Jones' head split in two, starting behind one ear and moving across the top of his scalp. The back of his head and face peeled away as if they were being unzipped, making a horrible, ripping-Velcro sound. Then she saw an actual zipper running down Jones' head, neck, and chest—she couldn't look any lower. His skin and clothing peeled next and what emerged from them was almost too hideous to bear, but Louie couldn't tear her gaze away.

Something like a head appeared. Formed from a misshapen oval the color of snot, yellow-green snot ejected from a deeply infected sinus, with things that seemed to be eyes, but twelve of them—little beads of purple light set into the infected snot mass. Below the head, his hulking body seemed far wider and lumpier than Jones appeared, like lime Jell-O gone terribly, terribly wrong. Louie heard a high-pitched noise over the growl and gradually realized she was screaming.

"Hush." Even though the head was no longer Jones, somehow the voice was still his. "Stop screaming for Spryxl's sake."

Louie stopped screaming. Hearing Jones's voice come out of that green lump brought her back to herself at least for a moment. *I'm dreaming again. I'm still in bed with Buddy and I hit snooze one too many times and I'm dreaming.* She grabbed a hunk of the skin on her arm between her thumb and forefinger and gave it a sharp twist.

"Ow!"

"What in Spryxl's Name are you doing?" asked the Jones lump.

"Pinching myself." Louie winced.

"Why?"

"That's what you do to wake yourself up from a dream. I've seen it in movies."

"Well, stop it. It's very disconcerting to watch a human inflict pain on itself. We prefer to do that ourselves."

One more sharp twist that hurt like hell. *Crap. Not only is my boss some kind of alien, but I'm going to have a wicked bruise on my arm from pinching myself so hard.*

Louie always thought of herself as slow to react in a crisis. Her friend Mac used to joke if they were on the Titanic, she would throw people into the lifeboats while Louie asked everyone if they were really, really sure it was an iceberg, because she hadn't seen it, and it might be just a rumor. But Louie never faced a situation like this before. She discovered, to her immense surprise, her mind became focused and clear.

"So it isn't a joke. You are an alien." As she spoke the words out loud, Louie realized she believed this herself ever since she pulled the strange document out of the cardboard box in the Archive Room two days ago. It was the only explanation that made sense of the last three years at PPP3. She felt momentarily elated, as she always did when the pieces of a puzzle started to come together—not all the way, but reached the critical mass, and then her mind would realize, *yes, you will solve this one, you are solving it, it will be solved, you will achieve closure and you can relax. And then you can start the next one.*

"From your perspective, yes, I am an alien. I am from another planet, the name of which is unpronounceable in any Earth language. For your convenience let us call it Spryxlburg," the Jones lump said.

"That's pronounceable?"

"It's close enough for humans. Spryxlburg is the home of the Grythylwecs."

"Okay. Why are the Garth—the Greth—why are you all here?"

"We thought PPP3 was our ticket to what American humans call Easy Street. When Sergio brought us this deal...."

This is a Sergio deal, then. "I saw his signature on the document. You don't have to tell me the rest. Sergio brought you the deal and claimed it would generate what, millions? Billions? Of dollars." Sergio was famous for this at the company—putting together grandiose deals that wound up drowning PPP3 in debt and sucking up everyone's time trying to clean up the mess.

"Trillions of Sprxl dollars."

"Of course, trillions of...your dollars. He promised you

could get in with very little upfront investment."

"Only one billion American dollars—which is like three Sprxl dollars."

"Right. That's the money that went to Paster to get him to take his whole family—where?"

"Also unpronounceable."

"Never mind."

"But for convenience sake, call it Arizona."

"Okay—wait, like the state?"

"Well, it's a warm planet, and everyone there likes golf."

"Right. Paster gets paid off on condition he takes his family to 'Arizona,' and never says a word. That's just so like him, to take the money and run. You get here and find out that the deal Sergio put together is, well…"

"As crappy as the products PPP3 sells."

"Exactly. The company doesn't make much money, it's under all kinds of investigations, and you're stuck in this little backwater of a planet."

"It's not Spryxlburg, that's for sure."

"Ooookay, I'll grant that. So what are you going to do?"

"Kill you."

"No, I mean about the company—wait, what? Why are you going to kill me?"

"So you won't tell anyone about our plan."

"I don't know your plan!"

"We are turning humans into cyborgs, creating the largest cyborg army in the galaxy."

"Dammit, Tom! Now I do know your plan!"

"Yes, that's why we have to kill you."

Louie tried pinching her arm one more time, a really wicked twisting pinch, like her aunt used to give her friends when they swore in front of her. Now was the time to wake up if she was going to, but her arm just throbbed. "Well, then, tell me the rest of the plan." *Might as well know it all before I die.*

"What rest of the plan?" asked the Jones lump.

"After you turn all the humans into this massive cyborg army, what are you going to do with them?"

"I don't know. Fight some other galaxy, I guess."

"You don't have a plan?"

"Sergio is supposed to be writing the plan."

"Sergio is writing the plan for using the cyborg army? Let me guess—he's bringing another partner into the deal."

"Yes, they are from—well, it's another planet with a name you couldn't pronounce."

"And they are putting up the money."

"Yes."

"And all you have to do is sit back and share in the plunder when the army takes over—some other galaxy you haven't determined yet."

"That's right."

"That's a Sergio deal, all right. Well, I'm a lot less worried about the future of humanity because I have yet to see a Sergio deal actually produce anything. Has it started?"

"Has what started?"

"The army. Have you started turning people into cyborgs?"

"Yes. We started with the staff in Human Resources."

"You mean Paul?" Paul Webb was the Director of Human Resources, or Chief Human Capital and Office Party Officer, under the new title system.

"Paul, yes, he is now a cyborg. The whole HR staff has been migrated."

"Migrated? Wait—this is the big migration project we've heard whispers about?"

"Yes."

"We thought that was for our data management system!"

"Well, data management is involved. Migration takes a lot of IT support."

"So our Chief Information and Killer Apps Officer—"

"Yes, Sergio brought him from our partner planet."

"I knew it! I knew he wasn't human." *Knowing the rest of the IT staff, they'd be thrilled to learn their boss was an alien.* "Wait a minute—the whole HR staff? What about Michelle?" Louie attended Michelle's memorial service the week before. Sadly, she was one of the few company employees to attend. Of course, the fact that it was held about three hours away in a small town, at Michelle's parents' church, the Temple of the Believers in WalMart, a cult that recently exploded into popular consciousness, might have kept a few people away.

"Michelle's migration was unfortunately incomplete."

"You told us she died in a car accident!"

"Well, it was an accident."

"In a car?"

"No. Migration has its risks to humans, we are finding out. That's why we moved it out of the country."

"Where to?"

"I really can't tell you more. I already have to kill you. I really don't want to have to take any additional prejudicial action. The paperwork is a nightmare."

Louie felt a mixture of astonishment, fear, and vindication…. she knew something crazy was going on, and here it was. These aliens were stupid but brutal, and she knew her next move meant taking a giant risk. But she couldn't think of anything else to do. She needed to buy some time to think of a way to stop them. *Why do I want to stop them? There's a surprise.* But what came out of her mouth next surprised her more.

"Let me help."

"Help?"

"You know if you leave it to Sergio, this plan to take over some other galaxy will never get done. Give it to me, and I'll have it done in a week. I am the Chief Strategy Officer, you know." *And I need to make sure you don't kill me, or decide it would be easier just to turn me into a cyborg.*

"One week?" At least two of Jones' eyes focused on Louie.

"One Earth week, yes. But I have some conditions."

"You insist on conditions when I have said we will kill you?"

Louie worked with Jones long enough to be pretty sure that even though he was an alien, he was, deep down, a prick. And she knew pricks were easy to back down, at least in the short term.

"Yes. I won't do this unless you grant me these conditions."

"What are they?"

Louie relaxed a little. He wouldn't ask if he hadn't already made up his mind to give her something.

"One, you send me to the new migration project location—I assume you mean that little factory in Eastern Europe Paster bought before he split—so I can see the operation for myself. Two, you give Michelle's family compensation for her loss. One million American dollars."

"Compensation? Why, when eventually they will all be migrated, too?"

"Because it is one of my conditions." Louie knew pricks never explained and lost respect for an opponent who did. "And three..." Louie paused. She was pushing it, but she had to try.

"Yes?"

"Sergio does not know that I am helping you. He does not know why I am going to Europe, and you keep him away from me until my plan is done."

Jones sneezed, and Louie jumped. *Even aliens get allergies when they live in Seattle long enough.* Then he spoke. "Europe is under Sergio's scope of authority. He'll wonder why you are going there."

"You'll think of something to tell him. If you want a real plan, that is."

There was a moment of silence. *Shit. I pushed him too far. I'm going to die, or be cyborg-ized.*

Then Jones spoke. "I will have my assistant set up your travel. You have your one week."

"One Earth week. From tomorrow." *What the hell? If I'm going to die anyway, it might as well be after eight days instead of seven.*

"One Earth week, from tomorrow. You may leave now. This meeting is over." *That's how pricks always tried to show they were in charge, by having the last word.*

Louie needed to say one more thing to Jones before she left. "Don't you think you'd better, um, zip up before I open the door?"

"Oh. Right. Yes." The zipping up process was almost as horrific as the unzipping, with all his green lumpy flesh needing to be stuffed back into the too-small human skin, and Louie looked away. She could feel tears burning behind her eyes. She had one week—no, eight days—to do more than put together a plan. She had to save the human race.

Nine

When Louie left Jones' office, she expected his assistant and everyone else nearby to be staring. The whole unzipping and zipping back up process had seemed so, well, noisy, and then there had been her screaming. But no one paid any attention at all. She glanced over her shoulder and caught Jones' eye—one of only two of them now, thankfully—and he gestured toward the edge of the door—oh, she saw it now. *Weather-stripping. Of course, they'd soundproofed the CEO's office when they remodeled it for him.* Well, at least she wasn't going to have to waste time explaining her screaming to anyone.

Although Jones mentioned he would set up her travel with his assistant, Alice, Louie knew he would immediately forget having made any such promise. "Hey Alice." She tried to sound normal, but to her own ears, her voice sounded like she was talking into a tin can. "He wants me to go visit the eastern European operation ASAP—like tomorrow. Can you get me a flight?"

"Sure thing, Louie." Alice was one of the few normal people working around Jones. Louie really, really hoped she didn't turn out to be an alien, too. "What's the rush?"

"Oh you know how these guys work—never a plan, only a string of crises." Louie cast around for a plausible one. "Sergio is playing fast and loose with the rules again, and Tom wants me to sneak in and see what's really going on." That was always true. No matter what Sergio's hand was in—*I wonder how many hands he really has?*—he always tried to get away with something.

"But I know you hate to travel, so it must be serious if he's making you get on a plane tomorrow," said Alice.

"Actually, I wanted it to be right away." Louie needed to

make this sound less interesting, or Alice would start talking to the other assistants about it. "I'm having the house fumigated, so I've already arranged for Buddy and the cats to stay somewhere else for a week, and I was going to have to be in a hotel anyway. Might as well do it in Europe, on the company dime."

That sounded plausible. Louie often talked about the old house in an old Seattle neighborhood she was renovating, and all its problems. But it made her realize she was going to have to find a place for Buddy and the cats. She'd call her aunt—Louie hated to ask her aunt for favors, but this time she had no choice.

"Right on." Like most of the staff, Alice was always ready to take a little extra from the company whenever the opportunity presented itself. "Hey, if you want, I can use Tom's frequent flier miles and upgrade you to business class."

"Hell yes, leg room is always appreciated. But I didn't know you can transfer those things."

"Oh yeah, about six months ago we got him on a plan where any company 'executive' can use them and with all these C-titles floating around, even you are an executive!"

Louie smiled in spite of the knot in her stomach. Alice's kindness in taking care of her made Louie feel tears pressing on her eyes again.

"Someday I hope I can tell you how much this means to me right now." Louie's voice quieted, and Alice's face became quizzical. *Damn, I'm making it interesting again.* Louie exaggerated a sniffle. "I love you, man!"

Alice laughed and turned back to her computer. "Do you want me to set up your hotel, too?"

"No thanks, I'm staying with Jack." *What the hell? Where did that come from?* She and Jack had become close over the last few months, through their increasingly long email and Skype chat conversations, but she knew staying with him was a bad idea. This trip should look as normal as possible, and bunking in with the Director of Quality Assurance and Underling Morale for European Operations on a business trip was anything but normal. Alice stared at her. "I mean, I'll call Jack and have him make the reservations from there. They get a better deal as locals."

Alice shrugged. "Okay, let me know if you need anything else."

"Thanks." Louie scooted back to her office before she could run into anyone else. She called her aunt to set up the pet care. Louie's Aunt Emma moved to Seattle from their hometown, a little place east of the Cascade Mountains called Zillah, to stay close to Louie when she went to college. Often Louie longed to have more distance between herself and her aunt, but she couldn't deny it helped to have a trusted critter-sitter nearby.

"Hello?" Emma picked up the phone on the fourth ring, as usual.

"Hi, Aunt Emma."

"Louie? I just came in from working at the bookstore. I saw that guy there, you remember, the one who was in my poetry class." Louie's aunt always answered the phone and picked right up in the middle of the conversation she thought she'd been having with Louie since the last phone call. Most of the time Louie didn't really listen, she just made "mm-hmmm" and "oh, wow" sounds at what seemed like the appropriate places. But today she interrupted.

"Em, I need you to look after Buddy and the cats for me."

"You do? Why?"

Louie thought for a minute and decided it was better to manage as few lies at one time as possible.

"My boss is sending me to Europe for about a week. We have some issues over there and he wants me to go in 'under the radar' and do some fact-finding. I have to leave tomorrow."

"Why is he sending you so soon? Why doesn't he give you time to get ready? He takes advantage of you, he really does."

Oh Aunt Em, if you only knew. "It's okay, I don't mind as long as the kids can stay with you; I know you'll take good care of them." Louie's stomach clutched again. When she dropped Buddy and the cats off at her aunt's, would that be the last time she ever saw them?

"I love them, you know that. My cats will be thrilled with the company."

"Great, thanks. I'll drop them off this afternoon after I get home. About five?"

"Well, I'll be at my exercise class until at least then."

"Okay, five-thirty?"

"I'll try to be home."

"Thanks, Aunt Em. I love you. I have to get back to work."

"Louie? Are you okay?" Louie's aunt was typically unaware of anyone's part of the conversation except her own. Now all of a sudden her motherly instincts kicked in. *Hell, if Aunt Em is noticing your emotional state, you really have to get a grip on yourself.*

"I'm fine, just a little frazzled with getting ready for this trip."

"Okay. Did I tell you about what happened at the bookstore? This man came in, you know the one I mean, what is his name? The nice one. Anyway…"

"Aunt Em, I have to go back to work."

"Oh, of course dear. I'll see you tonight."

"Thanks, Em." Louie hung up the phone. She looked at the clock on her computer. It was just before noon. She could gather up some papers and her laptop, get something to eat, go home and pack. It wasn't like she was going to get any other work done today—it wasn't like any other work mattered, anyway.

Louie printed the eticket confirmation Alice sent, shut down her laptop, and began putting some papers in her briefcase. She stopped when she felt her fingers touch the sale agreement. She was glad she'd taken it with her out of Jones's office, although she didn't recall doing so. She packed it in between other stuff that she could use to make her cover story of checking on the European operation plausible. Although she didn't trust that it would ever really work, that agreement was the closest thing she had to real proof of what was happening. She'd better keep it with her at all times.

As she was getting ready to leave, her phone rang. She looked at the caller ID—it was an area code 202 number—Washington, DC. She picked it up.

"Mac?"

"Louie! How the hell are you doing?" Mac was calling from her current job in the State Department. State cherry-picked her after she published her paper on the uses of late-night television for pro-democracy propaganda. They made her an offer she couldn't refuse, not that she would have looked for a reason to refuse it. Mac took an immediate dislike to the new regime of Jones and Eastwood, and she leapt at the chance to go back East, where she grew up and still had family.

"I'm fine, a little hectic—"

"Good, good! Hey, I read about the latest Sergio craziness. What's the inside scoop?"

Mac worked with Sergio long enough to remain obsessed with his incompetence. Louie could hardly blame her, being pretty well obsessed with him, in her own way. The wires picked up a press release PPP3 sent out to announce yet another manufacturing partnership, this time with a toy factory in Macao. The partnership was old news, but the wires picked it up now because this factory's CEO was being accused of setting it up just to launder drug money, which not only was illegal, but also pissed off the mafia who wanted all the drug money laundered through their Macaoan casinos. And of course, PPP3 proudly proclaimed its use of a "state of the art, highly ethical manufacturing plant" to make its latest crappy plastic device. So now they were being dragged into the mob story. No products were ever made, but rumors flew that PPP3 took in some Macao money as "transfers in kind" from the partnership anyway.

Still, Louie didn't have time to go into all this now. And Mac was one of the handful of people in the world who Louie really trusted. And she was at State..."Mac, I—"

"Yeah?"

"I can't go into it now, but I might need your help."

"You got it. What's up?"

"Sorry, Mac, I can't give you the details now. I'm going to the European operation tomorrow—"

"You are? Why? You hate to travel!"

"Yeah, but I have to go, and when I get there, I'll call you, okay?"

"Okay, sure. Are you in trouble?"

"I—I'm afraid we all are, Mac."

"Oh Louie, what have Jones and Sergio done now?"

"I'll talk to you tomorrow."

"Okay—call my cell, I've got a bunch of meetings on the

Hill but I'll get back to you as soon as I can."

"Thanks. Hey, Mac?"

"Yeah?"

"Nothing, I just wish you were still here."

"Are you sure you're okay, Louie?"

"No, but I'm sure I have to go."

Louie hung up. Jack popped into her mind again then, not because she thought he could do anything, but because after that escapade with him, when they'd first met at the company conference in Seattle the previous fall, she felt she could trust him. At least he wouldn't immediately assume she was crazy. She hoped. Or at least he would tell her if she was crazy, if she'd lost her mind. Jack knew something about dealing with the impossible and the absurd. It struck Louie just how impossible and absurd this whole thing was. Her boss an alien, the color of bad lime Jell-O? Despite the number of times— at least hundreds—Louie and Mac complained that Jones was so out of touch with reality he must be from another planet, they were just kidding, weren't they? Like people saying "I'm going to kill you," because they are so angry with someone, but they don't ever really mean they're going to kill that person. Do they? Louie shuddered recalling Jones' statement about killing her. He certainly seemed serious enough.

More frightening, because it was even more unexpected, was her apparently immediate decision to try to save the human race, distant and incomprehensible as humans were to her, as often as she'd railed about their faults and foibles...and the idea that she had the skill or intelligence or courage to do it. Now that was completely absurd, and probably impossible.

I should be having a nervous breakdown. I should be curling up under my desk in a fetal position, forsaking all speech, staying there until—well, until the world ends or they turn me into a cyborg. But for some reason, she wasn't. She was getting ready to take on these alien pricks, and it even felt good. *I guess I'm doing this for Buddy.* She pictured the little dog waiting for her. *I doubt cyborgs know much about how to take care of dogs.*

She picked up her stuff and grabbed her coat and walked to the elevator. The familiar hallway, with its familiar beige walls, beige carpets, cheap office furniture, harsh florescent lighting, bad art on the walls—it all seemed very strange all of a sudden, and at the same time, very dear. Louie didn't know when she would see it again. She dropped her stuff in a pile by the elevator, and ran back to her office. *Where is it?* Panic blurred her vision, making it hard to search. She rifled her desk drawers, rummaged through the stacks of paper on her shelves. *There it is.* She grabbed it and pressed it between her hands. It was just a silly photo, one of her and Mac, at Mac's going-away dinner. They were at a table in a restaurant, leaning into each other's arms, grinning like young girls. Louie remembered the waiter who took the photo at Mac's request. The moment he'd captured was special, the two of them on their last day as the dynamic duo of PPP3. Louie put the photo in her coat pocket and walked back to the elevator, punched the button, picked up her stuff, and when the doors slid open, she was relieved to see it was empty, so she could cry all the way to the parking garage.

Ten

Louie remembered when Jones and Sergio arrived at PPP3, about three years earlier, shortly after the sudden sale of the company and disappearance of its founder. She'd just arrived at work that morning when her phone rang. She'd looked at the caller ID. It was Alice, Paster's executive assistant.

"Hi, Alice. How can I help?" Louie usually answered calls this way, a joke to herself, given her typical inability to make anything good happen at PPP3.

"Louie, there's a command performance. The Board chair is about to make an important announcement. Can you be in the large conference room in five minutes?" Alice sounded more tense than usual.

"Sure, I can cancel my meeting. But what is it? Do you know?"

Alice whispered, "I'm not sure, Louie, but I think they've hired a new CEO."

"What? The search committee's only met once. They haven't even reviewed resumes yet..."

"That's right Louie, the large conference room in five minutes." Alice's voice turned formal.

"Oh, he walked in, huh? Okay, sorry. I won't put you on the spot. I'll be there." Five minutes later, Louie sat next to Mac in the large conference room.

"Mac, do you know what's up?"

"New CEO," she whispered. Leave it to Mac to know before most people.

"But how...when..."

"Well, I heard—"

A sudden bang made Louie jump.

"Is this on?" The Board chair was one of those small men who tried to make up for lack of stature by becoming an even bigger asshole than their normal-sized counterparts. He used to be Paster's lawyer, but wrangled his way onto the Board, and quickly leap-frogged over the kindly ex-banker who was in line for the Chair when the old guy died of a heart attack. He dressed in impeccably tailored suits that reminded Louie of those plastic discs you colored and then shrunk in the oven—same details, miniature size. The Board chair tapped a hand-held microphone. Every tap made a loud bang through the speakers.

BANG! "Is this on?" *BANG!* "Is it on? Can you hear me?" *BANG!*

"Is he deaf or an idiot?" Mac whispered.

"Yes! We can hear you!" someone shouted from the back of the room, finally loud enough to be heard over the loud banging.

"Okay, well then—" *SCREEEECH!* "What the fu—?"

The Board chair wandered too close to the loudspeaker and generated a wicked feedback howl. Now the room filled up, and the employees were rolling their eyes and murmuring. "What a chucklehead," Louie heard from someone behind her. Finally the Board chair seemed to be a safe distance from the speakers, and convinced himself that the microphone was working.

"Welcome to this special—" *BEEP!* "Okay, what the hell!"

Alice walked up to him and whispered, "Sir, that's the conference phone. Someone just called in. You requested an open conference line to the Eastern Europe operation, remember?"

"Oh, yes, right. Well, then. Welcome, everyone, to this special announcement from your Board. I am Calvin Allemonde, your Board chair." He paused for the applause he fully expected. The room stayed silent. Allemonde coughed.

"Okay, well, as I said, welcome to this special announcement. As you know, Chief Executive Officer Paster resigned, ahem, suddenly about a month ago. To spend more time with his family." A knowing chuckle passed among the crowd. Everyone knew the Paster family members hated one another with the kind of passion reserved for those bound by blood, money, and vicious greed. If they were spending more time together, it could only end in death and destruction. "And you know the Board takes our responsibility to hire an excellent Chief Executive Officer very seriously. We know this organization needs an excellent Chief Executive Officer who is committed to excellence, who has excellent depth of experience in pursuing excellence, and who will ensure that this organization maintains and improves the standards of excellence it has so excellently pursued over the years."

"Oh my god, it's a freak show," Mac muttered under her breath.

"I am pleased to announce we have found such an excellent man. May I introduce Mr. Thomas Lee Jones."

Louie focused on the man standing beside Allemonde. He was tall, with greying brown close-cropped hair, clean-shaven, and a pale complexion. Louie was terrible at guessing people's ages but, if she had to, she'd peg him at about sixty. He wore an expensive looking suit that didn't exactly fit—a little too short in the sleeves, a little too tight across the shoulders, a little too long in the trousers. His tie was slightly askew. *An absent-minded professor?*

"Thank you, Mr. Chair." Jones' voice was gravelly and sounded older than he looked. *Maybe he's a smoker, or a drinker. Or both.* "Now I'm sure you are wondering how I was selected for the special honor of being your Chief Executive Officer. Well, I've known Chair Almond—"

"Allemonde," Allemonde whispered, looking grumpy.

"Sorry, Chair Allemonde. I've known him for eons, er, years. When he called to tell me he was launching a search for a new CEO for your wonderful organization, I said, Almond, my friend—"

"Allemonde!"

"Right, I said, Allemonde, my friend, I'm recently retired, and my wife wants me out of the house!" Jones chuckled as if he were the first middle-aged white man to ever make that joke. It took him a few minutes to realize no one else was laughing. "So, Almon-I mean, Calvin, I said, so Calvin, why not hire me? I love a challenge!" Jones smiled broadly and scanned the room. "And so suddenly, Almon—Calvin saw the sense it made, and here I am!" Allemonde jabbed him in the arm. "Oh, and it's a deep honor that I feel very deeply to be here. I look forward to serving you all, and making this organization so much more excellent than it has been up to today. Thank you very much."

Allemonde took the microphone back. "And Chief Executive Officer Jones, did you want to introduce our new Vice President?"

"Oh, yes, right. Eastwood, where are you?" A thin, dark man emerged from a shadow in the corner. *Now when did he come in? I'm sure I didn't see him there—*

"This is the new Vice President for—for—um—" Jones turned toward the man, who whispered something in his ear. "Right, Vice President for Special Initiatives, including new titles for all executives at the company. Mr. Sergio Leone Eastwood."

"That's not a real name," someone whispered.

Mac nodded. "It's his name, though. I saw it on the IT order to get him a security ID. It's crazy. Louie, what do you think?"

But Louie didn't answer. She stared at the new Vice President.

"Thank you, Chair Allemonde and Chief Executive Officer Jones," He spoke with perfect English diction. "I, too, am deeply honored to be here, as Chief Executive Officer Jones commented. I know this may be something of a surprise, to be told of two new executives in one day. But I can assure you that the Board has gone through a very demanding selection process in which they carefully considered all the possible synergies and convergences that such a move would provide to the organization. And we have been charged with maximizing those convergences and synergies in such a way as to not only benefit said organization, but also to provide new and potential opportunities for the constituencies we choose to service."

Everyone in the room stared at him.

"Huh?" Mac grunted. "Anyone know what that means?"

Louie barely heard anything. All of her attention focused on his eyes. They were black. Her stomach tightened into a knot. *He's bad news. Very bad news.*

BEEEEEP!!

The sound made everyone jump. "Someone hung up on the conference line to Europe," whispered Mac. "Jeez, they should learn to put that thing on mute."

Eleven

After a start-up history that included selling out of the trunk of his car, working his way up to his garage, a rented storage unit, and then a surplused elementary school, Paster finally made enough money to move PPP3's headquarters into a relatively new office park just outside Seattle. Cheap enough to bring the elementary school furniture with him, even now, fifteen years later, some employees were still stuck with guest chairs in their offices suitable only for visitors weighing less than eighty pounds. The office park was in a suburb just off the freeway, less than three turns after the exit, a Paster Principle for locating your business. Never make a customer turn more than twice, or they're likely to get lost and find your competition instead, he would say. It was lost on him that his customers were all finding his products on late night television, and the only people driving to headquarters, other than the staff who worked there, were vendors peddling insurance, new copy machines, or coffee supplies.

A few years before Paster sold out and moved away, he'd started a legendary battle between the Coke and Pepsi vendors for the staff lounge soda machine contract. Over six months, Paster kept them at each other's throats, switching from one to the other, to the point where the staff seeking a beverage with their lunches never knew on any given day if they'd be able to get a Coke for a dollar or a Pepsi for seventy five cents. Oddly, this generated one of the very few official complaints about Paster to Human Resources. People tolerated his dirty jokes, his temper, and his propensity to fire someone on a whim; but one employee was damned if he was going to go another day without his Pepsi.

The employee's name was Mr. Sack. He had a first name,

but no one called him by it. Mr. Sack worked as the controller for
PPP3. At the time of the Great Pepsi Battle, Mr. Sack was about
fifty-five years old and looking forward to retirement. He was a gruff
old geezer, short and wiry, with grey hair thinning on his head and
thickening in his ears. He spent most of his time reviewing expense
reports for inaccuracies or policy violations, anything that might give
him a reason to deny reimbursement. Paster loved him for that. If
Mr. Sack showed up at your cubicle with your expense report in his
hand, his reading glasses sliding down his nose, and his trademark
cough, you simply took your report back and fed it to the shredder. It
didn't do any good to argue or debate. Mr. Sack did not engage in the
battle if he was not sure he'd already won.

Mr. Sack bought a Pepsi every day to drink with the lunch
his wife packed him at home. She made him a ham and Swiss cheese
on cracked-wheat bread sandwich, included a five-ounce bag of
Fritos, and a piece of fruit. Usually it was an apple, but in the
summer sometimes Mrs. Sack would get creative and include a
peach or nectarine—Mr. Sack would usually be disappointed in its
condition by the time he ate, a single bruise being enough to put him
off eating the entire thing. Mr. Sack would open his lunch bag at his
desk, lay out his sandwich, chips, and fruit, and then head to the staff
kitchen vending area for his Pepsi. The first day after the Coke
machine appeared, because the vendor convinced Paster he'd
recognize a twenty-percent higher kickback, Mr. Sack had been fine.
He'd calmly returned to his desk and eaten his lunch as the rest of his
staff held their breaths. The second and third days were much the
same. The fourth day, Mr. Sack went to Paster's office after lunch.
He'd come out and gone back to work. The fifth day the Pepsi
machine was back.

But not for long. Paster realized he could play the two
vendors off each other and the Coke machine came back a few days
later. Mr. Sack visited Paster again, but this time he'd come out of
the office red in the face. As the weeks went by and the battle raged,
Mr. Sack grew redder and thinner. Soon he could not eat his lunch.
His coworkers feared for him, but did not want to risk getting in the
middle of the battle. They'd watched from the sidelines and clucked
their tongues. Once, a young assistant in the office, a temp who'd

only been there a couple of days, got disgusted and went to the mini mart down the street. She'd returned with a cold Pepsi and placed it on Mr. Sack's desk as he sat there staring at his ham and Swiss. "For god's sake, you can get these anywhere, you know." Then she'd turned to the gathered staff. "You are all imbeciles, really." She'd packed her few temp-like personal items from her desk and left, never to be seen at PPP3 again.

As she'd left, Mr. Sack muttered something to himself, and walked to the Human Resources Director's office.

"What did he say?" asked one staffer.

"I think he said, 'that's not the point,'" replied another, "but he might have said, 'I need a joint.'"

"You're ridiculous, Mr. Sack wouldn't smoke a joint," the first employee scoffed. Mr. Sack emerged from the Director's office a few moments later. The Director visited Paster. The next day, there was no vending machine at all in the staff kitchen. The staff all noticed its absence when they gathered in the kitchen to discuss the Human Resource Director's email that morning, announcing his early retirement.

It was events like this that led some of the longer-time staffers to reminisce nostalgically about how much better things were before PPP3 got too big for the elementary school. They did not believe that the office park setting, with its low-slung, modern buildings, tall glass windows that would not open, air conditioning that was always too cold in the summer and heating that was always too anemic in the winter, even its semi-bucolic setting backing against a greenbelt filled with invasive blackberries, scraggly old evergreens, and goldenrod, they did not believe this was an improvement. Neither did Mac, whose allergies were set off by the goldenrod. Louie didn't like the commute across Lake Washington to her Seattle neighborhood, but other than that, she felt PPP3 was the sort of company that would be out of place anywhere, so it didn't much matter if it was uncomfortable in an elementary school or mismatched into a suburban office park.

Louie often thought of PPP3 as a haven for mediocrity. Anyone who had too much ambition would move on quickly, to some place or business where ambition was recognized and rewarded. Anyone who didn't want to do much of anything could find a nook or corner and stick at PPP3 for a while. If they were savvy enough, they could do just enough, horde just enough information, to stick for a very long time.

There were exceptions of course. Without them, the company would have gone under years before. There was Mac, who seemed unable to work at anything other than warp speed, until she burned out like a rocket suddenly emptied of fuel. There was Alice, the assistant who would be assigned to whichever executive was currently floundering, and she would quietly and efficiently do his work for him until the floundering ceased or the executive was fired. When it was all the Paster family as executives, Alice worked for whichever son-in-law needed her most, but everyone knew she really worked for Paster. She was the only one immune from the family squabbling and backstabbing, and everyone assumed she had something on them or on Paster himself, but they didn't begrudge her a little blackmail because she was always ready to smooth things over or plug a hole in their own dikes if necessary.

Louie lasted because she didn't scare anyone. None of the Paster sons-in-law felt a glimmer of interest in her, so she didn't threaten the daughters. Despite her discomfort with the new Jones-Sergio regime, she never rose far enough above the background noise for them to feel threatened, either. Her weekly meetings with Jones on planning or strategy or market research were usually perfunctory. If he could assign her something he would. If she had a problem he'd dismiss it as quickly as possible, and the only times their meetings lasted the full hour scheduled was when he wanted to show off a new big idea or grand scheme. Louie learned quickly that he only sought an audience. She obliged outwardly while rebelling internally, and often let herself imagine the conversations she should be having with Jones, if she was brave enough.

You'd better get Mac out from under Sergio, if you want to keep her around, and trust me, you do, she's the smartest employee you have, and her research is going to put her in high demand out on the job market.

What are you letting Josef get away with in the Eastern Europe operation? You're going to have a sweatshop scandal in the factory there if you don't make him do his job.

If you make me produce another market research study and implementation plan you know you won't ever use, I'm going to quit.

But despite the belief of most PPP3 employees that Louie wielded some sort of influence with Jones, she never held those conversations out loud. She did try, once in a while, to sneak some recommendations into her market analyses. "Americans are more concerned than ever with the working conditions of the people who make the items they buy," she'd write. Or, "research shows that high-performing sales organizations are the ones that invest in retaining their best people." She always delivered the analyses on time, as assigned, and with full plans for implementation based on the findings. Like Paster before him, Jones always put them on his bookshelf and did exactly what he'd wanted to do anyway.

PPP3ers were used to bad leadership. The smarter among them knew they were and would always be a small company with big pretensions as cheesy as their products. Paster watched Starbucks and Microsoft take off over the years, and remained convinced Seattle was the right place for PPP3, too.

"A hotbed of innovation," he called the area, while making terrible business decisions that killed the most innovative ideas PPP3 generated. But the Jones-Sergio regime surpassed even Paster in creating an ever-widening gap between what the company could do in reality, and their fantastical expectations for it. Jones even joked about "taking over the world" and "conquering this planet, I mean, this industry." Their deals multiplied, PPP3's revenues kept sliding. Jones seemed entirely in Sergio's thrall. As deal after deal fell apart, Jones' ambitions only increased.

Mac had been beside herself at the waste of resources. Louie dutifully prepared more research reports to support new strategies. The rest of the employees grew ever more cynical. And the beat went on.

Twelve

Louie's bad feeling about Sergio had been confirmed soon enough, when he fired dear old Mr. Sack. Mr. Sack clung on at PPP3 like so many of its ninety-eight employees. It was funny, there had always been ninety-eight employees for as long as Louie'd been paying attention. If one left, another arrived. If a position was created in one department, someone in another department got fired. That's what happened to Mr. Sack, finally, and Louie was the only one who refrained from making the obvious joke about his name. Not because she was particularly kind or sensitive, though that's what most people thought. Because she didn't see anything funny in the situation.

About three months after arriving at PPP3 with Jones, Sergio had returned from one of his mysterious international deal-making trips, this time to South America, or so the rumor mill claimed, with the announcement that he'd hired a new crony, with the improbable title of Special Assistant to the Vice President for Special Initiatives. Speculation raged through the company about who would get fired to make room, to the extent that Jones sent an all-staff email reassuring everyone that PPP3 could afford a ninety-ninth employee, or even a one-hundredth, if it came to that, and any superstition to the contrary was just that—utterly absurd superstition.

Fifty-five minutes later, Mr. Sack's parting email went out to the same all-staff distribution list. Louie knew why. Her office was close enough to Mr. Sack's cubicle to have seen Sergio's assistant deliver his expense report from the trip to South America, and to have seen the papers handed back to her with a shake of Mr. Sack's head. Unallowable, undocumented expense, she heard him mutter to the hapless assistant. In tears, the assistant stopped at Louie's door.

This happened every day; some PPP3 staffer or other with a problem that was none of Louie's doing, a problem she couldn't solve, stopping by her office to ask her to undo or fix it. Most of the time all she could do was offer a sympathetic ear, and afterwards she would renew her resolve to simply turn these help-seekers away, though she never seemed able to carry it through.

"What am I going to say to him?" the assistant had asked Louie.

"Let me see the report." When Louie saw what Sergio was trying to bill to the company, what prompted Mr. Sack to reject the entire expense report, she frowned. "That's all? Oh, for chrissakes, Sergio can cover that out of his own pocket. No need to make a fuss." The charge was for something called a 0356 cable, in the amount of thirteen dollars and ninety-five cents. The assistant left, not entirely reassured. *What a prick. Sergio, buying some cord thingy for his big flat screen television home theater set up, or whatever, and trying to pass it off on the company.* The next day Mr. Sack was sent packing.

"It was a ploy," Mac insisted. "Sergio wanted that position—his Special Assistant to the Special Needs Vice President, or whatever the hell his title is—and despite what Jones says, Sergio knew someone would have to go to make room. Who better than the one person in the company who would question his crazy expenses? So he throws a little dubious expense in there, knowing Mr. Sack will bite—and then *bam!* Mr. Sack himself is bitten off and spit out."

"I don't know, Mac. Is Sergio that devious?" Louie frowned at Mac.

"Deviouser, is my bet, and before you say anything, Louie, I know 'deviouser' isn't a real word." Mac turned out to be right, as usual. Over the next few months, as Sergio pitched deal after deal for PPP3, and each one fell apart more or less spectacularly, anyone who openly questioned Sergio's incompetence either quit, retired, was fired, or, in one especially sad case, died. Each time, Jones insisted no such thing was happening, right before it did. "Jones is a prick, but Sergio—he's an asshole," Mac said, after Mr. Sack's cake and Pepsi going away party.

Thirteen

Mac started at the company when she was only twenty-two, working part-time as a receptionist while she earned her MBA. Eventually she'd worked her way all the way up to Vice President of Sales and Customer Service; then she was dubbed Chief Experience Officer by the Jones regime. On her way, Mac had worked in almost every department, and her unassuming appearance —and the fact she was a girl— meant that the men in charge didn't take her seriously enough to censor themselves around her. She knew where all the closets were that hid all the skeletons, knew who the skeletons were when the flesh was still on their bones, and knew why they'd been turned into skeletons.

Louie and Mac bonded over a prick. In fact, Louie didn't know that word until Mac came into her life. *Leave it to a lesbian to teach me about that part of the male anatomy.*

The prick in question was Paster's son-in-law, Truman, called Idiot Boy by other PPP3 employees behind his back. Having married the youngest and most multiple-substance-addicted Paster daughter, they'd always tinged his nickname with a dose of pity, even after Idiot Boy turned from stupid to mean. In Louie's second year at the company, Idiot Boy, proving that, among his other shortcomings, he had no gaydar, came on to Mac.

The scene outside the women's bathroom was predictable. A nearly deserted hallway—neither Idiot Boy nor Mac realized Louie was working late that night—the clumsy yet aggressive advances, which included the proud showing off of an erect yet rather small male member. The expression of disgust followed by a resounding slap across Idiot Boy's face. The sound of that slap roused Louie from her office and brought her to see what was going on, just as

Mac went on: "If that's not enough to get my message across, I'll hit you a little lower, and I mean a very, very little, you prick—"

Idiot Boy, taking offense not at the threat of violence—which actually inflamed his desire further—but at the insinuation that his proudly erect member was not of sufficiently impressive size, raised his hand to strike Mac. Louie walked up behind him, and asked what was going on, which gave Mac the chance to duck. Idiot Boy's fist landed harmlessly against the wall. Mac kneed him in the groin and grabbed Louie by the hand, striding in her high heels down the hall back to Louie's office while Louie scrambled to keep up, as usual.

"What was all that with Truman, Mac?" Louie asked, after Mac pulled the office door shut and locked it behind them.

"Oh, never mind him. He's a prick on his way to becoming an asshole, and I just refused to be a step on his path." Mac shuddered. "Thanks for coming when you did, creating a diversion so I could take him down, Lou."

"I didn't do anything."

"Sure you did, Louie. Right place, right time—that's always something. And I owe you one. Mind if I stay here in your office a while? Until the coast is clear? I don't want to risk hurting my knee if I have to do that again."

"Of course, Mac. Stay as long as you like. I've got a ton of stuff to work—"

"Great," Mac cut her off. "Now tell me your story. What's a nice girl like you doing at a place like PPP3?" They'd gone on to talk for hours that night. Louie always felt slightly abashed, like an imposter who'd gotten away with her act, knowing that Mac thought she'd rescued her that night. In fact, Louie really hadn't known what was going on in that hallway. She struggled to read most interpersonal situations with any kind of accuracy. But she was grateful to Mac for taking her under her wing, and set about trying to earn the trust Mac placed in her during that first battle. She took Mac's lesson to heart.

"Right place, right time." And she devoted herself to trying to be there for Mac from then on.

~ * ~

About three months before Louie discovered the mysterious sales agreement, while they worked late together, Mac took Louie into her confidence.

"Lou, I've been working on something."

"What's that, Mac?" Louie figured it was the new sales campaign, or something equally mundane.

"A paper."

"Like a newspaper? A newsletter for the company or something?" That didn't sound like Mac, but one never knew.

"No, a scholarly paper."

"Scholarly?"

"Yeah. I've been taking some classes, you know, toward a Ph.D."

"What? When? How would you have the time?" Mac was the smartest person Louie knew, but she didn't show it around the company very much. Mac went about her business intimidating others with her work ethic and sharp tongue, but Louie knew there was a seriously brilliant brain in there.

"Tuesday nights, mostly. Didn't you notice I always left early on Tuesdays?"

Louie felt embarrassed. Too many of her own Tuesday nights spent in the Archive Room for her to notice Mac's change in routine.

Mac brushed away her blank look with an unconcerned wave of her hand. "Anyway, I've been working on this paper about how late night television can be an effective tool for propaganda. You know, like for the government and the military? It's fascinating, really, what you can get people to buy when you bombard them with messages, some obvious but most subliminal, during the times when they are sleepless. Well, if you can get people to buy stuff, you could get them to do other things, too, I figured. So I started looking up the research, and doing a little of my own."

Louie's eyes widened in surprise. "You mean those focus groups? I thought those were on our new sales campaign."

Mac laughed. "Yeah, well, I slipped in a few extra questions. It's okay, no one got hurt. And I discovered a few pretty interesting things. It turns out this professor of mine has contacts at the State

Department of all places. He told one of them about my research. The guy was interested. He emailed me the next day, in fact."

"He wants to read your paper?" Louie could sense where this was going.

"That too, yeah. But he offered me a job, Lou. A job at State."

"I don't know Mac, that's great, but—" Louie paused and considered. "First of all, we can't get by without you here. But also, it makes me a little nervous to think of my government being interested in selling me stuff on late night television."

Mac's eyebrow shot up. "Me too. The thing is, I guess there are other governments already doing this kind of thing. Peddling their wares, if you want to put it that way, to their people—and others—on late night television. I checked it out. Do you ever watch late night television, by the way, Lou?"

"Me? No way. I know what PPP3 sells on there, and I don't really want to see the other plastic crap we compete with." *And I'd rather read a good book.*

"You ought to watch, sometime, just as an experiment. It's incredible, what's out there," Mac said. "According to this guy, State thinks we can't be left out."

"Even if it is somehow good for the country," Louie forged on, "that still leaves reason number one. We can't run this place without you. Especially now that Paster's gone and we have Jones and Eastwood playing Keystone Kops with the company." Mac had recently been assigned to work under Sergio, as his "right hand," despite the fact that he was supposed to be focused on international expansion and Mac was clearly in charge of domestic sales. Louie knew it grated on her for that reason, but also because she was so much smarter than Sergio. Jones played it off as a kind of quasi-promotion for Mac, but Mac and Louie and everyone in the company knew better. Mac was babysitting, plain and simple.

"Well, it's giving me a chance to visit Europe," Mac said. "I've been working at a distance with our guy there—what's his name?"

"Josef?" Louie tried to picture the two of them working together, Mac and Josef.

"No, the other guy," Mac shook her head. "Jack. Jack Smith. He's a good one. Josef's just a Sergio flunky. Jack takes his job seriously."

"What is his job?"

"Oh hell, who knows? Kind of like yours and mine, whatever needs doing."

"Well, at least stick around long enough to get that trip to Europe." Louie felt her insides slip with the knowledge that it was only a matter of time before Mac decided to take this guy at State up on his offer.

"It's Eastern Europe, and that's barely Europe at all," Mac chuckled, and changed the subject.

Fourteen

Louie recalled meeting Jack for the first time at the annual inventors' conference put on by PPP3. A tradition that went back to the early days of the company, the conferences were recognized as great window-dressing by the founding CEO, Jerome Paster. Sergio and Jones kept them going but, because they didn't really know anyone else in the industry, the conferences devolved into long, dry sessions of speeches by Sergio and Jones. No one from outside PPP3 attended anymore. All the staff dreaded the conferences. No one wanted to spend this much time on useless presentations and strategy discussions for such a small, lame company. Still, it was a command performance to show up and be a good audience, especially if you reported directly to either Jones or Sergio. Louie arrived the morning of this one with a feeling of dread in her stomach. As soon as she'd walked in the door to the conference room, she heard her name.

"Louie! Come sit by me!" Sitting next to Mac meant they could at least share the pain of sitting through the boring speeches, and make mocking comments under their breath. This time they'd talked about Sergio's latest trip to Europe, which, apparently, he hadn't told Jones about until he was back.

"Why in hell does Tom let him get away with it?" Louie fumed.

"I don't know, but I have a feeling Sergio keeps lots of secrets from Jones."

"That's probably not too hard to do, knowing Tom. I need coffee, Mac. I'll be right back." Louie stood and turned toward the back of the room, where the old coffee urns used at PPP3 meetings for as long as she could remember were set out with some stale pastries that looked almost as old. As she turned, she collided with someone equally oblivious to his surroundings in the primal hunt for caffeine. "Oh, sorry," Louie mumbled, and ducked around the man—she'd noticed his red jacket, but little more—got her coffee, and went back to Mac's table.

"Hey, there's Jack!" Mac pointed as Louie sat down. When Paster opened the Eastern European factory in a little town near Prague—to avoid some taxes, or so he said— Jack was hired to teach English to the factory workers. While Louie sipped her coffee and nibbled her stale doughnut, Mac whispered to her. "He's probably jet lagged as hell, poor guy. Sergio only told him he had to come to this conference a few days ago. After he gave him his new title—Director of Quality Assurance and Underling Morale for European Operations."

"But no increase in salary, right?" Jones and Sergio were both notoriously cheap. The whole idea of manufacturing in Eastern Europe puzzled most of the people in the company, since the labor wasn't as cheap as in Latin America or as unregulated as in Asia. But Jones wouldn't kill it, and they'd kept Josef Tiso as the local Vice President. Now Jack reported to Josef. "And shit, everyone here knows Josef is, you know, connected." Louie heard the stories about the Eastern European mafia, how it moved into the vacuum when the Berlin Wall came down and the Soviet Union became Russia again.

"Exactly. They think Jack will just do what he's told, and not ask too many questions, but I think they're in for a surprise. There's more to Jack than meets the eye," Mac said.

Louie looked toward the door. "Which one is Jack?"

"Oh, that's right, you haven't met him yet. He's the one over there, in the red jacket."

Of course. Louie stifled a groan. *The guy I nearly took out on the way to the coffee table.* A slim man, with boyish good looks, she knew Jack was about forty, with a reputation for being easy-going, and not making waves. He kept his curly brown hair close-cropped and his glasses made his face look innocent, despite the glint in his brown eyes. He dressed like he just got off a plane—more comfortable than businesslike—in jeans, sneakers, and red fleece jacket. He heard Mac calling him and his tired expression lifted a little. He made his way through the gathering throng over to their table, carefully protecting his coffee cup.

"Jack!" Mac greeted him with a big hug. "Congratulations on the big new job!"

"Do you say congratulations to a man who's just been put in charge of the asylum?" Jack grinned at her.

"No." Louie shook her head. "I think the proper expression, in that case, is welcome to the nut house."

Jack laughed as Mac turned to her. "Jack, this is Louie. She's our planning—I mean, Chief Strategy Officer. You've heard me talk about her."

"I, uh, I think we've met, actually." Jack held out his hand for Louie to shake. "Good to meet you more formally, Louie. Everything Mac said about you was completely flattering, by the way."

"Nice to meet you, Jack. And don't believe a word of it. I'm actually a raving bitch, everyone here will confirm it, if you ask them privately." *Where did that come from? I'm not usually such a smartass with people I don't know.*

Jack looked Louie in the eyes, and held her gaze for longer than most people would.

"That's a relief," he finally said. "If I'm going to spend the next two days with you, I'll be much more comfortable knowing you're a raving bitch up front." Just then Jones stepped to the front of the room.

"Welcome to the annual inventors conference sponsored by PPP3. I would especially like to welcome our colleagues and partners from abroad. As you know, we are engaged in a concerted effort to expand our operations around the world. Thanks to the extensive knowledge and experience of my special assistant, Sergio Leone Eastwood, we are considering the potential for new operations in Latin America, Asia, Spxs...." Jones coughed. "I mean Australia. While we do not have any deals in place yet, we have a great deal of confidence that they will soon be generating the growth PPP3 needs to be successful well into the next decade. As a way of recognizing his efforts, I have a special announcement regarding Vice President Eastwood. Sergio, where are you?"

Sergio made his way to the front of the room, looking like a jittery marionette. Louie wouldn't be at all surprised if he peed his pants.

Jones continued. "In order for Vice President Eastwood to continue his fine work in expanding our presence around the world, he needs to be in a stronger position to negotiate on our behalf." Louie looked at Mac. What was Jones about to do? Then she realized that Jack, sitting on the other side of her, tensed up, his hands gripping the sides of his chair and knuckles turning white. *Is he even more worried than we are?*

"I am pleased to announce that I am appointing Mr. Eastwood as Vice Chair and Chief International Expansion Officer. Congratulations, Sergio!" As Jones reached out to shake Sergio's hand, an uncomfortable silence stretched in the audience of about seventy-five of PPP3's most dedicated, or cynical, employees. Louie felt Mac kick her ankle under the table. She felt, more than seen, Jack slump in his chair, as if in defeat. Someone finally took pity on the two men standing at the front of the room, looking around for a response, and started a tepid round of applause.

"Holy mother of dog," Jack whispered. "I didn't realize he would move this quickly."

"What's that?" When he'd turned toward her, she'd jumped a bit. *His eyes, weren't they brown before?* They seemed to be a strange foggy grey, with tiny pupils. Suddenly the grey eyes focused on her face, softened back to brown, so quickly she wasn't sure that she'd seen anything at all.

"I said, Sergio moves up fast, doesn't he? Maybe we should sit back and try to ride his coattails." He winked at Louie, but he hadn't looked at all amused. *Oh. He's one of those—make a joke anytime things get uncomfortable or crazy. Well, there are worse qualities. And he is pretty cute. No wonder Mac's taken him under her wing.*

At the first break, Mac grabbed Louie's sleeve. "Let's use the bathroom one floor down, so we can talk. Jack, we'll be right back. Girls gotta go to the powder room together!" They took the back stairs. "What the hell does Jones think he is doing? Does he really believe Sergio deserves a promotion? Vice Chair of Whatever the Hell That Means?" Mac ranted as soon as they were out of earshot of the rest of the crowd.

"I don't know." Louie shook her head. "I honestly don't know. Sometimes I think Tom is just as fed up with Sergio as the rest of us, and then he goes and pulls something like this."

"Well, I wasn't going to tell you until later, but I got another call from State." Louie remembered the night Mac told her about the job offer from the State Department, and their interest in her research on the uses of late-night television-based propaganda.

"And?" Given that morning's announcement, Louie knew Mac's answer before she asked.

"Louie, I have to take it. I can't continue to work here and support that...weasel." Mac might have meant Sergio or Jones, Louie didn't know for sure, though it didn't really matter.

"Of course you do, Mac. I'm amazed you held out this long." Louie swallowed hard. She'd known this was coming, but didn't want to let herself really face the possibility of working at PPP3 without Mac. "But oh hell...don't go, Mac. What are we going to do without you?" They both started to cry.

"Louie, you should come with me."

"I don't want to live in DC. I want to stay here. It's home." *Or the closest thing I have.*

"I know, but Jones knows that, too, and he's going to continue to take advantage of you, while he promotes Sergio the loser."

"Sergio the Vice Chair, you mean. Vice Chair of Darkness, I say. Well, I can find something else here."

"You can, but you won't. You're attached to this place, for some reason I can't figure out."

"Well, I—" Louie wondered, for the millionth time, why she didn't leave. It was almost as if she was waiting for something to happen, and she needed to be here and be ready. "I'm just a big chicken. I've got my little house, Buddy, the kitties, my cozy little life. I don't want to uproot it all." They left the ladies' room and walked back toward the stairwell. Jack came around the corner.

"What's the matter?" Genuine concern filled his voice.

"Why?" Mac turned away, just a little.

"You're late getting back, and...your eyes are red. Both of

you." Jack studied them.

"Oh, I just have allergies or something," Mac sounded as nonchalant as she could then blew her nose into her handkerchief.

"Both of you?" He didn't look like he believed her.

"It's Seattle, everyone here has allergies." Mac straightened her shoulders. "Come on, we'll be noticed if we stay away too long."

As they'd headed back upstairs, Mac whispered to Louie. "I have to take Jack to dinner tonight. I'm going to tell him I'm leaving. Come with me. I can't do it alone."

"Sure, no problem. I'll call doggy day care and have Stuart keep Buddy for a couple extra hours."

"Thanks, Lou. I'm really going to miss you."

"Let's not talk about it until we have to." Louie wasn't sure how she made it through the rest of that day. The talks had been dreadful, the room stultifying. Her heart felt heavy with the knowledge that Mac was leaving, and that Sergio solidified his status with Jones, and that she was trapped, even though she knew it was by her own choice. Occasionally, when there was enough noise to cover, Jack would whisper a joke or comment to her. Once, she laughed out loud and turned it into a cough before her boss noticed. It was only later she'd realized he was doing it on purpose, trying to make her feel better, even though he hadn't known why she was upset. Very sweet of him, and although normally she'd rather be by herself, Louie noticed she was actually looking forward to dinner, at least a little.

Fifteen

Mac and Louie took Jack to dinner at a little bistro not too near the company, the place they went when they wanted to make sure they wouldn't run into anyone they knew. They asked for a table in the back corner. Candlelight made the ochre colored walls glow, and the scents coming out of the kitchen made them hungry.

"This is on me." Mac patted Louie's hand. "I'm starting with a beer. One for you, Jack?"

"Sure. Louie?"

"No, thanks, although tonight I'm sorely tempted."

"She always says that, but I've never seen her go through with it. I've never seen you actually have a drink, Louie." Mac chuckled as she spoke.

"Alcohol gives me migraines, you know. Cheese, chocolate, alcohol—all the really good stuff in life gives me a major pain." Louie provided her stock answer. Jack studied her face, which made Louie a little self-conscious. She'd been about to ask if she had spinach in her teeth or something when Mac spoke.

"Okay, well, you know me. I can't keep a secret or pussyfoot around. Jack, I told Louie this morning. The State Department has been after me ever since I published that article on the propaganda uses of late-night television. I'm going to accept. After seeing Sergio, the weasel, promoted to Vice Chair, I don't have any reason to say no to them any longer."

Jack paled. He stared at his beer, and then looked at Louie again.

Mac's smile wavered. "Jack, I'm really sorry to leave you. This is going to be a tough road, with Sergio doing all kinds of crazy deals with his new crazy title, Jones looking the other way, and

Josef—who knows what Josef will do? Louie will help you all she can. Won't you, Lou?"

Jack captured Louie in his gaze. *What the hell? It's like he's testing me somehow.* "Of course, Mac. Not that I can do much."

"Don't let her fool you, Jack. Jones trusts her. She can slip things into her conversations with him, make sure he gets the right information." Louie noticed Mac looking at her, too.

"But Mac, after today, I don't think even that will help. Jones has thrown his weight behind Sergio." Louie stole another glance at Jack, who'd caught her eye.

"And there's a substantial amount of weight to throw, ain't there?" *Another joke? Well, he's trying.*

They spent the rest of the meal telling stories and laughing about Sergio and Jones, in the way people do when they are facing something extremely unpleasant, and they don't want to cry about it. They laughed a little too hard and a little too long, until finally it was time to go home. Mac excused herself to go to the ladies' room, and Louie felt the need for some fresh air. She and Jack headed outside to wait by the cars.

"Louie, I'm really glad we bumped into each other today." Jack tucked his hands into his pockets and rocked on his heels.

"Sure, me too." Louie still wasn't sure what to make of this guy. Sweet, funny, and he disliked Sergio—all in his favor. But something about the way he looked at her made her a little, well, self-conscious. Again she wondered if there was something in her teeth.

"Do I have something in my teeth?"

Jack laughed. "No, why?"

"You keep looking at me like I do."

"I do? I'm sorry, I wasn't aware…"

"It's okay, I'm probably imagining it. What color are your eyes?"

"My eyes? Brown, I guess, why?"

"No reason. It's just that…well, it's been a long day. I need to get to day care."

"You have a kid?" Jack seemed shocked. "Mac never said."

"No, no. My dog, Buddy. He spends the days at doggy day

5

care."

"What kind of dog is he?"

"He's a blind, cranky, bossy mini-Schnauzer. I'm pretty sure he's from Mars."

Jack laughed. "Why Mars?"

"Because when I first met him, he jumped right up on the chair with me, put his paws on my chest, and lifted his nose to the sky as if he'd just conquered me. Which, of course, he had. There was something about that pose that reminded me of the little Martian on the old Bugs Bunny cartoons. A little guy, but he believed he was in charge of everything and everyone. That's Buddy."

"Well, I'm sure he's waiting for you. You'd better take good care of him. I have a feeling you're going to need him someday."

"Someday? I need him every day. I have two cats, too, and they are my babies. Buddy is my—he's my best friend."

"Good, with a best friend, you're never really alone, are you?" Jack turned away, shaking his head like there was a buzzing in his ear.

Mac joined them outside. "What are you two talking about?"

"My dog, of course. What else do I ever talk about?" Louie grinned.

"Oh god, she's on about Buddy, the world's most amazing blind dog?" Mac chuckled.

"Don't start—you and your pugs. You're just the same." Louie continued to stare at Jack.

"I know, I know. Well, we'd better get everyone home. We have another all-day session tomorrow. Seventh circle of hell." Mac gave Louie a quick hug before they parted for the night.

As Louie drove home that evening, she couldn't stop thinking about Jack. *What was up with that guy, anyway?* Eyes that change color, staring at her, making her laugh in spite of her bad mood, then that comment about needing Buddy some day. *Well. Mac wants me to help Jack out—what was it she'd said? There's more to him than Sergio thinks?* Any enemy of Sergio's was a friend of hers, so she'd step up. *Leave it to Mac, she always has something up her sleeve. She must've known we'd hit it off.* But there was something else to it—something that seemed bigger than Mac, or Jack, or any of them—something that seemed right, but strange, and a little scary. *Oh, I guess I'm just not used to making new friends.*

Sixteen

Louie recalled two disturbing incidents that took on increased importance in hindsight, and intensified her vigilance, now that she'd found the sales agreement and was headed for PPP3's European operations. The first took place on the second night of the inventors' conference, the day after she'd met Jack. Jones threw a fancy dinner at the posh "athletic" club, membership in which was a perk for the CEO of PPP3. Oh sure, it had a gym, a pool, and a plethora of Stairmasters, elliptical trainers, and rowing machines, even a small stack of free weights. But these were used in a ratio of one to one hundred compared to the dining room, banquet rooms, catered meeting rooms, drinking lounges, and bedrooms.

Tastefully decorated in shades of terra cotta and espresso, with soft lighting and round tables covered in white linen, the banquet room came to life with the sounds of clinking silver flatware and bubbling conversation. Jones stood and tinkled his crystal wineglass with his salad fork.

Oh crap, he's going to start talking. When she arrived at the banquet room, wearing her best little black dress but still slightly disheveled and red-eyed after sneaking a couple of hours in the Archive Room, she'd seen the three sights she dreaded most— middle-aged white men nearly choking on their own self-importance, trophy wives circling the room, bragging about their cherubic children, and place cards. *Hell, assigned seating. Who am I stuck between?* It could have been worse. On one side of Louie's chair was one of the two female PPP3 board members, who was slightly less impressed with herself than the men, and was known to let loose with a four-letter word or two after a few glasses of wine. On the other was the board member's ancient husband. Claude was about one hundred and ninety nine years old at the time, and his ability to drone on endlessly about the good old days of his youth as a young engineer at a big local aerospace company was only surpassed by his tendency to leer suggestively about eighteen inches below a woman's eyes. Occasionally, he'd even been known to cop a feel or pinch an ass, behavior that was usually overlooked because no one wanted to tell an ancient man to knock it off. Worst of all, Mac hadn't been there. She'd said there was an emergency at the office, but Louie knew she didn't want to deal with Jones and Sergio that night. Louie wished she could blow off the event like Mac did.

Great. Two glasses of wine from now, and I'll be hearing great Anglo-Saxon swearing on one side, while fighting off the world's oldest lech on the other. Why is it again that I don't drink? Louie tottered a bit on the high heels she wasn't used to, and took her seat. *Oh that's right, the killer migraine that comes from it. Well, some nights, it almost seems like it would be worth it.* Jones extended the pre-dinner drinking by launching into one of his patented "five-minute" speeches that lasted an hour. *They'll have even more alcohol on empty stomachs.*

"Welcome members of the Board, our international partners, and our special guests," Jones began. "I'd like to introduce each of you who are here tonight."

Louie scanned the room. Her gaze stopped and lingered on Jack. He'd been stuck between a trophy wife and the CEO of a small manufacturing firm in Quito, Ecuador, who spoke the fifty words of English he knew with a heavy accent that made him virtually impossible to understand. The trophy wife tried to flirt with Jack while the Ecuadoran explained something in what looked like an intense, almost intimate whisper. Louie grinned at Jack and rolled her eyes.

Just then she felt a pinch as the old man slipped his hand under her ass. Louie did not hesitate, she did not look away from Jack; she just jabbed Claude as hard as she could in his ribs with her elbow. "Try that again and I'll hit a little lower next time, old man," she hissed, as he gasped and grabbed his side. Fortunately everyone but Jack had been watching Jones. Jack's brown eyes twinkled as he mouthed something at her.

Lice mob? Huh? she mouthed back. He'd shaken his head and tried again. *Oh. Nice job.* She grinned at him.

After Jones finally finished talking, the waiters brought out the plates of food. As one reached to put a plate piled with a roasted chicken carcass in front of her, Louie asked if there was a vegetarian option. "Let me check, honey," he mumbled and put the plate in front of the old man. The rest of the table was served, and everyone started eating. Louie excused herself and wandered into the hall, looking for a waiter. The first three she saw were all working other events. Finally she saw the same one who tried to give her the dead chicken.

"Oh my god. I completely forgot. I asked the kitchen. They weren't told about any vegetarians."

"That's okay. Could I just have the side dishes, without the chicken?"

"They've all been served," the waiter shrugged. "I don't have any left."

"But surely you have one plate left, because I didn't get any?" Louie's stomach rumbled.

"No, they've all been served. I'll make sure you get dessert, though. You'll love it—dark chocolate mousse." The waiter beamed cheerily.

Louie swallowed. "Can't have chocolate either, I'm allergic."

He looked stricken. "I'm sorry, we weren't told about any special needs—"

"It's okay." Louie tried to fake a smile to distract from her noisy stomach.

"No, wait." The waiter dropped his voice to a conspiratorial whisper. "I have an idea. Come with me to the kitchen." He took Louie down the hall and through a door into a service hallway, then through another door into a huge kitchen, then around the corner into a little storage area with a small cooler.

"Staff food, sweetheart." He reached into the fridge and pulled out a plastic container. "This is leftover from a party last night. It's divine. Risotto, with pumpkin, sage, and pine nuts." He pulled out another container. "This is to die for. Young green beans in a light butter herb sauce. And—" he reached for a foil packet behind him on a little counter, "The best toast you'll ever have, made from this amazing focaccia."

Louie's stomach relaxed in gratitude. "I'm Louie. If we're going to eat together, you should know my name."

"I'm Adam. Fabulous to meet you. Now, you sit over here while I heat this up." Louie settled herself on a barstool in the corner. The food made Louie's stomach warm with satisfaction, and the conversation made her grin. Adam described himself as a flaming queer in real life, but said he toned it down for his job serving the rich and powerful at the club.

"I saw that old fart pinch your ass, and saw the jab in the ribs you gave him. I must admit, it was a thing of beauty. I thought I'd cry I was laughing so hard inside." Adam laughed, a boisterous sound that begged her to join him. "Want to be my bodyguard when I go clubbing? I could use someone who is unafraid to whack an elderly lech now and then."

"No thanks. I've got a more than full time job as it is, although there are quite a few days you could lure me away for nothing more than the promise we'd have fun together." Louie spoke around a mouth full of risotto.

Adam cocked his head, listening. "Your crew is finishing up dessert. You'd better get back in there."

"You can hear that from here?" Louie could only hear the bustle in the kitchen.

"Waiter's ears. Years of practice. But wait. Speaking of dessert, would you prefer a sublime carrot cake or an insouciant key lime pie? Here, take a little of both." He put two bites on a plate and handed it to her. "Eat fast and get back in there so your boss doesn't know you spent the whole event in the staff kitchen instead of schmoozing those VIPs he spent so much money on."

She gulped down the sweets and arrived back in the banquet room just as Jones stood. At least the old man slept in his chair, so she wasn't risking another ass pinching. She slipped into her seat and caught Jack's eye.

He raised his eyebrows. *Where were you?*

She shook her head. *Tell you later.*

Hell, he mouthed.

What?

Help. He looked at the Ecuadoran, at Sergio, at Jones, and then pointed at himself. *More help.*

More what?

Meeting. Help.

Oh. Okay. Louie nodded. Jones finally finished thanking everyone and people stood, swallowing one more gulp of wine, milling about. Louie noticed a partially finished glass of wine next to the old man's plate. She picked it up and headed across the room. Sergio corralled Jack, Josef, the Ecuadoran, Jones, a few other very self-important people, and was clearly trying to get them to go to the lounge for more deal making. Louie moved to just behind Jack's shoulder, touched his arm, and whispered to him. "Follow my lead." He nodded and she moved to place herself between Sergio and Jack. She held the glass in front of her torso and spoke louder than was strictly appropriate. "Well, I'm going to walk back to the old ranch. Got some more work to do. Just came to say goodnight to you all!"

Sergio looked startled, and Josef suppressed a grin. Jones was too buzzed himself to pay attention. "No, I mean it." Louie threw a little slur in there for good measure. "I'm shwalking, I need the shfresh airsh. You all have a wonsherful evening." She raised the wineglass as if she was toasting them, allowing some to slosh over the edge of the glass to trickle down her fingers. The Ecuadoran smiled warmly at her. "Goodshnight." She walked away. *Okay, Jack, come on, take the cue.*

She made it down the hall and all the way to the lobby before hearing footsteps behind her, and turning. "About bloody time. Could I have been more obvious?" But it wasn't Jack; it was Adam, the waiter. "Sweetie, I just wanted to say goodnight." He hugged Louie. "This was the best night at work I've had in a long time that didn't end in me going home with the cutest guy in the room."

Louie laughed. "I'd say me too, but I haven't dated in years."

"Oh sweetheart, that has to end! Here's my card. Call me. I know some guys who know some straight guys. Or maybe they know some guys who know some guys who know some straight guys.

Somehow, we'll get you a date!" He kissed her cheek. "Gotta go back and be professional, honey. Good night!"

Louie was touched by Adam's impulsive invitation to friendship. As he turned, Adam almost crashed into Jack. "Excuse me, handsome." He grinned and whispered to Louie, "Hey, maybe tonight's your lucky night, sweetheart! I didn't see anyone in that room cuter than this one. If only he played on my team..." He turned back to Jack. "Unless she's your sister or something, if I were you, I'd take her home tonight, my friend." And then he disappeared around the corner.

Louie turned beet red.

"What the...who is that?" Jack pointed toward the hall.

"That's Adam. He made me dinner." Louie could not help but smile.

"Huh?"

"It's a long story, I'll tell you later." *Change the subject, before I die of embarrassment.* "So, it took you long enough to catch up. Perhaps my drunk-woman-about-to-leave-on-her-own-far-too-wobbly-feet act was too subtle?"

"Hey, I had to convince them that I really am chivalrous enough not to let you walk back alone in your...state, despite their insistence on involving me in their high-level negotiations, during which, of course, my job would be only to nod enthusiastically."

"Well, I have now trashed my reputation as a teetotaler just to get you out of enthusiastic nodding. Come on, we'd better split before they see us." They stepped out into the cool night air.

"It was worth it, believe me," Jack pulled his coat tighter against himself. "Something about a deal where products from Ecuador would come to Europe and then be sold on the web with a cut to Seattle and I'd had a couple of glasses of wine and my head hurt and there was just so much Spanish going on..."

"You're right. It was worth it to get you out of that. Although I'm not sure it compares, drama-wise, to getting your ass pinched by a hundred and ninety nine year old man, being fed the best meal of your life by a flaming gay waiter, and then pretending to be drunk in order to save your friend from, um, another meeting." *Friend? Already?*

"Okay, you win on the drama, but only because the Ecuadoran never tried to pinch my ass. Otherwise we'd be even." Jack took deep breath. "The air feels great after, what was that, two million hours listening to the smug entertain the vain."

They walked quietly for a while. No rain, a few clouds, a cool breeze, just enough to put a bit of a chill in the air, all in all a lovely autumn night for Seattle. Even with the city lights, a few stars managed to wink from the sky. Louie felt overtaken by emotion, and a flash of intuition, and before she knew it, she'd spoken out loud.

"Jack. Are you going to tell me why you're so sad?"

He looked at her. "What do you mean?"

"You are sad, aren't you?" Jack stayed silent. "You joke a lot, but there's a sadness inside you, too." *Now where did that come from? It'll serve you right if Jack tells you to fuck off.*

His response seemed to confirm her fear, as his eyes flashed. "What are you talking about?"

"Is it a relationship? If it was work, you'd be angry, or upset, or frustrated, or even in despair, but not sad, I don't think. You lost someone, didn't you, Jack?"

"Yes, I lost someone, but no, I wasn't in a relationship. Who told you I was?"

"No one told me anything. It's just a feeling. Who did you lose?"

"I looked for...a relative of mind for a long time. But I never found her. And I am sad. Because she's... dead." Jack tilted his head back, as if considering those few persistent stars.

"I'm so sorry. Oh Jack, I'm so sorry. Was she a close relative?"

"I don't want to talk about it, Louie."

"Okay, but sometimes it helps..."

"Not this time. Not now. Please drop it." His voice went cold. Louie saw Jack's eyes change color again, and he put his hands over his ears, as if to shut out some unwanted noise. *Shit, I really put my foot in it.* Jack sped up until he'd gotten well ahead of her. When she finally caught up with him, he was sitting on a little iron bench at a bus stop. She sat down beside him.

"I'd love to love Seattle, like you seem to," Jack admitted.

"Because I love grey areas. I mean, isn't all of life on this planet a kind of grey area? But, too many bad memories, I guess."

"I don't love love it," Louie shrugged. "It's just the closest thing to home I've found, and I love the idea of that."

Jack thought for a moment, as if he was deciding something. "She was my sister. I've lost her three times. I lost her, just like you said. That's what freaked me out. When you said 'you lost someone.' I remembered the last time I was here in Seattle. It seems a lifetime ago, when I tried to find her, and realized I never would. I had just been thinking to myself, I lost her." Louie put her hand on his arm as he went on. "I'll tell you the whole story someday, but not tonight, okay? I just can't. I have to… there's a buzzing in my head."

"It's okay. You don't ever have to tell me if you don't want to." Louie squeezed his arm to comfort him.

"Will you tell me something?" Jack turned to study her face in that disconcerting way again.

"Sure. What do you want to know?" Louie waited.

"How did you know I was sad? I thought I was hiding it pretty well there."

Louie considered for a minute. "I'm not sure. Maybe because I know what it's like, though. Missing family. Permanently. Oh hell. How do you ever know anything?"

"I don't ever know anything myself, so I'm the wrong guy to ask. Can I ask you something else?"

"Sure."

"Did you get that waiter's phone number? He was damn cute."

Louie laughed. "I did. I'm sure he'd love to get a call from you, if you ever decide to swing the other way." *He's joking again. But this time it's to distract himself, not for me.*

"I have a better idea." Jack tapped Louie's shoulder and pointed across the street. "See what's right in front of us?"

"Oh my god. I didn't realize we'd walked that far already."

"It's Mecca, it's Shangri-la, it's the fountain of youth, it's Atlantis." Jack pointed, real awe in his voice.

"It's coke, it's heroin, it's booze, it's freakin' nicotine," Louie responded. They looked at each other.

"It's Book Bargain Basement," they almost sang in unison.

"Why are we still sitting here?" Jack tugged her to her feet. "C'mon. Let's run!" He pulled her across the street as they dashed for the front door of the biggest used and remainder bookstore in the city.

Book Bargain Basement was a haven for two book lovers like Louie and Jack. When they found themselves inside it that night, they just stood for a moment, staring at the stacks, wondering where to start.

"What do you want to look at first, Jack? Your call, since you're the guest," Louie said.

"I never know," Jack shook his head. "I live in a place where this vast selection of books in a language I can actually read is...completely absurd and nearly impossible. Let's just go this way." So they started toward the nearest stack on the left. The sign read "Books About Music."

"Look! A graphic novel-type history of the Clash," Louie pointed.

"Too cool. How about this unauthorized biography of Lady Gaga?"

"Jack, you can't be serious."

"Okay, then, here's a book of psychedelic rock concert posters from the sixties."

"That's better." Louie laughed. They continued on like this for a while, wandering the aisles, picking up anything that looked interesting or unusual or silly, trying to make each other laugh, trying to forget the sadness of their earlier conversation, until they found themselves in the kid's section.

"Hey look, the original *Wizard of Oz*." Jack held up his newest find. As Louie turned to see what he held, she felt a sharp bump on the back of her head.

"Ow! Shit, what was that?" She'd turned back to see a book on the floor. "That book hit me in the head, Jack!"

He seemed unconcerned. "Uh huh. You sure you didn't take a glass of wine or two?"

"Very funny, you are. Ouch!" Another book bounced off Louie's shoulder, landing on the floor. "Okay, tell me that one didn't hit me!"

"I wasn't looking, Lou."

Smack! "All right, sonofabitch, who are you? Where are you?" Louie saw a third book on the ground, and so did Jack. Then he looked serious. "Louie," he'd whispered. "Where did those come from?"

"That's what I've been asking you!" She heard the shrillness in her voice. "Who is throwing books at me, Jack?" Three more hit her, one after the other, in the small of her back. "What, are they just flying off the shelves?"

"Shhhh. Louie, shhh." Jack craned his neck to see around the shelf.

"What shhh? What is going on?" Another one caught her across the left ear. "Ow! Dammit—"

Jack grabbed her hand and started to walk quickly. "Louie, be quiet, don't draw any attention, follow me, let's go. Now."

"Okay, but don't you think flying books are going to draw attention? What is going on here?"

"Just follow me and be quiet." Jack pulled Louie through the store as fast as she could walk without breaking into a run. Behind her, books were cascading off the shelves as if they were trying to get her before she could escape. Through Jack's hand she felt how tense he was, how serious, even scared. She put her head down and followed him. Soon they'd turned a corner to get out of the kid's section. One last book flew and hit her in the rear. *Nice. My ass is really taking a beating tonight.* But she'd kept following Jack as they worked their way out of the store. *Was that a crow that flew out the door behind us? Pretty bold, these city crows, flying right into big stores like that.*

When they got back to the sidewalk, Jack turned south and broke into a trot, pulling her along with him.

"Jack, high heels, remember?" Louie tugged at his hand, trying to slow him.

"Louie, suck it up. We have to get out of here, now. There's a bus. We're getting on it."

She looked at the number. "That bus goes out to the suburbs. It goes way out there. Way out the wrong direction if we're trying to get back to your hotel."

"Good. Get on it. Pay the fare. I don't have any money."

"Jeez, Jack, okay." Louie paid the fare for both of them and followed Jack all the way to the back of the bus, mostly empty at that hour. He sat down and turned to look out the rear window. "What are you looking for?" Louie demanded. "Is somebody following us?"

"No, I don't think so. I think we got on in time. Plus he won't expect this."

"No doubt, it took me by surprise. But who are you talking about, Jack? Who won't expect this?"

Jack looked at her as if he was just remembering who she was. "Who what?"

"Who did you mean when you said 'he won't expect this'?" *Had his eyes turned that funny color again?* Louie couldn't tell for sure.

"Oh, um, you know, that waiter. I thought I saw him following us." Jack relaxed. "I thought maybe he was going to ask me out after all. How awkward would that be, huh, a gay waiter asking a man's man like me out?" His grin was unconvincing.

Louie stared at him. "Do you think I'm that much of an idiot? Fine. Don't tell me whatever craziness you're engaged in at the moment if you don't want to, but please, Jack, don't treat me like I'm stupid."

"Sorry, Lou." Jack watched the road unfold behind the bus.

"Sorry my ass. I'd be furious with you except something is telling me that you may have saved my life. How absurd is that? Flying books, suburban buses, mysterious men following us. I should be pissed as hell."

"You should be, you really should. I'm probably just drunker than I thought," Jack replied.

"Okay, fine, leave it at that. I only hoped you'd trust me a bit more. But obviously not. So fine."

"Louie —"

"No, it's okay. Just tell me how far out into the frickin' suburbs we have to go before we can get off and turn around and head on back."

"How far out does this route go?"

"Far enough to be an expensive cab ride back, Jack."

"If I promise to pay you back?"

"You really want to ride all the way to the end of the line?"

"I do, I really do. Consider it sightseeing. Mac offered to take me sightseeing while I was here."

"I'm sure she was thinking the Space Needle, the waterfront, maybe a ferry ride. Not a completely absurd bus ride to Tukwila. In the dark. Of course there isn't that much to see anyway between Seattle and Tukwila. So we might as well do it in the dark, right?" Louie said.

"Sounds perfect. And look...." Jack paused.

"For dog's sake, you're a shoplifter, too?" Jack still held a copy of the *Wizard of Oz* in his hand.

"I guess so." Jack grinned. "Let's read it out loud as we go, shall we?"

It didn't take long to get through the little story L. Frank Baum penned a hundred years before. *And it's so different than the movie.* Louie felt herself relax in Jack's company.

Seventeen

The other incident Louie recalled, as she drove home across Lake Washington the day she discovered Jones was an alien, happened not too long after the flying books chased her and Jack away from the bookstore, onto that long bus ride to Tukwila. She hadn't connected the events at all at the time, but now, the memory took on a sinister cast.

A late fall afternoon, one of those crisp blue-sky days that make it almost worth tolerating the rest of the eleven and a half months of rain in Seattle. Louie always thought of it as the Emerald City, since she'd first heard it called that, well before she moved here for college and her Aunt Emma followed her, before she'd even seen the movie of the Wizard of Oz. Louie's house was a typical old Seattle bungalow, sturdy but badly made over in the height of the bad-taste-seventies, and it sat in a typical old Seattle neighborhood, slightly shabby, always humble, not yet sucked into the fancier neighborhoods' urge to join the big-city party. Peter, her neighbor from down the street, was almost thirteen, going on almost thirty, in the way kids that age often are. Sometimes nothing was more important to him than the next soccer game—hell, the next chance to score a goal or even get his foot on the ball. Other times he was asking the toughest questions about life, death, love, and evil. He'd always been a sweet kid, and Louie was a little afraid for him now that he stood on the edge of adolescence.

On this day Louie, worked in her yard, focusing on one monster clump of clover she tried to get out by the roots. She hadn't noticed Peter riding by on his bicycle. She heard the screech of brakes on tires and heard a voice she didn't recognize say, "Hi." When she looked up the sun was behind him so she couldn't clearly see his face, and for a second, she'd thought it was some gangly teenage hoodlum about to give her trouble. This old neighborhood was trying to gentrify itself, but hadn't really made it yet.

She opened her mouth to say something like, *Hey, did you see my giant Rottweiler anywhere nearby? He seems to have slipped away again. He's missing lunchtime, and boy, is he mean when he's hungry,* when she recognized Pete's bike.

"Pete? Hey, what's up?"

"Oh nothing. I was just riding." Peter's voice came out with a kind of squeak. *Yup, he's vacillating between tenor and bass. Poor guy.*

"Okay. Want to help me pull weeds for a while?" Louie laughed. She meant it as a joke. What almost thirteen, almost thirty year old, boy would say yes to that invitation?

"Sure." Peter sat down beside her. *Uh oh. He's either sick or something's eating at him.* Peter lived with his grandfather, who was awfully nice, but not always in tune with the priorities of teenagers. Louie started to explain which of the jumble of plants in front of them were weeds and which were "real." She gave Pete her dandelion tool and showed him how to use it to pry up the roots. Soon he flung weeds, dirt, and the occasional "real" plant all over.

"Hey, there, that's great enthusiasm, but you're making a bit of a mess. Try to go slower, you'll get more roots that way."

Pete slowed down for about, oh, ten seconds and then he went back at it. *Hmmm, it's like he's pissed about something. Well, that's my motivation for weeding half the time. You can take it all out on the weeds and they don't talk back. You don't want them here, you just rip them out. No negotiations, no permission, no need to make deals.* After a few minutes he stopped and stared at the sky for a bit.

"How's school, Pete?" Louie tried first.

"Fine."

"And your grandpa?"

"He's good."

Story of my life. Men who are troubled but won't tell me why. I spend my energy getting it out of them, then trying to fix it. Oh well, Pete deserves it. He'd helped her out many times when the other kids in her neighborhood acted up, or when she needed a little extra muscle around the house or yard. Plus their conversations were terrific, and Louie didn't have that many people in her life she could say that about. And, to be completely honest, Peter took as much care of his grandfather as he took of Peter—more, in some ways. This was a kid who didn't always have much time to just be a kid. Louie could relate.

"So, then, what's up? What's got you attacking those weeds like they were evil aliens come to take over the world or something?"

Pete's eyes widened. "You know about that?"

"About what?" Louie'd asked.

"About the aliens who are trying to take over the world?"

"Is this in one of your games, Pete?"

"No, I saw them. Well, I saw one of them, anyway. I'm pretty sure I did."

Louie looked at him, trying to see if he was joking. He looked absolutely sincere and a little scared. "What did he—it—the alien look like?"

"He just looked like a guy, at first," Peter shrugged. "A little guy, kinda skinny, with black hair. He was parked across from your house."

"My house? Here?"

"Yeah. I was riding by on my bike on my way to soccer practice and I saw him in the car."

Louie's stomach twitched with a touch of fear. Who would be parked at her house, even if he—it—wasn't an alien? "What kind of car was it?"

"Don't you want to know how I know he was an alien?" Pete sounded annoyed.

"Of course I do, but first I want to know what kind of car it was."

"It was a big, black Lincoln. That's why I first noticed it—nobody in this neighborhood has a car like that."

"A black Lincoln? Like a Town Car?"

"Yeah," Peter answered.

That's it. The shuttle service from the airport to town used Town Cars as their special "limo" service. It was someone who'd come in from the airport and was looking for an address. She said as much to Peter.

"No, the shuttle doesn't use black ones. Theirs are all silver or tan." Peter was a bit of a car buff. He would know. "Plus, this one was older. Like from the seventies or something. But mint condition."

A black mint condition nineteen-seventies Lincoln Town Car parked across from her house? This was starting to sound absurd. "Okay, then, tell me how you figured out this guy in the Town Car was an alien. Did he have an extra eye?"

"What?"

"An extra black eye, right in his forehead. You know, like on that Twilight Zone episode where the bus crashes, and they all go into the diner, and they are trying to figure out who the alien is? And it's the counter guy? He takes off his hat and shows his extra eye?" Pete and Louie would always get together on the long weekends when the Sci-Fi channel would run Twilight Zone marathons. This was one of their favorite episodes.

Peter looked a little hurt. "You don't believe me? I'm serious, Lou, this guy is an alien. When he saw me watching him, he started the car, and drove away. Real fast. Like he knew he wasn't supposed to be there. So I followed him."

"Pete, you didn't!"

"Sure I did—I wanted to see where he would go next."

"But he was driving a car and you were just on your bike. You couldn't keep up with him."

"He drove slow, though, like he wasn't sure where he was going, and I could cut through yards and alleys and stuff. I followed him for a while."

"And?" Louie very much wanted to know what came next.

"After he drove around a bit, he pulled into the loading dock behind the hardware store on Sixty-third Street—you know that one?" Pete looked nervous as he spoke.

"Yeah, I know it," Louie kept her voice relaxed.

"And then it was so weird—he pulled out something that looked like a cell phone, only it wasn't, and he talked into it, and then pushed some buttons on the dashboard—and then—" Pete stopped.

"And then?" *Come on, Pete. I have to know.*

Peter looked around. "Well, when I told Mark at school, he said it was impossible. He laughed at me."

"I won't laugh, Pete, I promise. You can't leave me hanging here, you have to tell me."

"And then the car sort of turned into this, um, pod thing, and it flew away. Straight up," Peter finished.

"Mark should know that's not impossible, a car turning into a space pod," Louie replied.

"No, it wasn't that—he said nothing can take off straight up, except a helicopter. A pod would have to go at an angle or it wouldn't get enough lift."

"Oh." Louie stifled a laugh. *Of course. These kids demand their fantasy aircraft obey at least some of the laws of physics.* "Pete, you know this whole thing does sound pretty strange. Aliens are usually only in movies and books."

"Yeah, but this one was real. I'm sure of it. And...."

"And what?"

"I didn't want to tell you, because I thought you'd think I was crazy or something. But I decided I had to, because, well, it just seems not good that alien guy was looking at your house."

"Yeah, I was thinking that too, Pete."

"So you believe me?" He made direct eye contact with her, as if looking for her third eye.

What could she say? Peter never lied to her before, at least that she knew of. He must have seen something that worried him, to tell her a story like that.

"I believe you saw something very strange, and it has you worried. I'm really glad you told me about it." They went back to weeding.

Now Louie worried, too. If it was what she thought, it meant Sergio's surveillance went back a lot longer than she'd realized. It must have been him—skinny little guy, black hair. Who else would drive the most ostentatious, stand-out-in-the-neighborhood-like-a-sore-thumb car like that? Come on, a thirty-year old black, mint-condition Town Car? *What a prick.* But he'd been there, on her

street. What did he already know about her? And how was she going
to fight him?

Eighteen

Meeting Jack, the dinner with Adam the gay waiter, the scary episode at the bookstore, and Peter's story—all these things happened only months ago, but now seemed as far in the past as when dinosaurs roamed the planet. *When all we were worried about was Sergio's new title, and Mac's departure, and what would happen at PPP3. Not about saving the human race from slavery or destruction.* Louie knew she should take a gamble and contact Jack. A cell phone call was traceable, but email would leave a permanent written record. Besides, she needed to hear Jack's voice and let him hear hers. So she called Jack from the car, on her way home to pack for her flight to Europe. She listened to his phone ring, hoping his insomnia would make him answer, even though it was so late there.

"Hello?"

"Jack?"

"Louie?"

"Yeah, it's me."

"Louie, are you in trouble?"

"Yes. Yes I am in trouble. I'm in the biggest trouble of my life and I'm going to share it with you, and pull you right into the middle of it. Jack, I'm sorry to do this to you, but I have to tell you something you will think is impossible, and it will put you in danger, but you have to believe me. I need your help."

"Where are you?"

"In the car, on my way home."

"Are you sure it's safe to go home?"

"I have to get my dog and take care of the babies—Wait, you haven't even let me tell you why I'm in trouble."

"Sorry. You're right. Go ahead. But keep your eyes open and

be careful, for dog's sake. What happened?"

Louie took a deep breath and plunged right in. "Jack, Jones is an alien. So is Sergio. They bought PPP3 because they thought it could make money. When they figured out it wouldn't, they decided to take over the planet, and turn all humans into an army of cyborgs."

"Why?"

"I don't know, they don't know—they don't have a plan beyond creating the cyborg army. Sergio is supposed to come up with one, but you know how that will go. Why aren't you asking me what I had to drink, or what I smoked, or whether I'm crazy?"

"Because I know you don't drink or smoke dope. I know you're not crazy, and my whole life has prepared me to accept the absolutely absurd and nearly impossible as true."

"Jack, I'm coming to the European operation." *To you.*

"When?"

"I'm getting on the red eye tonight. I'm taking Buddy and the cats to my aunt's, and then I'm getting on a plane. I go through Amsterdam and arrive in Prague in the morning."

"I'll meet you at the airport. You'll stay with me."

That was odd. Jack had the same first thought as Louie. But it was a bad idea. "No, get me a hotel room. This has to look like a normal business trip. Why don't you ask me why I'm coming there?"

"You're coming here because you think the answer is here."

"Yes, but how do you know that?"

"Because my whole life has prepared me to accept the absolutely absurd—"

"Yeah, okay, whatever. Get me a room in the hotel Sergio and Jones stay at when they come. Don't say anything to Josef, okay?"

"You'll tell me more when you get here?"

"Sure, but I don't know that much more."

"Louie, if what you are saying is true—"

"If! You said if! You do think I'm nuts."

"No, I don't. I just mean that what you call trouble may be really serious danger. Be careful when you get home, will you?"

"I will, I promise. But I don't think—"

"Don't underestimate them, Louie."

"Come on, you know Sergio as well as I do. These guys aren't that bright."

"Stupid they may be, but that doesn't stop them from being brutal."

"Great, thanks for the encouragement."

"I'm serious. Be careful, dammit."

"Yeah, I will. Hey Jack, do you think bullets will kill them?"

"Why, do you have a gun? You don't seem the type."

"No, I hate guns."

"Then it doesn't matter, does it?"

"Not now, no—but in the final battle—you know, like in the movies—"

"Don't think too far ahead, Lou. Just get home, get the critters settled, and get on the plane."

"Okay. Jack?"

"Yeah?"

Louie paused. "Thank you. I'll see you—is it tomorrow? Or the next day? The time difference always confuses me."

"Just get on the plane, Louie. And be careful."

Nineteen

Louie stopped at the doggy day care to get Buddy. Blind as he was, Buddy knew the sound of her footsteps coming through the door, or maybe it was her scent he recognized—either or both, he always ran to greet her with a body full of delight, expressing his joy by simultaneously wiggling every part of himself, from nose to tail.

"Buddy! Is it really you?? Oh, my best dog!" she always said and he responded with his sharp little barks, jumping up into the air, trusting she would be there to catch him. Stuart, the owner of the doggy day care, would fill Louie in on Buddy's day.

"You're early—what's up?" Stuart wondered.

"Was he a good dog today?" Louie didn't want to answer Stuart just yet.

"Isn't he a good dog everyday?" Stuart scratched Buddy behind his floppy Schnauzer ears. Louie was always glad the previous owners left Buddy's ears long, sweet for scratching and kissing.

"You know what I mean. Did he snap at anyone or snarl at the other dogs today?"

"He was fine—well, there was one episode."

"Tell me."

"It was about ten o'clock this morning—" Stuart started.

Louie's stomach lurched. That was when the horrible unzipping in Jones's office had begun. "What did Buddy do?"

"He just started howling. Does he ever howl at home?"

"I've only heard him howl twice and both times he was deep asleep and dreaming, and he just let out a little low howl. At the time I thought it was equal parts eerie and adorable. He was awake when he howled?"

"Yeah, wide awake. He'd been playing with Arthur, trying to get the newspaper squeaky toy away from him. Then he just dropped the toy, sat down, pointed his nose toward the sky, and started howling. Kind of quietly at first, but louder and louder, and I couldn't get him to stop for what seemed like forever. Then he stopped as suddenly as he started, and just began to shake. I pulled him to me and held him close, but he shook and shook, and growled. Somehow I knew it wasn't at me. I've seen him when he's cranky at me, and this was different. He eventually calmed down but was unsettled for almost an hour." Stuart's concern showed in his face.

Louie knew exactly what had happened. Buddy's "episode" corresponded with her conversation with the alien Jones. Her little dog knew. Dogs know things and Buddy knew this. She wanted to hug him tight and never let him go. Leaving him behind on this trip was likely to kill her—she shook herself. Thinking the word *kill* reminded her of the trouble she was in. She needed to keep Buddy safe, that was the main thing.

"Wow, that's weird." She tried to sound less worried than she felt. "Well, you know dogs. They have some connections to alternative universes. Or maybe there was an earthquake somewhere on the Pacific Rim."

"Sure." Stuart stared at Louie for another minute then looked down at Buddy. "See you tomorrow, Buddy."

"Actually, I'm going on a business trip. I'm going to leave Buddy with—" Louie stopped. She'd known Stuart for years and trusted Buddy with him every day, but now she questioned whether she wanted anyone else to know where Buddy was going to be for the next week. "I'm going to leave him with a friend."

"Okay. Well then old Buddy old pal, I'll see you later, alligator!" Stuart's corny sense of humor always reassured Louie, and she needed it today. She grasped Buddy's leash and walked him to the car, stopping once so he could have a good piddle on a shrub. He'd been going to this doggy day care so long she didn't need to steer him around the obstacles any more—he just knew when to zig left or zag right. She boosted him into the car and clipped the doggy seatbelt to his harness. Buddy stood in the back seat, whining. Usually he spent the drive home flopped down on his blanket, chin hanging over the edge of the seat, tail wagging whenever he heard Louie's voice. Tonight he was up.

Louie always believed in being honest with her animals, even if she wasn't sure they understood. "You know, don't you? Well, my friend, I'm in some trouble. My boss is an alien, and so is at least one other person—well, being—running the company. They are doing terrible things. I've got to try to stop them. That means I have to go away for a while. You and the kitties are going to stay with Aunty Em. You have to keep them safe, Buddy—" Louie heard her voice choke. "You have to keep them safe, and keep yourself safe, so that if somehow, despite the fact that we have barely a snowball's chance in hell, if somehow Jack and I do pull this off and save the world and all, I can come home to you and we can get the pack back together."

Buddy sat down on the seat. He became quiet but he wouldn't lie down. As they pulled around the corner onto Louie's street, Buddy stood up again and began to growl. The hackles rose on the back of his neck. Now Louie recognized exactly what Stuart described—this was not Buddy's *I'm annoyed leave me alone or I'll bite you* growl. This was low in his throat, almost unearthly. This was a look-out-there-is-danger-ahead growl. It got louder as they pulled into the drive.

"Okay, sweetie," Louie tried to calm Buddy down. "I get it. They are here, aren't they?" *Sons of bitches, they are at my house.* She felt terror and anger start to take hold as she thought of the kitties. *If they hurt the babies*...gun or not, she'd find out what kind of weapon would hurt these monsters.

Buddy paced in the backseat as much as his seatbelt would let him. She reached back and unclipped it. "I'm going to open the door for you, Buddy. When I do, you jump out and run." Buddy never jumped out of the car on his own before—without sight, he always waited for her to come around and boost him down. Louie didn't know why she believed he would jump out on his own now, but she was convinced he would. She hoped he would run down the street as he always wanted to when she kept him on the leash. She hoped he would run until he was out of sight, so she could deal with the monsters. When she was done, she would find him. She knew he wouldn't go too far.

Louie reached around from the front seat and opened the back door. Buddy vaulted out, his growl now positively unearthly. And he ran—but not away, as Louie hoped. He ran right for the front door.

"Buddy, no! Stop!" She thought she was screaming, but no sound seemed to come out of her mouth. Buddy was at the front door, clawing at it and growling. Louie steeled herself. Whatever was in her house, she and Buddy were going to find it together.

Opening her door, Louie expected to see another giant snot-green blob of lime Jell-O gone bad. Instead, she saw her living room, looking just like she'd left it. Buddy ran inside and started sniffing his way around the room, into the dining room and kitchen, down the hall to the bedroom. Louie kept one eye out for green snot, one eye out for her cats. She didn't see either and wasn't sure whether to be relieved or even more worried.

Then she heard a thump, a whimper, and a growl coming from her bedroom. "Buddy!" She ran down the hall. Buddy trapped something in the corner by her bed. Louie saw a black talon reach out and take a swipe at the dog. She lunged across the bed and grabbed Buddy's collar and yanked him back. The talon took a chunk of his ear. Buddy growled and writhed, trying to get back at the thing. Louie grabbed his collar with one hand and the thing with the other. Her hand closed around something that felt a little like a bird's leg, but cold, and slightly slimy. She pulled.

Up came the oddest creature she'd ever seen. It was jet black and iridescent, like crow feathers, but at the same time slimy, like a motor oil slick on a mud puddle. It was about two feet long from the part that seemed to be its head to what seemed to be its feet. Louie held one of those feet, from which extended two long, sharp talons. The thing started to hiss from what looked like a cross between a beak and a lobster's claw coming out of its neck—or whatever you called the part that joined its head-like thing to its body. Below the beak were four little buttons—were they eyes? They looked sort of like the eyes on a housefly, and Louie wondered for an instant how she looked to this thing.

"That hissing is creeping me out, thing," Louie hissed back

at it, trying to keep Buddy an arm's length away from it. He wanted to kill it, that was for sure. "Why don't you shut the fuck up or I'll let my dog loose and he'll tear you limb from limb."

The hissing stopped. Did the thing understand English? Was it really afraid of Buddy? The four eye-things seemed to be trying to focus on Louie's face. *Like it's trying to capture my image and transmit it somewhere.*

"Who sent you? Why are you here? Where are my cats?"

The thing just stared at her, eye-buttons trying to focus, faintly whirring.

"You want me to set my dog on you?"

No answer. Still sprawled across the bed, holding the monster with one hand, Louie noticed the eye-things seemed to shift focus to a spot slightly above and behind her. "Oh, you want me to look behind me, do you? Like I haven't seen that trick a million times in the movies."

Buddy wrenched out of her grasp, but instead of lunging at the thing she held, he leapt on her back. She heard the sound of hissing from above, and she felt the impact as whatever it was crashed into Buddy and sandwiched him between it and her.

Louie screamed and rolled over, using the thing in her hand like a baseball bat, whipping it around with the intention of smacking whatever it was off of Buddy and herself. As she rolled over she saw the other thing was a second, somewhat larger version of the first. The one in her hand smacked into the one on top of Buddy with a dull, sick thump and then a crunch of bone on bone. Their head-parts collided and black goo oozed out of their necks.

No, they turned into black goo, almost like they melted. Louie grabbed Buddy and pulled him out of the growing, oozing mess, which became a giant puddle of dirty oil on her bed.

Buddy stood panting by her as she watched the puddle. The things almost entirely dissolved, just eight little button eyes remaining to stare at them. Louie felt the same brief intuitive flash—that they transmitted what they saw to someone else—and then the eyes became goop, too.

She dropped to her knees and put her arms around Buddy. His ear bled and he trembled. She checked him all over for any other signs of injury, but didn't find anything. She whispered in his ear. "Buddy, I think you saved my life by trapping that first one. If they'd both been able to come at us at the same time..." He turned to lick her cheek. She thought maybe he said thank you, too. "Yeah, well, the pack fights together." She kissed the top of his head. "Let's go find the babies."

Louie found her two cats hidden in the basement, behind the clothes dryer. "Good babies. You guys found a great spot," she cooed. They crept out when they heard her voice. "It's okay, the evil things are all gone." Louie hoped she was telling the truth.

As Louie cleaned Buddy's torn ear, her rage took over. Hadn't she made a deal with Jones? And he sent those things to kill her anyway, endangering her animals. This went way beyond prick—this was asshole territory. He needed to know his little plan failed. She picked up the phone and called his office. Alice answered.

"Alice, it's Louie. Put Jones on now."

"Louie? Are you okay?"

"Oh yeah, Alice, I'm fine. Just fine. I need to talk to him right now. I don't care what he's doing."

"Okay, he's in his office. Here you go."

The line clicked twice and then Louie heard Jones' voice. "What's the problem?"

"What's the problem? You mean besides those evil fucking crow bat monsters you sent to my house to kill me and my dog?"

"What are you talking about? Slow down. You are clearly hysterical."

"We had a deal, Tom. You give me a week, I give you a plan, and you don't kill me. You welched."

"Welched? What is that? Some human thing? I don't know what you are talking about." Jones sounded bewildered, but Louie remembered he often feigned confusion in executive meetings, trying to trip someone else up.

"When I got home, I found two ugly black bird bat monsters in my house, and they tried to kill me and my dog."

"Describe them. What did they look like?"

Louie described them as best she could. "And then when I

smashed their heads together, they melted into a pile of black goo on my bed. You're getting the cleaning bill, by the way."

"Black goo—like a dirty oil slick?"

"Yeah, like that."

"And the eyes, what did the eyes do?"

"Now that you mention it, they stared at me, and for a second I thought they were transmitting something. Why?"

"Fucking Sergio," Jones sputtered.

Louie used that phrase herself often, but couldn't remember ever hearing Jones say it before. Not with much emotion, anyway. "Sergio?"

"Those were Sergio's reconnaissance scouts. But I assure you they wouldn't have tried to kill you unless you attacked them first."

"Oh really? And what would they consider an attack?"

"Well, touching them in any way, making any noises —or noticing that they were there."

Alien reconnaissance scouts are a touch oversensitive, I guess. "Well, I noticed them all right. Tom, I told you to keep Sergio away from me and that he wasn't to know about this trip. What did you tell him?"

"I didn't tell him anything. My guess is he started the surveillance on you a while ago. You went home early and surprised them. I hope I see these hours on your timesheet as vacation, by the way."

Asshole, indeed. "Right, Tom, you'll get my timesheet as soon as my week is up, it'll be the first thing on my to-do list. So the transmission—Sergio will know that I smacked the bat things around."

"Yes, he will have seen that."

"What will he do about it?" If she couldn't stop another attack, at least she wanted to anticipate it.

"I don't know. But if I were you I wouldn't wait around too long to find out."

"Tom, you have to call him off."

"You are giving me orders?" Jones sounded petulant.

"No, I'm just reminding you of the conditions you agreed to.

Tell him something that will keep him away from me for the next seven days. Unless you'd rather wait to see if he comes up with a plan of his own for this giant cyborg army you're building, with your reputation as a galactic leader on the line…"

"All right. I'll tell him you are off limits. But he will be suspicious. Now I have to go meet with a delegation from…let's call it North Dakota."

"A cold planet?" Louie was starting to get the hang of this.

"Yes, to humans it would be very cold indeed."

Jones hung up and Louie put the phone down. She wasn't sure how long Jones could keep Sergio away, but she figured the immediate danger was over. She'd better get a good meal, get her thoughts and things organized, and get the critters over to her aunt's.

Twenty

As she packed her things for the trip, Louie remembered another old conversation with Jack, typing her question into the Skype chat box on her laptop, trying yet again to avoid work she'd rather not do.

"Can you believe in hell if you don't believe in God?" Soon her Skype icon flashed with his reply.

"Why, don't you believe in God, Louie?"

"Well, I've had experiences that are, I guess, sort of spiritual. Once when I was in college I was listening to a talk about some priests and their housekeeper who were murdered in El Salvador. It was the usual terrible story and meant to rouse us students to some kind of semblance of involvement in political action, you know, the way our profs kept trying in the eighties to get us to act like they did in the sixties, or really like they wanted us to believe they did in the sixties, but probably didn't. Anyway, I was listening to the horror story about the murders, and all of a sudden I was taken by this feeling."

"Feeling? Like what kind of feeling?"

"This feeling that even though I couldn't forgive the murderers, there was something bigger, something that could forgive them."

"Something like God?"

"I don't know, just something that was bigger than me."

"So, do you believe in God, Lou?"

"I don't think there is a God like a person, like God the father or mother or whatever. Not a God who alternates between watching out for us and punishing us. Not a God who is a who, you know?"

"So what do you believe in?"

"That's harder."

"It usually is."

"Huh?"

"It's usually harder to know what to believe in than what not to believe in. It's easy to rule stuff out. Harder to rule stuff in."

"Oh, like the null hypothesis."

"Right. But, Lou, you still haven't answered the question. What do you believe in?"

She'd paused. "I believe in two things. One of them is love."

"Some people say God is love."

"I don't need love to be God. I just need love to be there."

"Do you really think love is possible?"

"I think love is necessary. Love is the Great Spirit. Love is what is bigger than any single one of us. You can't love by yourself, you know. There has to be someone or something else to love."

"Oh, I can love myself."

"Stop it, Jack. That's disgusting."

"Not the way I do it…it's really a beautiful thing."

"Well, that explains it."

"Explains what?"

"Why you have to wear those glasses. You're slowly going blind."

"Not so slowly, let me tell you. I'm having a great time destroying my eyesight."

"Okay, okay, I give. You win this round of the Completely Inappropriate Conversation Olympics."

"That's all I ask—just to win one round, occasionally. What is the other thing you believe in, Lou?"

"Hell."

"Wait. Don't you have to believe in God to believe in hell?"

"Why?"

"They just seem to go together, you know, like peanut butter and jelly, milk and Oreos, pickles and ice cream."

"Pickles and ice cream?"

"If you're pregnant."

"Or in hell."

"Ba da bum. But you're dodging the question again, my friend. How can you believe in hell but not believe in God?"

"I don't know, Jack, but I can. I think hell is the place we make when we deny love."

"Oh, hell on Earth."

"Hell wherever we are, whenever we decide something else is more important or more real than love."

"I like that."

"You like hell?"

"No, I like the idea that nothing is more important or more real than love."

"Me too, Jack. Me too."

Twenty One

Keeping up with his wife turned the being who, on Earth, would be known as Thomas Lee Jones from a homebody into an interplanetary tycoon, or at least a tycoon wannabe. On his home world of Spryxlgysm, Jones grew up the only son in a family of women, five older sisters and his mother. His father was not absent physically but long since gave up trying to have a voice or presence in that brood, long before Jones was born as the last of the six children. As a result, Jones grew up without a father, instead having something more like an older male pal, and a fairly unreliable one at that. His mother and sisters alternatively smothered him with love and gentle clucking disapproval of anything he tried if they hadn't arranged it for him. Soon enough he'd found himself following his father's lead and disappearing into the feminine miasma. They planned for him to take over his father's business, selling what on Earth would be called "junk" before the nineteen fifties and "antiques" after. He was alone with his dad only during their drives around in the hovercraft snagging items other Grythylwec put out as trash. Grythylwec, generally snobbish beings, chased the latest trends with a predictability that made them beloved by marketers. They trashed a lot of pretty good stuff regularly. It also meant there was little market for even gently used items, so Jones' family lived on the edge of poverty, albeit with pretty nice stuff.

Jones was always particularly fond of a certain piece of furniture with a flat frame and a relatively hard cushion he and his father scored on one junking trip. The cushion was covered in a sturdy fabric that was only slightly stained and musty smelling, and the best part about it was the frame was convertible. It could be laid out flat and the cushion spread across it for use as a bed, or folded up for use as a couch. The Grythylwec word for this kind of piece was pfhoootahn, and they indulged in a brief but intense love affair with the pieces, infatuated with their purported versatility, so that millions were made. The pfhoootahns quickly proved both heavily cumbersome to actually convert and not that comfortable for either seating or sleeping, so the Grythylwec moved on. But it was one of the few recently trendy things in the family's house, and Jones loved it. He was always looking for spare covers for the cushion and bringing them home, much to his mother's and sisters' annoyance and his father's profound indifference; his secret favorite was a cover printed with the Spryxlgysm version of horses and cowboys, green jello-blobs riding hideous copper-colored six-legged beasts with four snouts but strangely kind brown eyes. He'd never put it on the pfhoootahn, though, never showed it to the women in the family, knowing they'd hate it. He'd kept it in his room as a private treasure.

In a strange way, Jones' pfhoootahn cover was the catalyst for his interplanetary career. He'd gone on a rare solo junking trip in the hovercraft, his father being ill with a version of food poisoning brought on by a bad batch of takeout Grythylwec food the night before, a dish that humans could easily mistake for chop suey. Jones decided to detour to the upholstery shop dumpster, to see if it held any pfhoootahn covers that day; it didn't, but the shop owner's daughter was out tossing some other of yesterday's trends into the dumpster, and she'd cornered Jones when he'd stepped out of the hovercraft.

"You're the junkman's boy, the one who pilfers our dumpster."

Jones could hardly argue the point if he'd been inclined to, but something about the way she said it seemed to make him bolder rather than shyer.

"That's me. Is there a problem?"

She'd narrowed her eyes at him. "You take the pfhoootahn covers, right?"

"Yeah," the young Jones tried to sound nonchalant.

"Follow me." She'd led him down a grungy back alley to a concrete-type structure and keyed open a padlocked garage door, slid it up with a tremendous amount of creaking and grunting, some of it made by the door, and Jones followed her inside, blinking in the dim light.

As his eight purple eyes adjusted, he'd seen a warehouse-like space filled with rows upon rows of pfhoootahns, made of all kinds of materials, and racks and racks of covers. "What the—" he'd sputtered.

"Been hoarding 'em a while," she'd answered, "because I have an idea."

He'd turned to look at her, and caught his breath. In that place, in the low light filled with dust motes, her green mass was stunningly lovely. The determined look in her multiple eyes set off the blobs of her face area, and the slight flush of excitement tinged her green with the yellow of watered-down beer. Jones fell hard in that instant. The Grythylwec didn't waste time with dating or courting or pre-mating rituals, so within the hour they'd been hitched and the union consummated. Grythylwec sex, being universally indescribably disgusting, won't be portrayed here. Suffice to say, it blew Jones' mind.

His wife took the place of his mother and sisters. Only her opinion mattered, and he would follow it, and her, slavishly. Her opinion was that other beings on other planets were so inferior to the Grythylwec, they would have a much longer infatuation with the pfhoootahns, and she had a plan to deliver them to those places. Jones would help, of course.

The scene at home was gratifyingly histrionic. Jones' mother took to her room, distraught. His sisters took turns yelling at him for getting hitched to a complete stranger without any arrangements or notice—worse, to the daughter of a tradesman. Never mind a trade like upholstery was considered at least two huge Grythylwec steps up from junking. They all hoped when Jones got hitched, he'd leap the family into the trendy set full on. Worst of all, this woman, what was her name? was taking him far away to peddle new —!— pfhoootahns on other worlds.

After the female hubbub finally died down, Jones' father said only two things to him. He asked, quietly, "Was the hitching good?"

Jones had the decency to blush a little when he nodded.

His father nodded too. "Good, because it's gotta last a long, long time." Then he'd slapped Jones in the region humans might think of as a shoulder and gone back to bed.

Jones' new wife, in the meantime, got busy making arrangements for him to join her on her first interplanetary sales trip. If it disturbed him to find everything set up in her name, he didn't show it. His stomach-like organs might have clenched a little, but the prospect of another hitching session helped him overcome it as he went along.

The journey lasted longer than either of them planned. When they arrived with no hitching since that first time, and his wife itching to set up deals, Jones realized he was going to have to carve out his own business or go mad with frustration. He'd snuck off with some of the pfhoootahn covers and found a buyer and withstood the shit storm when he got back.

While he'd made the sale, the woman doing the buying turned on something she called a television. She got it from another salesman returning from the next planet over, a place called Earth.

"Horribly provincial," she'd claimed. "The native beings there don't even realize they are not alone in this galaxy, but this television thing they've got is mighty keen." The show was one about three beautiful Earth women who took orders from a man's voice in a box.

A man's voice alone could control three females! Jones was amazed and stayed to watch the entire show. He remembered one name from the credits—Thomas Lee Jones. When, thirty Earth years later, a company hired him for his business skills, much to the chagrin of his wife, and sent him to run a little scam operation on that same provincial little planet Earth, that was the name he decided to take.

Maybe it was something about how Mount Rainier loomed over everything. Maybe it was how Seattle residents stayed up too late from all that coffee they drank, and insomnia made them gullible. After one conversation with Paster, Jones believed whole-heartedly that PPP3 was the potential goldmine Sergio promised.

Sergio cut a deal with the disgusting lord of the Kleptogarrh to keep the capital flowing. Jones shuddered at the thought of the lord's huge black bulk. But whatever it took, he couldn't go back to his employers—or his family—as a failure. More importantly, he couldn't let his wife be right after all, that she was the one with business sense. Jones sweated in the human body his company gave him, that of a recently "vacated" college professor. Unfortunately it didn't fit exactly right, and had an annoying tendency to split its zipper whenever Jones felt emotions that expanded his molecular structure, such as the frustration and fear triggered by encountering a serious obstacle to his dream of returning to all the women in his life as an unquestioned hero.

Twenty Two

Louie always kept two cats. Even when she was growing up with Aunt Emma, it was just something they did, making sure there were two cats in the house. Louie named her current pair Thing One and Thing Two. She'd adopted them together about seven years before, when Emma's two cats suddenly disappeared, and Louie had given Em hers. Well, "given" was a strong word. She'd brought George and Martha to Emma's house to help her through her grief. Somehow, they'd never come back home with Louie. After about three months, Louie accepted the situation and went to the county animal shelter.

Louie hated going there, only partly because she knew she'd want to take the animals home. She hated the whole idea of unwanted animals, and the county shelter was one of the worst places for them to land. Seattle also boasted several great no-kill shelters, run by devoted volunteers, and Louie gave them a fair amount of her salary every year in donations. But she adopted from the county shelter because it was basically pet prison. It was dark and cramped and loud with sounds of mewing cats and barking dogs. Even the volunteers there gave Louie the creeps. Especially the one who took charge on Saturdays.

It was a Saturday when she'd gone to adopt two new cats. Sure enough, he'd been there. He wore the little green volunteer's vest like it was a drill sergeant's uniform and treated the people who came to adopt animals like they were his rookie recruits. Worse, he treated the cats as if they were his to dispose of, benevolently or maliciously, as he saw fit.

When he saw Louie walk in, he immediately latched onto her. "Are you here to adopt a poor little dog or a poor little cat today, ma'am?" he said in his oily, smarmy voice.

"I'm here to see the cats, and take two home, but—"

"Oh, how wonderful of you! You'll come right with me, this way!"

"No, I'd rather look at them alone—"

"Nonsense! You'll just pick out the cutest two, and believe me, they aren't the two you want."

Oh god, here we go. Louie shuddered.

"You want the two I'm about to show you," he'd continued. "They are a little scruffy looking, but I've tested their attitudes, and they'll be the most compliant little kitties you've ever had. No trouble at all."

She followed him into the room with the cat cages, fighting the nausea that always threatened to overcome her in that kind of place. *I'll ignore him and see who's here.*

As they turned a corner, she saw two cats sharing a cage. A big white fellow and a little orange tabby, the tabby curled up with her front legs around the big white cat, as if she clung for dear life, her eyes squeezed shut. The white cat stared at Louie with golden eyes.

In that instant the deal was done. "I'll take those two," Louie pointed them out to the head volunteer.

He walked back a few steps to see where she was pointed. "Oh no, dear, they aren't for you. They are a couple of terrors. I've taken them out of their cage, and tried to hold that big white monster and give him a cuddle. He bit my nose! Made it bleed, little beast! And the little orange one just howls if she's not right with him." He'd dropped his voice to a conspiratorial whisper. "Between you and me, I don't think they'll make it. They only have a day or so left on their ticket, and I'm not sending them home with anyone."

"I'm taking them," Louie insisted.

"I don't think so." He'd leered at her. "Who is wearing the green vest here, honey?"

"I'm getting my carriers from the car. Have them ready when I get back."

She walked out to the car and pulled out the two carriers. When she went back inside, he blocked the entry to the cat area.

"Where do you think you're going with those?" His eyes glittered.

Louie let herself get angry. *Okay, gloves off.* She put the carriers down on the floor, and walked up to him until her face was about two inches from his.

"What is your name? Oh, there it is, on that green vest you're so proud of. 'Rusty.' Well, Rusty, let me tell you something. I am going to go back there and put those two cats in these carriers. I'm going to take them home with me. When I get home, I am going to write a letter to the shelter director. I am going to tell him that Rusty is the best volunteer in charge he's ever had, and he needs to make sure to keep you around. Unless, Rusty, unless, that is, you try to stop me. In that case, I'm still going to go get those cats, even if I have to knee you in the balls to get to them. And I'm still going to write a letter. But if you try to stop me, the letter will say this— Rusty, your volunteer in charge on Saturday, groped me in the cat cage area. He pushed me right up against the cages and grabbed my boobs. He threatened to kill the cats I wanted to adopt if I didn't let him do me right there. I kneed him in the balls, grabbed my cats, and ran. Mr. Shelter Director, I do not want to make trouble for the shelter by calling the police. You all do fine work and it would break my heart to do anything that might cast it in a bad light. But I am coming back next Saturday, Mr. Director, and if Rusty is anywhere within ten miles of the shelter, I will call the police, and the Channel Five News, and Mrs. Rusty. And I will tell them all the story of how he tried to feel me up in the cat cage room."

Rusty's eyes became huge, and he dripped sweat. "You wouldn't dare," he whispered in a hoarse voice. "You bitch."

"That's right, Rusty. I'm a raving bitch, and now you are going to step aside and let me get those cats. Right?"

Rusty stepped aside. Louie picked up the carriers and walked back into the cat cage room. The big white cat stood up, staring at her with golden eyes. The little orange cat sat beside him, blinking at her.

She opened the cage and spoke to them. "All right, little ones, it's okay. I'm taking you both with me, but I have to put you into these carriers to get you to your new home safely. That means you'll be apart for about half an hour, but still very close to each other. Okay?"

The white cat raised a paw, showing the previous owner cut off its front toes—declawing, they called it, but it was really amputating each toe from the last joint.

"Guess you're going to be an indoor cat, sweet thing." She smiled as the soft white paw touched her nose ever so gently. She scooped him up and put him in a carrier and closed the little door. "Now you, sweet thing number two."

She expected the little orange tabby to howl at being separated even for such a little time from her big friend, but the little cat blinked at her again. Louie'd placed her gently in the other carrier and closed its door, too.

"Now, we have to do one more thing before we go. Be patient just a bit longer." Louie walked around the cat cage room, and opened every door. "Guys," she'd said, "this is only temporary, but it's likely to get old Rusty there fired for letting the cats out during the day. If you want to add a touch of drama, one or two of you hide under something for a long enough time so that they think you've escaped entirely. And set up a howling to beat the band, please, so the director will hear you in his office."

For a moment, they all seemed to look at her, and then at each other. Then a skinny grey cat, with green eyes, jumped down out of his cage and set up a holler. Two black cats followed, and a little calico scooted into a dark corner under a table. Soon the cages were empty and the noise turned into a din.

Louie picked up the carriers, walked out past a red-faced and furious Rusty, and put the kitties in the car. They stayed silent the whole time. She looked back toward the shelter in time to see the director run into the lobby and start shouting at Rusty, who shouted back.

"Better split, things," she said, and drove away. *Thing One and Thing Two.* She said the names out loud. "Thing One"—and the little orange tabby stood up in her carrier and mewed. "And Thing Two"—and the big white cat rolled over on his back and showed her his tummy, as she glanced at her rear view mirror to see them in the back seat. She laughed. "Okay, that's not the order I thought you'd be in, but I get it. She's the brains, you're the brawn. I think we'll get along great."

~ * ~

Louie recalled that day as she sat on the plane flying across the Atlantic Ocean. It was the last time she remembered having the courage to fight for something. Since then, Thing One and Thing Two lived up to their names, wreaking havoc in her house, waking her up an hour before dawn, demanding food, dashing across her bed, howling at one another. Every day they did something that made her laugh, no matter how low, stressed, or tired she felt. They even accepted her little blind dog, Buddy, with relatively good grace, especially once they realized he couldn't see them. Thing Two especially loved to tease the little dog by reaching out and smacking him on the back when he walked by Thing Two's perch on the living room ottoman. The dog would turn to find who touched him, and Thing Two would leap over his head to the chair, seeming all the while to chuckle at Buddy's attempts to locate him.

Louie wondered if she would ever see any of them again. She hoped she'd done the right thing, leaving Thing One, Thing Two, and Buddy with Aunt Emma, and taking off to go halfway across the world, trying to save a human race she didn't always care for all that much. Maybe she should have just packed up her little family and headed for the hills, let the rest of the humans shift for themselves. Some days, it seemed like most of them would be seriously improved by being turned into cyborgs. Like Rusty, the shelter volunteer. Like the guy in the next seat who spread his bulk well over the arm that was meant to separate them, or the one who bonked her on the head when he hoisted his overstuffed rolling carry-on bag into the overhead bin. Or the woman across the aisle, trying to get a stewardess's attention over the noise of her squawking, puking toddler.

Yes, on many days, if someone told Louie she'd be asked to choose between hiding out with her babies in some remote cabin somewhere and saving the human race, she would have found it tough to decide. *Oh, who am I kidding? Cabins and critters of course. It would've been no contest.*

To help tune out the screaming toddler and her own gnawing

fear, Louie pulled her iPod out of her backpack and put the headphones on. She scrolled through the music list until she found some blues, which seemed right, and settled back in her seat as she heard the voice of Blues Boy King come spilling through the ear buds.

Twenty Three

On the long flight from Seattle to Amsterdam, listening to B.B. King's *Live from the Cook County Jail* pouring from her earphones, Louie remembered the first live concert she attended. She read in the paper that B.B. was coming to Seattle and decided to buy tickets she couldn't really afford. She'd used the excuse of giving them to her then-boyfriend for his birthday, but although he knew who B.B. King was, it was obvious to them both the gift was really for Louie. Back then, she worked at the writing and math tutoring center at one of the local community colleges, making barely above minimum wage, and still dated the wrong kind of guy.

The night of the concert, Louie'd had a crappy day at work. Her boss at the tutoring center was a terminally chipper middle-aged woman named, improbably, Zinnia. Zinnia was always on Louie to improve her manner with the students she tutored. Many of the students who came to the center were international students who needed help with the perverse mechanics of academic writing in English; Louie liked working with them a lot. But there were always a few who just didn't want to do their own homework, and they'd treated all the tutors as their personal servants. Louie dreaded seeing one in her queue. Their entitled attitudes put her on edge, and she inevitably wound up snapping at them. Zinnia's uncanny ability to walk by her little cubicle at the moment some privileged entitled kid would finally push Louie into making a smart-ass remark resulted in regular lectures to Louie about her "attitude." "You collect more flies with honey than vinegar," Zinnia would say in her singsong ex-hippie voice. *Right*, Louie would want to reply, *and who wants to excel at collecting flies, anyway?* But she'd bite her lip, because the tutoring gig was all that stood between her and the twin horrors of depending on her boyfriend or living out of her car.

On the day of the concert, Zinnia, with her usual sense of timing, walked by just as Louie let loose on a particularly annoying student. This one, a pretty young blonde, had been rolling her eyes and sighing at every suggestion Louie offered for improving her case study on a young coffee company that just opened its first store in Seattle. When Louie tried once more, asking "Now in this paragraph, what's your topic sentence?" the blonde replied, "I don't know, why don't you just rewrite it for me?"

"Because that would be cheating, not tutoring, and because even if I did, it wouldn't change the fact that you are as dumb as a bag of hammers," Louie said just as Zinnia walked by.

"Louie, please come to my office," Zinnia chirped with a frown.

Damn, I'm in for another lecture. Louie followed Zinnia down the hall and stepped into her office as Zinnia instructed.

"Close the door, and sit down." Louie did both.

"Louie, I heard you insult that student."

"Did you also hear her ask me to write her paper for her?"

"No, but even if she did, that is no excuse for being rude."

"Even if she did? Don't you believe me?"

Zinnia made a small sound of exasperation. "What I'm saying, Louie, is that it does not matter what she said to you. What matters is that every student who comes to the tutoring center should leave with a smile on their face."

"His or her face." Louie could not stop herself.

"What did you say?" Zinnia almost lost her chirp.

"Every student is singular, so you can't use 'their,' you have to say 'his or her.' And face is singular, too. You could say 'all students who come to the tutoring center should leave with smiles on their faces.' But you can't say 'every student' and 'their face.'" Louie paused. "It's incorrect."

Zinnia coughed delicately and leaned forward in her chair. "Louie, I think you should take the rest of the day off. Please reflect it as vacation hours on your timesheet. Come back tomorrow with a better attitude." Louie looked at the cat-shaped clock on Zinnia's wall. Already four pm, time to go home anyway. *Clowns to the left of me, jokers to the right.* Louie left Zinnia's office in a cloud of frustration.

Traffic had been terrible, and when she'd finally gotten home, Louie's boyfriend still wore his house-painting coveralls.

"Hey, why aren't you ready?" Louie'd tried to keep her voice light.

"Ready for what?" He knew she hated it when he answered her questions with a question.

"For the concert—remember, tonight's B.B. King at the Paramount!"

"Louie, we have plenty of time."

"Wrong, the opening act starts in an hour and a half, and you know how hard it is to find parking—"

He cut her off. "No one cares about being there in time for the opening act. Do you even know the name of the band?"

"That's not the point. The point is, if we left now, we could get there in plenty of time and be relaxed for the start of the show. Instead, we're going to be rushing, and tense, and—"

"You're no fun to be around when you're like this, you know."

"Like what?" Louie didn't really have to ask. They'd had this fight many times before.

"When you're tired, or nervous, you try to control everyone around you."

"I don't!" Even then, Louie realized she did.

"You do. You tell me what to wear, when to get dressed, what route to take to the theater—you know you will, when we get in the car. If you had a bad day, suck it up and don't take it out on me."

And the evening went on like that, with Louie picking on her boyfriend, and developing a pounding migraine, until by the time they got to the theatre she thought her head would explode. She'd known it wasn't his fault, and she'd even wondered if Zinnia had a point. Maybe she did have a bad attitude. Maybe she was too judgmental, too controlling, too hard to be around.

When they'd finally found a place to park, Louie'd walked from the car to the theater in that kind of stony silence she sank into when she knew she should apologize, but felt too bad about herself to do it. "Okay, all right, we're here already," her boyfriend snapped as they headed toward the theatre. She'd been unable to respond. "Fine. Don't say anything. Happy birthday to me, I guess."

After rushing to get there in time for the opening act, Louie'd been annoyed to find it was terrible—just a lot of exceptionally loud guitar playing by some young skinny kid who let his hair hang around his face and didn't say a word to the crowd. In return, the audience mostly talked through his set. Louie'd settled into a pit of self-loathing. At the intermission she considered leaving, going home, catching a cab, whatever it would take to get out of there. But she knew she couldn't, this was her birthday gift to her boyfriend, and she needed to stick it out.

Then B.B.'s band took the stage and started to play. Louie didn't know if the house adjusted the sound level but suddenly it wasn't too loud at all, it was perfect. And the band was in a groove, and the leader began whipping up some enthusiasm in the crowd.

Are you ready to have a good time?
Yeah!
I said, are you ready to have a good time?
Yeah!
I can't hear you, Seattle!
Yeah!
I can't hear you, Seattle!
Yeah!

Then the King himself walked on stage with his beautiful Gibson guitar, Lucille, and the crowd really went crazy. And as he played, Louie's headache literally melted away. By the time he got to *How Blue Can You Get*, Louie thought the world was a fine, fine place. By the time he started his second set with *The Thrill is Gone*, she'd loved everything and everyone in that world again, and with *Rock Me Baby,* she'd believed even she could be forgiven.

It was something about how Lucille became a second voice for him—and he'd said, "I don't play and sing at the same time, I never learned how"—*but she is him singing, and she is the voice of his soul. And that voice is beautiful. If humans can make beauty like that, maybe they are worth saving, after all.*
~ * ~

On the plane, remembering that night a long time ago, that moment she first experienced forgiveness, Louie let Blues Boy and Lucille rock her into a fitful sleep.

Twenty Four

Harsh florescent light illuminated the Prague airport, as in airports everywhere. The international arrivals terminal was newer, and clean, at least. Luckily for Louie, it was designed to be easy even for the directionally impaired to find the baggage carousels after going through passport control. Everyone spilling off the planes and congregating around the slowly turning black belts seemed tired. Louie reminded herself she'd essentially been up all night, and searched for a clock on the wall, trying to figure out what time it really was here.

She felt for her keys and found them, pulling them out of the pocket of her bag. It was just habit, she always reached for them first, whenever she arrived anywhere. Something fell to the floor and skittered across the shiny marble with a tinkling sound.

My house! The little silver house on her key ring somehow fell off. Rapidly, it got lost in the sea of boots and shoes tromping around the carousels. Louie tried to chase it as people unknowingly kicked it several times, until she finally lost track of it. She sat down in an uncomfortable bright blue vinyl airport chair, fighting tears. She remembered when she discovered that her Aunt Emma slipped the little charm into Louie's things, after a particularly tough Thanksgiving visit, when they came as close as ever to fighting. Emma had worn the house on her charm bracelet for as long as Louie could remember. Louie always told her aunt it was the house she wanted for herself one day, and she'd kept it since then as a kind of good luck charm. Now it was gone, now when she needed luck more than ever before.

Louie's frustration took over and she started swearing to herself. "Goddamn sonofabitch mother fu—"

"You look like you lost your best friend."

Louie jumped. She turned and saw Jack smiling at her.

"Oh Jack, I dropped my house, and it went under everyone's feet, and I can't find it." Louie tried not to let the tears escape.

"Your house?" Jack looked confused.

"My little silver house charm—it's been on my keychain forever, it brings me luck—and now it's gone."

"Well, welcome to eastern Europe, land of lost hopes and lost luck. In fact, that is the local motto. You'll fit right in here."

Louie smiled in spite of herself. "Thanks, Jack."

"For?"

"Meeting me, making me laugh—everything."

"Well, don't get all mushy on me just because you're jet lagged. We've got to go save the human race, you know."

"And we have to do it without my lucky charm. All right, which way out of this place?"

"Well, some people like to go that way, and some people like to go that way, but—" Jack grabbed her duffel bag and started off. "I like this way!"

Louie shouldered her backpack and followed him down the wide hallway, looking back once or twice to see if she could catch a glimpse of silver somewhere on the floor. Instead, she thought she saw a flash of black, but it disappeared behind a corner before she could decide whether it was real or a trick of the light. She was so focused on that, she didn't notice the large gentleman in a trench coat and mirrored sunglasses put down the newspaper he wasn't reading, and follow them out of the airport.

They went to Jack's car and loaded Louie's bags in the trunk. As Jack reached up to close the trunk lid, Louie saw that black flash again out of the corner of her eye. Now she recognized it.

"Jack! Look out!"

The bird-bat thing swooped down towards Jack's head, and he ducked just in time to miss the worst of the raking talons. The thing climbed back up in the sky, making a big arc, picking up speed for its next dive.

"What the hell? Get in the car, now!"

Louie yanked on the door handle. "It's locked, idiot! Push

the unlock button!"

"Have you looked at this car? It doesn't have an unlock button. It doesn't have anything electronic."

"I don't care how you do it, just unlock the door!" As Louie yelled, the thing made its second dive, this time right for her. She hit the ground and slid under the car. The thing crashed into the passenger window and shattered it. It bounced off and fell on the ground, about two feet from Louie's face. The black bat monster lay still just long enough for Louie to think it might have knocked itself out. Then its eye-button-things seemed to focus right on her face. She tried to crawl out from under the other side of the car, but she was lying face down, with her arms under her chest, and the back of her jacket was caught.

"Shit. Jack, do something. I'm stuck here."

Jack didn't respond. The thing's eye-buttons recorded or filmed her, Louie recognized. "Jack. Jack? I'm trapped here, where are you?"

Silence, except for the slight whirring sound the black monster made.

Then a screech as it flung its two talons toward Louie's face.

Then another screech that, in Louie's terrified state, sounded a lot like the Tarzan yell.

"Ahhh, ahaahahahaha, ahahahha!"

Then a thud-smack-crunch, as Louie saw her backpack come smashing down on the black monster thing.

The sound of her own heart pounded in her ears, as the thing melted into an oozy, oily black puddle, just like the ones on her bed.

"Louie?" Jack's face peered at her under the car, over the puddle of ooze. "Are you okay?"

"I think so, but my jacket is caught—"

Jack reached under the car, found the snag, and unhooked the jacket. "Okay, crawl on out."

"I think I'll go out the other side, so I don't have to go through that.... gunk."

"Good idea. I'll meet you over there."

Louie slid out the other side of the car as Jack came around. As she stood up and brushed herself off, she realized his left ear was bleeding.

"It got you, Jack."

"What?"

"Your ear. It's bleeding. The thing got you."

Jack put his hand to his ear and pulled it away, staring at his blood. "Crap. Do you think it's poisoned or anything? Do you think I'm dying?"

"I don't think so. One of them got Buddy's ear, too, and he was okay."

"Buddy, your blind dog?"

"Yup. Two of them were waiting for me when I got home yesterday—or the day before, or whatever—and Buddy went after them."

"I thought you might need him."

"I always need him. I'll tell you the whole story later. We should get out of here now."

"You're right. Here's your backpack—" It dripped with black oily ooze.

"Great, thanks. You couldn't have smashed that thing with something I didn't have to carry?" Louie curled her lip in disgust.

"I wasn't exactly thinking much further ahead than 'stop it before it tears Louie's face off.' And this is the gratitude I get for saving your life. Nice. Besides, it was the heaviest thing I could grab."

"How did you know it would be heavy? I carried it to the car myself." Louie cocked her head at Jack.

"Louie, how many books did you bring with you?"

"Just a few. I mean it's a long frickin' flight, and then I got another one or two in the Amsterdam airport—oh. You knew my backpack would be full of books." Louie wasn't embarrassed, exactly. In fact, she kind of liked being known so well by someone. Then she noticed something. *That's funny. I was pretty sure I zipped that bag all the way, and now it's open. The zipper must've slipped when Jack whacked the monster with it. Hope it doesn't break.*

Jack grinned. "Get in the car. At least now you can reach right in that broken window and unlock it yourself."

As they drove away, a black SUV pulled out and followed at

a discreet distance.

Twenty Five

Only a few hours later Louie found herself ready to give up. "Jack, I can't do this."

"Do what, Lou?"

"This. Fight Sergio. Fight Jones. Fight—all of them. Why would I, anyway? Just to save humanity? Aren't we all a kind of cyborg army anyway? I mean, don't most people spend their time just believing what they're told, doing what they're told, doing whatever is put in front of them?"

"You don't."

"Yes, I do. That's all I've ever done. What's in front of me."

"Well, then, it must be the way you do it. You make things better."

"Ha! Name one. One thing that's better around PPP3 because of me."

"Me."

"Right, that's what I said. Because of me."

"Me."

"Jack, don't fool around, I—"

"Me. I mean me. I mean, I am. Better. Because of you."

"Oh Jack. You know that's not what I'm talking about. Anyway, I give up."

"But you tried, Lou. And you have to keep trying."

"Oh sure. See where my 'trying' got us? Jack, if it hadn't been for your friend Gil, we'd be—"

"Don't say it."

"Dead. We'd be dead, Jack, because of my trying."

"Lou."

"And Gil is dead, isn't he."

"Lou."

"Just tell me, Jack. He's dead, isn't he?"

In Jack's silence, they both recalled the scene. After fighting off the bat-monster at the airport, Jack drove them to the center of town and they walked to a little coffee shop in the old square. It seemed best not to go directly to the office building in the factory town, he explained, given their encounter with the monster. They needed a spot to talk about what to do next.

"Tell me everything you know, Louie," Jack demanded once they were seated and each held a steaming cup of cappuccino to warm their hands.

"Everything? I have a master's degree in philosophy, Jack, I know a lot of useless shit. Shall we start with Schrödinger's cat? See, there's this cat in a box, and it might be dead, but it might not be dead—"

Jack nudged her shoulder. "About Jones, and about Sergio, and the migration project, Lou, as if you didn't know that's what I meant."

Louie leaned away. "Migration project?" She ran through their phone conversation in her mind. She didn't recall ever using that phrase with him. "What are you talking about?"

"When you called me, you said they were turning people into a cyborg army, you said that's what the migration project really was—"

"No, I didn't."

"You didn't?"

"No."

Jack sat back in his chair. "Shit. Are you sure you didn't say migration project? Because if you didn't, I've just given myself away, haven't I?"

"You have, and now I'm giving you about three minutes to convince me I should keep trusting you." A knot grew in Louie's stomach, but somehow she was sure he would persuade her.

"Now that's a line I've heard too many pretty women say to you, Jack," came a voice from over Louie's shoulder, smooth and deep, with no trace of the local accent, and every inflection of the American south.

"Gil?" Jack jumped, clearly startled to see him there, though he didn't seem displeased.

"Aren't you going to introduce me?" Gil swiveled a chair from his own table to theirs. Before Jack could answer, Gil reached out and took Louie's hand in his firm grasp. "I'm Gil Munroe, pleased to meet you. I'm obviously much more polite than my good friend Jack here." Gil was lanky, dressed casually in jeans and a wool jacket. His sandy blonde hair, twinkling green eyes, boyish face and warm smile made Louie imagine all kinds of things happening between them, made her shift in her chair, made her cheeks flush pink, and she knew, without a doubt, she was the thousandth woman to react to Gil this way. It made her a little angry.

But only a little.

"My name's Louie, visiting Jack here on business," she hastened to add, not sure why.

"Not personal then? That's the best news I've had all day," Gil grinned.

"How do you two know each other?" Louie wondered.

"Oh, you know, two Americans in this place, we were bound to run into each other, right, Jack? In fact, it was in that bar right over there, across the square."

Jack coughed. "That's a story Louie doesn't need to hear right now, Gil. We're kind of busy here, so if you don't mind—"

Gil laughed. "Don't worry, I wasn't going to tell her the worst of it. Although, as a journalist, I am obligated to tell the truth, it doesn't mean I have to tell the whole truth. And right now, Jack, my journalistic instincts are going to do you a huge favor." Gil dropped his voice and turned serious. "Don't turn around, but there are two goons over there, just outside that bar, and I think they're watching you and your lovely coworker, here. Lou"— she noticed he slipped easily into calling her that name, as if he were already her friend too—"you can look without drawing attention. See what I mean?" She looked, and saw nothing out of the ordinary, or at least what she assumed to be ordinary in this place she'd never been before. "No, where are they?" she whispered to Gil. "Right over there," he replied, and she followed his gaze in time to catch a fleeting image of black trench coat. "I'm not sure," she said.

"Maybe."

Gil let out a low whistle. "They're too good to be Josef's boys. Jack, what kind of trouble are you two in?" Jack's face looked pained, but he'd stayed quiet. "Oh, I see," Gil said. "The deep shit kind. Well, that's my cue to leave. I never stick around for trouble, as Jack can tell you, Louie. But if you get out of this square alive, well, tell him to give you my number so I can take you out for a drink." Gil squeezed her hand and strolled off the opposite way from where Louie had seen the flash of trench coat. She turned to look at Jack, who'd become pale and silent.

"Are we?" she asked.

"Are we what?" came the whispered reply.

"In the deep shit kind of trouble."

"If Gil is right, then yes, yes we are."

"And I still don't know why I should trust you."

"No, no you don't. But Lou—"

A hand came down on Jack's shoulder. "Mr. Smith?" said an accented voice. Louie looked up to see a man in a tan trench coat looking down at her. "You will please to come with me, Mr. Smith."

She turned to Jack to ask him what this was about, what she should do, but his eyes turned grey again, and he was not looking at her. "Gil," he hissed. "He wouldn't—" *Turn you in?* Louie's mind completed Jack's thought. Had Gil found the trench coated man and told him—what? Something about Jack? About Louie? She realized she was in a strange city, in a strange country, completely out of her element, and her only friend there was about to be taken away by — what did Gil call them—a goon, and not one of Josef's goons, either, some other goons who were far better at what they did. Louie still didn't want to know what they did, she only knew that trust Jack or not, he was all she had. She needed to act. Like her friend Mac. Action unimpeded by emotion, in this case Louie's fear. *What would Mac do?*

What happened next happened so fast, the business traveler standing near the cafe in the square would have missed it if he'd blinked.

Louie got up and turned away. She moved toward the cafe door, as if she needed to go inside and use the restroom. The goon started to pull Jack up by his coat, and then, out of nowhere, something—later that business traveler would swear, *I'm not kidding, it looked like a baseball*—whistled through the air and hit the goon in the head. Someone from the other side of the square yelled—again, the traveler would say, *I'm not kidding*—someone yelled "beanball! Warning to both benches!"

The goon was dazed and dropped his hold on Jack's shoulder, and Jack should've run at that moment—that's what the traveler would have expected—but instead he reached out to stop the goon from falling.

Louie turned away, looking in the direction of the voice, and took off toward someone else—*the source of the voice,* that traveler would opine. *She took off running toward the source of the beanball voice*—which meant, for a moment, she was all alone in the middle of the square, a perfect target, and Jack roused himself to run after her, but he didn't get there first. The source of the beanball voice, a tall, lanky man with sandy blond hair, reached her, and the next noise wasn't a baseball being thrown, it was a gunshot. The traveler would pause to explain that he knew it was a real gunshot because *it didn't sound like the ones in movies or television shows, it was a popping sound rather than a too-loud bang,* and then the blond man stopped dead, and looked down at himself, and started to crumple, and Louie tried to catch him, to ease him down, and then Jack was there too, and they'd been swarmed by people.

And here's the weird part, that traveler would tell his friends, *I know, you're thinking we haven't gotten to the weird part yet? But here it is—the blond man slipped out of the crowd, while the other two were talking to a police officer, and the goon stumbled after him, and the blond guy turned into a side alley, and then my Blackberry buzzed, it was the office and I had to answer it so that's all I saw.*

Neither Jack nor Louie saw that part, of course, and now they sat outside the police station, where they'd finally finished answering all the questions they could, a million times each. "He took the bullet meant for me," Louie said softly. "And now he's dead. And I give up."

"You need a bridge," Jack answered. "Sooner or later, everyone who comes here does. Follow me."

Twenty Six

Jack walked along in silence, finding his way among the streets and alleys, taking his time, on purpose. He wanted to give Louie time to calm down, to realize what she'd done so far. He wanted to give himself time, too, to think about what to do next. It was a giant cock-up, as usual, a cluster, was the expression he'd learned in America. *A cluster fuck.* She'd only been in the area for a few hours, and he'd already slipped and made her wonder if she could trust him, already run into Gil, of all people, and then Gil pulled the disappearing act, as always. They already fought twice—the first with the bat monster ended okay because he was ready, but the second one in the square with the goons was so unnecessary, if he'd been thinking and sent word in time. Now she thought she was done already, ready to give up, and he knew there was so much left to do before—before the end. So he walked her through Prague the long way, to the bridge.

Louie thought while she walked, too. About all the reasons why she should give up, or better yet, never should have tried. What was she thinking? Asking Jones if she could help, putting herself in the worst kind of mess, a cluster, that was the word Mac taught her, *this was a cluster fuck,* and it was all her fault. Like the Archive Project, like her bad boyfriends, like her whole life. She couldn't even hang on to a stupid good luck charm more than five minutes into this ridiculous adventure. Who did she think she was, anyway?

Prague Castle sits on top of the city like an old patriarch, silent and dominating, drawing everyone to court its favor sooner or later. Their walking had taken them around the long way, so they came from the top of the hill after a good strenuous climb. Louie walked down the cobblestones toward the castle, taking it in.

"Oh look," said Jack. "They're about to change the guards." The crowd of people gathered close to watch. "You see those uniforms? Guess what year they were designed." Louie opened her mouth to answer. "Wrong!" Jack called out, before she could say a word. "They were used in the film *Amadeus*, directed by Milos Foreman, and the people liked them, so they kept them. That was what, nineteen-eighty-two?" Louie smiled; just then she heard music. She turned around and behind the crowd in the entrance was a small group of musicians, a violin, a bass, and a flute, and they were playing and singing something lovely that floated on the air. While everyone else watched the guards perform their ritual in Hollywood costumes, Louie wandered closer to the music.

When she turned around, Jack was there.

"That was nice," Louie smiled. "I liked that."

"Don't do it again, though, in this crowd," said Jack.

"Do what?"

"Walk away without telling me where you are going. For a second I thought I'd lost you." *And panicked like I'd lost* her *again.*

"Jack, I was right here." Louie knew Jack was right, and it made her grumpy.

"Yes, but I wasn't."

"You are. You're right here, too."

"I am now, yes, but—never mind, Lou, just tell me before you wander away, okay?"

"What am I, a two-year-old?"

"No, if you were two you'd actually do what I tell you."

"What makes you think I won't?"

Jack gave up. They walked around the castle toward a viewpoint where the red roofs of Prague stood below like, well, really red roofs. Louie admitted it was a nice view.

"What do you want to be when you grow up, Jack?" she asked.

"Where did that come from?"

"Oh, you know, all those red roofs bring out the existential questions in me. Don't they do that to you, too?"

"Um, not exactly, but maybe, I guess, I can see that, sure."

"You're patronizing me."

"No! Teasing you, yes, not patronizing you, never."

"Then answer the question."

"Oh hell, I don't know. I don't have a plan. I just want to do good, you know, do something that helps people."

"Like saving the world from aliens who want to turn all humans into a giant cyborg army?"

"I suppose that'd count, if I could do it."

"It's a little late to doubt yourself now, isn't it? I mean we are in this so deep we can't get back out, even if we wanted to." Louie knew as she spoke she was talking to herself as well as to Jack. Quitting was as good as losing, and they had to at least play to a draw.

"I know, but jeez, Lou, since I got this job I've done nothing but let everyone down," Jack answered. "PPP3 is a total fuckup of a company, but I keep working for it, forgiving it in a way, and you know why? I think if I want grace for my own failures I need to give it, too."

Louie looked at him, at his face. "You're serious. You really don't see it, do you." Jack looked lost. "It's funny, you know, that you of all people don't see it. How you are a good influence on everyone you're around. How you make people and situations better than they were without you. How no one cares if you screw up now and then, because we can all see exactly where your heart is."

"Middle of chest, a little to the left?"

"Right. Exactly. I didn't really mean that as a straight line, but okay, I should have known you'd treat it like one."

"I'm sorry. It's just hard. You're right. I don't see myself that way."

"Jack, the thing about grace, if you believe in that stuff, is it comes whether you deserve it or not. It comes because someone or something wants to give it, not because you want it or need it or earn it. You can earn respect, you can deserve kindness, you can ask for help. But grace either comes to you or it doesn't. You can't do anything to influence it. The only thing you can do is recognize it."

They'd been walking more than an hour, and were about halfway down the hill from the castle, heading down the narrow road, stopping now and then to take in a sight or stand under an eave to wait out a sudden shower. Louie saw a bookshop and was drawn to it, as usual. All the titles were in Czech.

"What does that one say? Jack?"

Louie scanned the crowd and realized Jack had stopped and was standing on the sidewalk, about twenty feet behind her. She walked back to him.

"Jack?"

"Yeah."

"You okay?"

"I got it."

"You got what?"

"It, I got it, I recognized it. Just then. Just now. Right now. I got it. I see it. I feel it. It is there. I'm afraid to move, it might go away." He felt a sensation, almost forgotten, almost imperceptible, near his head, as if it were floating there.

"Jack? Do you have a fever?" Louie asked. It began to rain, then hail. "Let's go in here." Louie pulled him by the arm into the nearest doorway, which led into the dark interior of an old church. The musty smell of age greeted them, along with a handful of pamphlets telling the history of the church in Czech and English, and a sign that read, *Silence.*

Few people sat in the pews, praying. Jack stood just inside the door and stared at the altar. Louie stood beside him. She put her hand on his forehead. Not hot, but damp with rain. Maybe he was ill. She couldn't ask in here, *Silence.* She could only stand by him and wait. *Well, maybe that's all he needs.*

Neither was ever quite sure how long they stood there, in that dark little old church on the king's road. It could have been seconds or hours. Finally he just took her hand, gave it a slight squeeze, and led her back out onto the street. The sun had come out into a sliver of a gap between two steel grey clouds. They blinked.

He smiled. "Let's go, Lou. You still need a bridge, and then I need a beer."

Finally, right at sundown, they walked through an ancient gate and set foot on the bridge. The most beautiful bridge in the world, at least at that moment, to them both, with the knowledge that it all might be lost to the human race so soon. The statues of saints, kings, martyrs, and heroes along the sides of the Charles Bridge seemed to feel it too, seemed lean in, deepening the shadows. The few tourists still walking the bridge hurried their steps just a little, to get off sooner. Jack walked to a statue about halfway across and stopped, leaned on the wide stone railing, looked down in the water, waited for Louie to catch up, and then explained.

"This bridge was built by Karol II, Charles in the western world, and all these statues have stories. Of course these are reproductions, in the early eighties they moved the real ones into a museum, they were falling apart, and started restoring them. But the stories are still here. This one, for example. Carved in the bronze here at the base, there's a saint on one side, and a little dog on the other. The legend is, if you touch the dog, it brings good luck. See how the bronze is rubbed shiny there? It gets touched by hundreds, maybe thousands of people a day. On a summer afternoon, the line to touch the dog stretches all the way off the bridge. It's also supposed to be good luck to touch the saint on the other side, but most people would rather touch the dog."

Louie touched it herself, felt its cold smooth surface, remembered Buddy, back in Seattle, and made a silent wish. The sun dipped all the way below the horizon and they were in the dark. It seemed all the usual night lights were broken or dimmer than usual, and it took a while for Louie's eyes to adjust. When they did, she saw—or rather felt—it again. *Beauty like this.*

They walked on, back down into the old town square, found a pub, and sat at a table outside, despite the nighttime chill. Jack ordered a beer; Louie started to ask for a coffee, but then changed her mind. "I'd like a beer too. What the hell."

"Another *pivo, prosim*," Jack spoke to the waiter. "You won't regret it, Lou. The Czechs make the best beer in the world. Don't tell the Slovaks I said so." He grinned. "They still compete about everything."

The beer arrived. Louie took one sip and knew he was right. She savored the flavor and the way it warmed her insides, and shook loose a few things in her head, too, after only a few swallows. "Don't tell anyone back in Seattle, because I have a reputation to uphold." Louie thought of the beer, so that the rest of her sentence surprised her too. "But I think I'm falling a little bit in love…"

Jack choked on his beer and spit half of it out. Louie looked sideways at him. "Relax. I was going to say I'm falling in love with this city. But thank you for that. That was a Hallmark moment. For a split second you think I'm about to say I'm falling in love with you, and you choke. Beautiful. That's a moment I am going to remember on my deathbed. Thanks." Louie laughed a little. Then she surprised herself again by starting to cry. She felt her heart swell as she realized how she did feel about Jack. She felt…connected. And feeling connected felt good. It felt very good. Louie didn't want to ever stop feeling connected like this.

She realized Jack was staring at her, his face pale and drawn with worry. "Jack…"

"Oh my god, Louie, I'm sorry. I really hurt your feelings. I can tell because you're crying, aren't you. Stop crying…" he reached out to touch her cheek, to wipe a tear away.

"Do you want to know why I'm crying?"

"Yes I do. Do I? You look so sad. Maybe I don't want to know," Jack said.

"I'm not sad. I'll try to explain…but I have to use a lot of words to tell you. I know that won't come as a shock. So be patient because they are all important, these words." Louie took a deep breath.

"I grew up with my Aunt Emma, because my parents were killed in an accident a long time ago. I love her, but for as long as I can remember, I knew I didn't belong to her, and she didn't belong to me. Not really. Not like blood family. She's not really my aunt, you see. She told me once and I chose to forget it, or ignore it. But I knew it all the time. I'm not sure how I wound up as her obligation, but that's what I was. An obligation.

"When I got old enough I started creating a chosen family. That makes it sound too much like I did it on purpose. I didn't. I just became blessed with people who I am actually connected to, people who I love because of who they are, because we belong to each other. There are not very many of them but they are each very, very precious to me. In my chosen family, I have a wonderful sister. I cherish her."

"Mac," Jack stated, rather than asked.

"Mac. But..." Louie paused to swallow something, maybe her meal, maybe the threat of tears. "I've never had a chosen brother." She looked at Jack. "I'm asking your permission to choose you as my brother."

He looked back, but kept silent. Finally Louie needed to say something. "I promise I won't ask to borrow money or anything. You don't have to beat anyone up for being mean to me on the playground. I just would really, really like to think of you as... family."

Jack's left ear buzzed now. He tried to ignore it, and pulled Louie into his arms, as they both cried silently for a while. "Only if I could choose you as a sister," he finally whispered, some part of him feeling he'd done so a long time before.

Louie nodded. The buzzing in his ear increased to a roar and he wanted it to stop, so he made a joke. "And I will ask to borrow money. I will need a lot of it, I think." To his immense relief, Louie laughed, and the buzzing began to fade.

They went back to their beers, and when Jack spoke again, his tone was serious. "So, what do we do now?"

"I don't know, Jack. I really don't. Maybe we should just give up."

"Lou, you think you've lost already. But, the truth is, you haven't even been in the game, not really, until now."

Louie's mind turned back to Gil, and the baseball that probably saved her life, back in the square. It was absurd, a baseball in the middle of Prague, and she was sure he'd thrown it. Maybe she owed him something now, like she owed Buddy for saving her from the monster. Maybe she owed Mac, and maybe even Emma, everyone who'd cared for her, who'd tried to have her back. And there was Jack, still here with her, promising to be her brother, her family. Some kind of strength welled up inside—or maybe it was the effect of the beer. "Okay. I'm in the game, Jack, and I think it's time to change it."

"Then so do I," Jack said, "and for that, we each need another beer." Louie nodded and almost smiled. For some reason, maybe it was the strangeness of the place or the adrenaline still in her system or being with Jack, or maybe she was learning to accept the impossible and the absurd, but the headache she expected from drinking never came.

Twenty Seven

Mac grew up in a military family, but not the way most people would assume. Her mother was in the Navy, and rose fairly high in the ranks of Naval Intelligence. Mac's dad seemed mostly to go along for the ride, until he disappeared when she was about twelve years old. From then on, it was just her and her mom. Once, in a fit of early-twenties self-exploration and inspired by a college psychology class to trace all the family dynamics that influenced her, Mac asked her mother about her own childhood.

But her mom would only say, "It's like I showed up on this planet all alone one day, when I was just a little younger than you are now, and the Navy was the only home I could find."

If there was one thing Mac remembered from the time before her father left, it was the feeling of safety. The way being with him made her feel as if the world was an entirely predictable place, a place that would be the same tomorrow as it was today, at least in all the most important ways. Her father could give her this feeling just by being around. She couldn't pinpoint anything he did, any specific way of his that made it happen. It wasn't his easy laugh that was more of a giggle, it wasn't the way he'd grab her hand in his and swing it along as they walked somewhere together, it wasn't the funny hats he'd wear in the sun to protect his bald scalp from burning, it wasn't the spicy smell of his aftershave or his goofy sense of humor or his ridiculously bad taste in ties. She'd loved all these things about him, but none were the absolute source of the safety she'd felt in his presence. She knew this because after he left he still did all those things, presumably, wherever he was; but her sense of safety had been demolished, like that big football stadium the city of Seattle blew up twenty years ago, the Kingdome, *blown to Kingdome*

Come, the joke went, when Mac had watched it on television along with everyone else at work. Watching the huge structure implode and transform itself over the course of a few minutes from a recognizable thing to a cloud of dust and a pile of rubble, Mac had remembered the day her mother told her that her father was gone.

"Gone?" the twelve-year old Mac asked. "Like on a business trip or something?" Her mother laughed a small, cold laugh. "A trip, that's right. He's on some kind of trip, the kind he'll never come back from. It's just you and me now, kiddo." Mac's mom was wonderful, strong and devoted. But no matter how hard she tried, Mac never really felt safe again. She knew her world could implode, like that stadium, at any moment.

Though she didn't realize it, the experience of surviving the loss of her father when it seemed impossible to do so was one reason why Mac was ready, so many years later, when Louie called her from Prague.

"Hello, this is Mac."

"Hi Mac, it's Louie."

"Lou! What's up? Where are you?"

"I'm in Prague."

"You made it to the European operation. Are you with Jack? Is everything okay? Do you need help?"

"We're having dinner. Jack just stepped away from the table. Mac, are you alone?"

"Yup. Why the cloak and dagger? Your voice sounds funny. Louie, are you...are you drunk?"

"Maybe. I drank one, or was it two, beers tonight with Jack. But this is all too real, although you probably won't believe it."

"Hell's bells, Lou, spill it! If you're drinking, this is serious."

Louie told Mac about the sales agreement, the goons, the monsters, and the baseball. And they agreed on what Mac needed to do.

Twenty Eight

Louie and Jack drove to the PPP3 factory Paster'd bought, the one whose workers were Jack's responsibility as Director of Quality Assurance and Underling Morale for European Operations. Silence filled the car as the road twisted and turned through rolling hills covered in green trees, a landscape that spoke of a population too small and too poor to afford the technology that would completely decimate its natural lushness. Louie gazed out the window. *So different from home.*

Where she grew up, trees were lumber waiting to fulfill their destiny by traveling through a Mega Giant Home Improvement Discount Store on their way to becoming a new carport on a split-level ranch house.

"How long until we get there, Jack?"

"About two hours if we don't hit any traffic." Jack turned the car's radio on. *Here I am...rock you like a hurricane...*came pouring out of the speakers. Louie began to laugh.

"What's so funny?" Jack asked.

"Nothing. The Scorpions. That song. It just brings back some memories."

"Good memories? Then do tell. We could use some cheering up, couldn't we?"

"Good? I don't know. It was the closest I ever came to getting into a real fistfight. Happened in high school. It's a long story."

Jack thought for a moment. "Well, we have time. Unless it's a longer than two-hour story. Is it?"

"I hope not," said Louie. "I don't think I could stand thinking about high school for more than two hours." She settled into the seat and turned to look out the window. "I do have to give you some background, though." She looked at Jack out of the corner of her eye. Sure enough, he was grinning. He knew very well Louie couldn't make a story about herself short to save her life. Oh well, she forgave him for smiling at her. She knew it too.

"In my high school, there were three ways to be popular. You could be good looking, be athletic, or provide the beer for the parties of the good-looking athletes. Actually, that third group wasn't so much popular as tolerated. Well, I was never going to be pretty, and I don't so much catch balls as put my hands up to block them from hitting me in the face. That meant sports were out. And I never had enough money for beer. So popular wasn't in the cards for me.

"Beneath the popular kids and the tolerated kids there were two other groups—the stoners and the nerdy geeks. You'll know which group I was in when I say these two words. Debate Club."

"No." Jack rolled his eyes.

"Oh, yes. All three years. Second place in district championships my junior year. Jack, did you just roll your eyes?"

"Me? No, I'm watching the road. Concentrating on my driving. Yup, just watching the road."

"Good, because if you had rolled your eyes, I'd have to stop telling my Scorpions story."

"God forbid. Please, you must continue."

"Okay, well, where was I?"

"Debate Club. Junior year champion."

"No, not champion, second place. Please pay attention, Jack. Anyway, when football season rolled around, all the student clubs got to sponsor a post-game dance. When the Debate Club's turn came around, my crazy abusive high school boyfriend and I were put in charge of the music. We got a brainstorm. We figured we could save a bunch of money by pre-recording all the music, so we wouldn't need to hire a DJ. My aunt owned a decent turntable and cassette deck, and my crazy boyfriend kept a good record collection. We spent a marathon recording session in my aunt's attic putting together about three hours of music on two cassettes. It was brilliant, really, except for one major problem." Louie paused.

"What was that?" Jack took his cue.

"We hated the music that was popular then—this was nineteen-eighty-two. Our FM radio station was pumping out Olivia Newton John and Air Supply, Journey and Toto. We couldn't go there. So in the three hours of music we put together there was a lot of Sex Pistols, Dead Kennedys, X, some Bob Marley thrown in for spice. Then as the day wore on we started adding stuff from my aunt's collection—Louis Prima, the Andrews Sisters, Disney movie soundtracks. You know, like the *Bare Necessities* from the Jungle Book? I am not sure of many things in this world, but I am sure of this—it was the most eclectic set ever recorded for a small-town high school post-football game Debate Club-sponsored dance.

"You can imagine what happened. The Friday night of the dance, we fired up a really big boom box and ran it through the speakers in the high school gymnasium. About nine pm, the kids started streaming in. We cranked the music. By about, oh, nine forty-five the crowd was already thinning pretty significantly. The Debate Clubbers who sold tickets at the door pointed out to us, perhaps somewhat less kindly than was absolutely necessary, that more than a few of our fellow students demanded their money back. By ten pm, only a handful of people remained in the gym. Even the adult chaperones wandered off, probably to get away from the Dead Kennedys.

"I do believe my crazy boyfriend and I were dancing to the Andrews Sisters singing *Apple Blossom Time* when a young gentleman sporting a leather jacket, acid-washed jeans, and a mullet stomped up to us.

"'Play the Scorpions. I want to hear the Scorpions,' he demanded. It was apparent from his breath and demeanor that he'd drunk more than a few under-the-bleachers-at-the-high-school-football-game beers. 'I need to hear the Scorpions. Play the Scorpions right now, goddamn it.'

"Now, things probably would have been fine if I'd spoken first. I was ready to explain that all the music was pre-recorded, that we didn't have any Scorpions, so he would probably be better off simply returning to his muscle car and playing the radio.

"Instead, my crazy boyfriend spoke first. Well, actually, he laughed first. Then he made some rather ungentlemanly remarks about the sort of person who would so love the Scorpions. In fact, he said young men who appreciated the music of the Scorpions and their ilk were very likely to be, shall we say, sexually attracted to other young men who appreciated the music of the Scorpions.

"This probably unnecessarily inflamed the situation. In my small town, like most in America in the early eighties, the worst, the very worst thing you could call a teenage boy was a faggot. That's just the kind of place it was.

"The young man in question was short, but solid muscle. My crazy boyfriend was about six foot two, but skinny, with a permanent limp from an automobile accident that crushed his left leg. Blows were threatened. Fists were drawn back, arms cocked. If I'd had any street smarts, I would've run for the hills, or at least a chaperone. Instead, I stepped in between them."

"Louie. You didn't."

"But I did. See, I've always been a borderline idiot." *Maybe not borderline—maybe all the way over the line.*

"What happened?"

"I'll never forget it. The Scorpions dude looked me right in the eye and said, 'you think I wouldn't hit you because you're a girl?' And of course that's exactly what I'd thought. Exactly. I thought 'you're not going to hit me because I'm a girl. Now I was pissed, because the boys were being stupid; but even more, I was pissed because I'd been wrong. So I said—and, Jack, I have to say I think this is really one of my finer moments—I said, 'do you think anyone who likes the Scorpions could hit me hard enough so that I would notice?'

"Luckily for me, right about then, there was a commotion in the hall as the vice principal who was chaperoning the dance found some unauthorized person wandering out there. He kicked the kid out and shut down the dance. I think after all the refunds and expenses, the Debate Club netted about twenty-five dollars. So much for our big money-saving idea, huh? We blew it all on pizza at our next meeting. And, somewhere in my aunt's house, those cassette tapes live on. I'd love to find them one day and see how the set holds up."

Jack shook his head, touched his left ear, and frowned. Louie looked at him.

"Well, I think that's a funny story. Maybe I didn't tell it right..."

"No, it's hilarious, really. It's just—Louie, you called him your crazy *abusive* high school boyfriend."

"Did I? I suppose that's the name I've given him in my head all this time."

"Was he? Abusive? To you?"

"Yes, I guess he was."

"Then tell me his real name, because I have to go kick his ass. Right now."

Louie snorted. "Jack, I don't know where he is, but I think it is extremely unlikely that he is anywhere near this road. And, you know, we are on a mission to save the human race, and everything. I think that should trump personal revenge at this time, don't you?"

"I don't care. Tell me his name. Tell me his name and I will find him and I will kick his ass."

Louie took another look at Jack's face. "You are serious."

"As a heart attack. As a pissed-off drunk Scorpions fan. Louie, did this boyfriend of yours beat you up?"

"Once or twice. But that wasn't the worst of it. You have to understand—are you sure you want to hear about this? It's ugly stuff. Way uglier than a high school not-quite fist fight over the Scorpions."

"I do. Louie, you don't always have to make me laugh, you know."

Louie felt tears stinging her eyes. "What are you talking about?"

"You know exactly what I mean, I think, because you and I are the same. We both try to make people laugh, to keep them around. I'm telling you this, Louie, and I want you to understand. I care about you, and that means I want to know about your trouble. I want to know the ugly along with the funny."

"Well, as long as you admit the Scorpions story is funny."

"Knock it off, Lou. Tell me something real. Finish what you were going to say."

Louie took a deep breath. *Okay, he wants to know, so here*

goes. "I was going to say, you have to understand that I never would have called him abusive at the time. Remember I wasn't popular or pretty, and I had no money for beer. So between that and my need to rescue all the strays, I hit my dating years convinced that my job was to find the sickest puppy around and rehabilitate him with my love. Well, I succeeded in the first half of my quest. He'd ignore me in public, make out with other girls in front of me, always wanted sex, no matter what I wanted or how I felt. But I never thought about leaving, because each of these episodes was just proof that he needed my love more than ever, right?

"That night of the dance, something happened. I couldn't tell you exactly what. It felt like a visit from a kindly spirit, or something, you know, when you feel touched, and woken up. After the fight, I suddenly seemed to see the truth—that my boyfriend was a prick, too. I tried to break up with him several times. He would wait for me outside my classes, call my friends and threaten them, call me in the middle of the night and tell me he wanted to kill himself or me. I kept going back to him, just to give him time to get better, always promising myself when he was better I really would leave him."

Jack listened intently, almost as if he were remembering that small-town high school dance himself.

"Then one day I got a call from him—this time he was in the hospital, in the mental ward." Louie's voice dropped to a whisper. "He'd committed what they call a suicidal gesture—slit his wrists bad enough to bleed all over his bathroom, but not bad enough to actually die. And now to finish this story, Jack, I have to tell you something really ugly. About me."

She turned to look at him; her eyes were dry, but full of pain. "That's when I finally left him. When he was in the hospital with his wrists bandaged, looking like death on a cracker. I told him I would never see him again. I told him to leave me alone. I told him to get well, but to do it without me. And I walked out and I never saw him again.

"How's that for real, Jack? And very unfunny?" Louie waited for Jack's reaction. She looked out the car window—it was almost dark now, and she could only see her own reflection in the glass. Were the green trees still there? Or had the deepening blackness erased them completely?

After what seemed to her like an eternity, Jack finally spoke. His voice was thick. "Oh, Lou. Yes, that is very, very ugly and unfunny. But you, you are brave. You faced reality. You told him to leave you alone. You saved yourself."

"But I didn't save him, Jack."

"You couldn't. Louie, you were what, eighteen, nineteen?"

"Yes, but—"

"Even if you stayed with him until you were one hundred, you couldn't save him. You know that. He either saved himself or he didn't. It was always up to him." Jack paused for a minute, seeming to collect himself. "And if he did save himself, and he's out there somewhere, I'm telling you, I'm going to find him and kick his ass, Lou."

Louie breathed again, although up until that moment, she hadn't been aware of holding her breath. "Thanks, Jack. No one has ever said anything like that to me before." *And I had no idea how much it would mean to me when someone finally did. This chosen brother thing, I could really get used to it.*

"It's about fricking time then, isn't it?" Jack's grin threatened to return to the corners of his mouth.

"Jack, I have something else to tell you."

"What is it, Louie? You can tell me anything, you know."

She seemed to shimmer at him. "I'm starving. Can we stop for something to eat?"

Twenty Nine

"I don't know, Louie, I've been in this factory hundreds of times. If they are doing anything here other than making useless plastic gadgets, I can't figure out where or how." Jack stood in the entryway to the factory, the only place where the drone of machinery was quiet enough to hear each other.

A small office could be seen off to the right, with "Factory Manager" painted in Czech and English on the frosted glass panel. After greeting them, the little rotund manager went onto the factory floor to deal with some problem or other, asking them to wait a few moments, *prosim*. To the left a single restroom tempted, and though Louie remembered her aunt's advice to always use a restroom when you can, the general state of oily dustiness of the place led her to resist. In front of them, the large sliding corrugated metal door led to the factory itself, with its rows of machines and slow conveyor belts, and rubber pads where the employees stood for hours and hours each day, putting slot a into slot b, and dreaming of—what? The kinds of people who would buy the things they made here, things that had no real use? The chance to play with their children at the end of the day, or the chance to offer them a different kind of life than their grandparents lived, under the communists? Or simply the next pint of *pivo*?

"Let's check it out one more time, anyway," Louie said. "Maybe I'll see something you don't."

They put on their loaner hardhats, Jack's a canary yellow, and Louie's orange like life vests on an airplane. Neither fit well, and Louie resisted the urge to wonder if they would protect them from any real danger, other than a surprise inspection finding the factory out of safety compliance. The factory manager came back, leaving the large door open behind him, and beckoned them in. As they walked the aisles, keeping a safe distance from things that whirred, buzzed, whined, or grunted, Louie scanned for anything that seemed odd or out of place.

Like I would know what looks normal, with my vast experience in eastern European factories.

They walked up one line and down the other, the factory manager talking all the time, in Czech, but even if he'd spoken English, she wouldn't know what he was saying with the factory noise swallowing his small voice. They came back to where they started, and she exchanged a glance with Jack. He shook his head. *Nothing.* She made up a reason to walk around again. About halfway along the second line, something caught her eye. She stopped. Shook her head, as her dog Buddy did, when there were too many smells and he needed to cleanse his sniffing palate and start over. Looked at it again.

"Jack," she called, but he'd walked too far up the line to hear her. "Jack!" she tried again, running up to tap him on the shoulder. "Come back, let me show you this," she gestured so he'd know what she was saying.

He followed.

"There," she mouthed and pointed. "The instructions on that machine." His gaze followed her finger to the little laminated sign screwed to the front of the machine, to the left of the levers that controlled it. He turned back to her, shook his head. "There," she mouthed again, and gestured. But it wasn't there. What she'd seen just moments ago was gone. And that's when she knew.

"Never mind, tell you later," she mouthed, and they wrapped up their tour. Jack spent another half an hour with the manager, listening to his complaints about the lack of support from headquarters. He'd sent requests to Josef and Sergio for months now for new resources, Jack knew very well, he'd cosigned them, and where were they? He couldn't keep running the factory on such a shoestring, the Ministry of Labor always changed the rules, and he must comply, mustn't he? Or else they would be shut down.

Jack listened, nodded, promised to do his best, knowing he could do nothing at all. Finally they were outside again.

"I hate these visits." Jack pulled on his jacket. "I always walk away with a headache from all the noise and a crystal clear vision of how badly I am failing at my job." They got in the car and he started the engine. "The manager is right, he's been sending requests for months, and sooner or later the Ministry will come and do another inspection, unless Josef pays them off, but even so, they won't wait forever, and who will get blamed when things aren't what they are supposed to be? And all the people there, waiting for the day they learn the factory is closed down and they're out of jobs. What am I supposed to tell them?"

Louie was quiet. *If we don't defeat Jones and Sergio, you won't be telling your factory crew anything except where to go to get migrated. But I still don't know how we're going to do it.*

Jack went on. "I mean, every time I visit, they are all so nice to me, but I could never do a damn thing for them. I couldn't change their hours, I couldn't fix their compensation, I couldn't even get them new goddamn rubber pads to stand on. Did you see how worn down those were? Can you imagine standing there for eight or nine or ten hours a day, the pain you'd be in by the time you got to go home? How you'd carry that pain home with you, yell at your husband or wife or kids or dog, because your body ached in ways you hadn't thought possible even yesterday, when it ached more than it ever had before?"

"Jack."

"The manager and I, we came up with a plan together, for small compensation increases for the employees who have been here the longest," he went on. "We worked it out with finding some other ways to save a little, so it cost nearly nothing, but it would make such an impact on morale. Word got out, even though I told him not to tell anyone before it was approved, not to get their hopes up, but word got out somehow, and everyone was so excited. Then Josef got wind of it, even before I could give him the real proposal—at least I think it was Josef, because I got this email from Sergio, and it was copied to him: 'There are no resources available in the approved budget for increases this year,' Sergio wrote. 'Please desist any discussions regarding said increases, and propose other means of improving morale.' Right, like what? Door prizes for the ones who don't lose a finger in the machinery this month?"

"Jack."

"In two sentences, without even hearing the plan, he demolished it. You should've seen their faces when I told them, Lou."

"Jack, we need to focus on what we're fighting now. Old battles don't mean anything."

"Nothing I did here means anything. I was as useless at this as I was at—" he stopped talking, and stared at the road.

"At what, Jack?"

"Nothing." She saw the dampness in his eyes. *His sister,* she felt rather than knew. *Looking for his sister.* She put her hand on his arm. "Sorry," he spoke at her touch. "Went down the self-pity road there for a moment, but I'll come back."

They drove in silence for a while. "Hey," he brightened, finally. "What did you want to show me in there?"

"Jack, you took this job seriously, didn't you," Louie said.

"No, of course not. I just had a moment. I don't take anything seriously, as you should know by now."

"Yes, you did. That's good. Someone should. And taking it, and them—your workers—seriously, well, that's part of why you want to stop Sergio and Jones now, isn't it. They're a big part of why you're in the game with me, aren't they."

Jack smiled just a little as he drove. "So tell me what you found."

"The instructions on that one machine. What does it do?"

"I don't know, it probably cuts slot A or inserts slot B or something. That's part of the problem—I don't know anything about this business, and here I am in charge. Ridiculous, isn't it? Aren't I?"

"It does something more than that," Louie replied. "We walked by that machine, what, four times? The first two times, the instructions were normal—a little laminated page of Czech, I couldn't read it. The third time, it caught my eye because—" she paused.

"Because why?"

"It was in English. The words became English, they changed themselves to a language I could read. Like the sales agreement.

Keep your eyes on the road, Jack."

"I've never seen anything like that." he pointed the car straight again.

"Because you read Czech, enough of it anyway. I don't."

"What did the instructions say?"

"Nothing special, just how to run the machine. But..."

"But knowing how to run that machine is special enough to make it worth a magic set of instructions," Jack finished for her.

"Yup. And it had a little logo, did you ever notice that?"

"No. The manufacturer's logo?"

"Don't think so. It was a UFO, hovering over something that looked a lot like a castle tower."

"Prague Castle?"

"I don't think so. This one looked a lot smaller, older. You know this area, Jack. What's the nearest castle with an old, old tower?"

"There's another small village about an hour from here. It's known for its extraordinarily well-preserved castle tower, from the old Roman days. And that village is also worth knowing for another reason." Jack paused.

"What other reason?" Louie asked.

"It's the birthplace of one Josef Tiso," Jack answered. "His family practically owns the entire town."

Louie paused only for a moment. "When can we go, Jack?"

"You want to go to the migration site?"

"I do. That's where the game is. That's where he'll be, Jack. That's where we have to go. Tomorrow? Can we go tomorrow?"

"Tomorrow?" Jack considered for a moment. "I—well, I have some things I'll need to get ready. Day after?"

Louie calculated how many days that were left on her deal with Jones. "Okay, day after tomorrow. And you won't believe this, but now, I'd really like to check into my hotel and get some sleep."

Thirty

Louie checked into the hotel in the factory town after Jack dropped her off. It was fairly new, large, and modern looking; unfortunately Jones and Eastwood didn't like the quaint old smaller places closer to the center, and Jack took Louie at her word to put her where they stayed. The hotel was crowded with business travelers and it took about twenty minutes before the reception staff could get to her. The young woman who checked her in had the nicest smile and halting English, but finally they reached a mutual understanding of Louie's room number. She made her way to the elevator and found her room, slipped her key card in the slot, and opened the door to pitch blackness, lit only dimly from the light in the hall. She reached her hand to the wall, sliding it along, looking for a light switch; found a large flat one, and pushed it.

Nothing.

She tried again, and again, clicking and clicking, and no lights. She slipped further into the room, but the heavy door swung shut, leaving her with no light at all. She propped it open with her duffel bag, and made her way in the greyness to a phone on a writing table. Trying to guess at the right number for the front desk, she pushed zero, then one; then zero zero, then one one. The message in the small display screen on the digital phone was in Czech, so she had no idea what it said—maybe "push that sequence again and this phone will explode," for all she knew. As her eyes adjusted she could see a bedroom, sitting room, bathroom; she tried all the light switches she could find, and still nothing.

Damn, she sighed. *Pride-swallowing time.* She gathered her duffle and went back down to the front desk. She waited for the same young woman to be free, feeling that she needed a friend. "I'm so sorry," Louie began, though why she should be apologizing for the lights not working in her room, she couldn't say. "I'm so sorry, but there are no lights working in my room. Is it possible to get another?"

The young woman looked stricken. "Oh, no, I am intern."

Louie was puzzled. "That's okay, I just need a room with lights."

"No, no," said the young woman. "I am supposed to tell you. When you check in."

Louie stared. Was this a common occurrence in this part of the world, non-functioning lights? Should she have known about it somehow?

"You need to put card in slot," the intern went on.

"I did," Louie mimed the gesture. "I put my key card in the slot in the door to get in."

"No, in light slot," the young woman said. "I am supposed to tell you. When you check in." She dropped her voice to a whisper. "Do not tell please. I am intern."

"Oh, okay. Don't worry, I won't tell if you won't." Louie headed back to the elevator and her room, feeling entirely idiotic. Later Jack would tell her this was common in eastern European hotels, having to connect the electricity in the room by putting the key card into the master switch; it was a way to save energy, making sure idiotic American travelers didn't leave their lights on when they were out all day. When Louie got back to her room, she barely noticed the door was slightly ajar, and figured she just hadn't pulled it all the way shut behind her earlier. She put her duffel and backpack down, slipped her card into the slot on the first switch, and pushed.

Nothing.

What the hell, I'm doing exactly what the intern told me to do -

The hand over her mouth prevented her from thinking beyond that, as she felt herself freeze solid while someone held her arm twisted behind her back.

"Ssshh," whispered the voice into her left ear. "Tell me where it is, and I will let you go."

The sheer idiocy of that almost thawed her out. "How the

hell am I supposed to tell you anything, while you have your hand over my mouth?" she tried to say, but all that came out was "mghfmm frrrll mmff." She felt herself propelled to the bedroom, shoved so she landed face down on the bed; the hand came away from her mouth, and she felt a knee in her lower spine, pinning her there. Stupid, yes, but brutal they can be—isn't that what Jack had said? She felt fear return in a flood. "What? What do you want?" Louie twisted her head to the left so she could breathe.

"You know what it is. Tell me. And maybe I will let you go, though seeing you there on the bed, I am getting some other…ideas." An elbow shoved into her lower back, freeing the knee up to slip between her legs, forcing them apart. She flashed back to her high school boyfriend, to Jack's response, and she knew she wasn't going to let this happen. She knew she would fight. Like when Jones had unzipped in front of her, she found her mind suddenly clear. She caught a glimpse of black trench coat out of the corner of her eye. *Not an alien, then, most likely a goon. Maybe one better than Josef's boys. Better, but not unbeatable.*

"Okay," Louie said. "Let me up so I can give what he sent you here to get—you know he'll be royally pissed if he doesn't get it because you decided to have your little fun." She had no idea who "he" was, other than he was most certainly an asshole, and that her words would ring true to the goon. For a moment nothing happened; then she felt the pressure on her back ease; and as the knee between her legs moved away, she took her shot.

For some reason, she'd clasped her key card in her hand after trying the lights. Still there, she slashed it where she figured the goon's face would be as she propelled herself over onto her back. And, borrowing from Jack, she screamed as loud and as unearthly as she could—though it came out sounding more like Cheetah's squeak than Tarzan's yell.

The card hit flesh and carved a shallow red line out of the goon's cheek. The goon swore and flung his arm to block his face, while Louie ran for where she remembered the door to the hallway was.

The force of her stomach encountering the sink in the bathroom reminded her of how lousy her sense of direction could be.

At least the bathroom door had a lock. Louie threw it and sat in the pitch dark for she didn't know how long, waiting for the goon to pound down the locked door or shoot it open.

Then the pounding started, and she said a silent farewell to Buddy and Thing One and Thing Two, to Aunt Emma, to Pete, to Mac, to Gil, and of course, to Jack. The pounding stopped and she heard the goon's voice.

"Louie?"

"What?" she demanded. *Why the hell would the goon stop to talk to me?*

"Why are you locked in the bathroom?" the goon asked.

Now this was just annoying. *After chasing me in here, as if the damn goon didn't know...*but now she thought about it, that voice sounded familiar. "Jack?"

"Yeah, Lou, who else were you expecting?" It sure sounded like Jack, but still, it might be a trick.

"Prove it."

"Why?"

"Don't argue with me. You're either Jack, in which case you should be able to prove it easily enough, or you're the goon who wants to kill me, and then you can just shoot the door open and get this over with."

"Goon? Kill you? What the—Louie, are you all right? Let me in there, please!"

It really did sound like Jack. And the goon really had no reason to waste time like this. "Jack—" she opened the door and the light flooding in blinded her after so long in the dark.

"Louie." His arms steered her then helped her sit on a soft cushion. "What happened?" Her eyes adjusted, and saw Jack sitting next to her. She told him the story of the lights and the intern and the goon and her narrow escape, all in a rush, before she could remember to ask why he'd come back.

Thirty One

Louie cherished some very fond memories of growing up with her Aunt Emma. But she couldn't remember much before her twelfth year. She knew that her parents died in an accident when she was very young. She figured she must have blocked out most of her early childhood in order to protect herself from really feeling that loss. She and Aunt Emma never talked about it. It was almost like Louie woke up at age twelve, and Aunt Emma was there with her, and that's the way life was.

On her best days, Louie knew she didn't belong. On her worst, she was convinced she never would. Other people just seemed to have a code they spoke, a way of navigating the world, which eluded her. They weren't beset by doubts, or if they were, they didn't seem to show. They displayed a consistent faith that the world they would wake up in tomorrow would be the same as the one they woke up in today. Louie remembered one of her early lessons in faith, in her high school social studies class. They had been doing a unit on the Great Religions of the World, and a new boy was arguing the possibility of living without faith. Louie listened closely, always puzzled by religion in general. That's mostly what she did in school, listen. On the rare occasions when she spoke up, she regretted doing so immediately. Nothing like twenty or thirty of your "peers" staring at you like you'd just sprouted an extra head to make you wish for invisibility. That day, she'd listened to the boy arguing that faith was for losers and fools, for the lazy who wanted answers handed to them without work.

The teacher had listened, too, for a while. But in Zillah, like in so many small towns in America, questioning religious faith was not likely to go without correction, if not punishment. That's part of why Louie paid so much attention to the new boy's argument. She'd never heard anyone take on the accepted wisdom with such vehemence before. It made her wonder who this boy was and where he'd come from. Finally the teacher had spoken. "John, that was a very interesting point you just made." She'd smoothed her hands across the pages of the giant textbook, as if to remove any unwanted wrinkles in the societies described there. "But of course we all need faith, of which faith in Jesus Christ and his Lord is the best example. You can also think of it this way. It's like believing in gravity. If you lost your faith in gravity, you'd be lying in bed afraid to put your foot on the floor in the morning, because it might fly away."

There are four thousand logical errors in that argument. For one, if gravity somehow disappeared during the night, you wouldn't be "lying in bed" in the morning. But it stuck with her, as a way of describing what other people seemed to have that she lacked: that absolute confidence in the predictability of the world, the notion that there was an invisible force that held things and people in their places, just like believing in gravity. And even as Louie's sharp mind mocked the teacher's explanation, her heart ached. The new boy became her boyfriend. She'd done everything for him, and he'd been awful to her. All along she'd been trying, desperately, to find gravity.

Since she'd moved out on her own to go to college, Louie'd had a nagging sensation that at some point in her life, she really should try to remember those first twelve years. But that probably meant therapy, and therapy horrified her. Self-exploration in front of a witness who nodded thoughtfully and murmured mmm hmm, yes, tell me how that made you feel—well, that sounded pretty much like hell to her. So she'd put off that nagging feeling year after year.

One Thanksgiving at her aunt's house, when she was about to turn thirty, Louie gave in to an impulse and asked Aunt Emma a question.

"Em, did you ever celebrate Thanksgiving with my parents?"

Emma looked at her strangely. "Why do you ask?"

"I don't know, we're just sitting here eating Tofurkey and it occurred to me, were they vegetarian too?" Louie tried to laugh off a growing sense of uneasiness. Emma seemed to move far, far away in her mind. Louie realized too late that it must have been terrible for

Emma to lose them, too, and felt guilty for reminding her aunt of her own grief.

"Louie, let me tell you a story about your father. I knew him before the—accident," Emma said.

"Of course you did, he was your brother, right?" Louie replied.

"Not exactly."

"Then my mother was your sister?" Louie was confused. Hadn't she asked her aunt about this before? Hadn't they talked? Or had she always just assumed that Emma was her father's sister?

"Let me tell you this story, Louie. Be quiet and listen." Emma's eyes were vague. "Your father was very handsome, in his own way, and sharp and funny, but not all that bright. He loved music and would have really liked what you call jazz. Not the new stuff, not bebop and Miles Davis, that would have just confused him. But the old jazz, Duke Ellington and Dizzy Gillespie and those folks. That's who you're named after, the great jazz trumpeter and singer Louis Armstrong."

"My father named me after him?" Again Louie'd felt she should already have known all this.

"Well, let's just say your dad would have loved to know his daughter was named after Louis Armstrong. Your father's real gift was that he loved your mother, and would have done anything for her. That's why he got involved with that group; that was all her idea. I was in that group too. She never should have brought him there. He was too trusting, and he told—"

"What group? What are you talking about?" Louie's voice was urgent. Emma's eyes had suddenly come back into focus. They'd seemed to search for something and then landed on the mantle behind Louie, where a little trophy stood. "Um, that....bowling group. The one they were on their way home from the night of the—accident."

"My parents bowled?" *This is the big revelation? Leave it to Emma...*

"Louie, eat your dinner. I don't want to talk about it any more."

"I'm sorry, Aunt Em, I really am. I don't mean to bring back sad memories for you. But what did you mean, you aren't my father's sister? You're my mother's sister?"

"I'm not your blood Aunt, Louie. You just came to me, and I decided I needed to take care of you."

"We're not related?" *That's completely absurd.*

"Not by blood. But we are family."

A strange image appeared in Louie's mind. A dark night, a meeting, and a hiding place. Two black eyes burning into hers. Shouting, running, chaos. Another image—hiding behind a door, in a small space. Then a crash, a wave of dirt and darkness. Louie'd felt herself spinning into a kind of dark, black hole. Suddenly one side of her head started pounding, and she couldn't open her eyes without the light stabbing them like a knife.

"Louie." Her aunt's voice was soft. "Are you all right?"

"It's one of my migraines, Em. I—I think I'd better go lie down."

"Sure thing, sweety. Want me to bring you a damp cloth?"

"No thanks. I'll take my drugs and be okay in a little while." Louie'd swallowed her migraine pill, gone to her old room and laid down on her old bed, keeping the lights off. After an hour or so the throbbing pain and nausea started to ease, and she'd fallen asleep. Waking up hours later, in the darkened house, she hadn't been sure if the conversation with her Aunt was real or a dream. *Not related? Decided she had to take care of me? Then what were the last eighteen years of my life—a lie?*

Louie'd sat up. It wasn't the first time she'd faced a tough choice, but it might have been the toughest one yet. Confront her aunt and demand the whole truth? What if it was a dream? Those two black eyes came back to her, making her shudder. Life as she knew it was hard sometimes, but it was pretty much all right. She was about to finish graduate school, she loved Emma, she could see a future of some kind for herself. Why drag them both deeper into the past? She'd walked into the living room, where Emma watched television.

"Oh sweety, did the TV wake you up? I tried to keep the volume down, but the Wizard of Oz is on, and I couldn't miss it."

"No, Em, it's fine. I'm feeling much better."

"Good. Sit down here next to me on the couch and let's

watch this together like we used to do when you were younger. See, we're just to the part where Dorothy drops her house on the Wicked Witch."

"She doesn't drop her house on the witch, Em, the tornado does. Dorothy has nothing to do with it."

Emma giggled quietly. "That's what she wants everyone to think, Louie. You remember that, it's what Dorothy wants everyone to think. There is more to that girl than meets the eye!"

Louie sighed. They had this same argument every time they watched the movie. Aunt Emma was convinced that Dorothy really did have supernatural powers, that she was making everything happen while keeping up an innocent-Kansas-farm-girl front. Louie was never able to convince her aunt otherwise. But they both always shared a good laugh whenever Dorothy cried out, "Aunty Em! Aunty Em!" Aunt Emma would call back, "Yes dear! Here I am!" That night she'd added, "Dorothy, do you want some Tofurkey?" And the two of them collapsed into giggles on the couch. Louie knew then she wasn't going to ask again about her parents. *Let well enough alone.*

~ * ~

But Aunt Emma remembered. She remembered the first night she saw Louie, and remembered how she recognized her right away. She remembered Louie's father, that skinny, handsome, funny, not-too-bright fellow who followed his wife into such trouble. She remembered how he loved music, how he loved to laugh and make other people laugh. She remembered how his head splattered that night, and how his wife's eyes grew wide with terror before she, too, was dead. She remembered pretending to be dead herself, and thinking about how her own husband, who she loved more than anything, would have been furious to know she was there, with that group. She remembered how hard she'd worked to keep her involvement with the group a secret from him so he would not worry. She remembered wishing she had told him so he would know where to find her dead body, anyway, as she'd fully expected one of the shots flying around to hit her any second.

That night she thought about how hard she'd worked over the years to keep another terrible secret from her dear, sweet Louie.

Oh yes, Emma knew how to keep a secret.

But there was a trade off. When the time came, would Louie know what to do? More importantly, would she know who she really is?

While they'd watched the movie and laughed, Emma slipped the tiny silver house charm off of her bracelet and clutched it in her palm. When Louie'd gotten up to go to the bathroom, Emma had gone to the kitchen door and taken Louie's set of keys off the hook. She'd added the house to Louie's keychain. *Drop the house on your enemy, dearest, when the time comes,* she'd whispered.

"What's that, Aunt Emma?" Louie came out of the bathroom.

"I was just wondering if you were ready for pie. I thought I might go ahead and slice it, just in case."

"Oh Em. I'm stuffed."

"It's pumpkin pie."

"Well, maybe just a tiny slice," Louie had said, and they sat down at the kitchen counter to eat together.

Thirty Two

It had happened on Sergio's third trip to Europe, or maybe his fourth. Sergio kept himself on the move, making it hard for anyone to keep track. On prior trips, he spent all his time behind closed doors with Josef, occasionally giving a nod to Jack if they met in the hall on the way to the toilet, or while getting coffee. Each time he passed Sergio in close proximity, Jack got a cold shiver. He wondered if Sergio knew who he was, too and on that third trip, or maybe the fourth, he found out.

Sergio was in Josef's office for several hours. Jack thought he was probably on the way to the toilet again. But this time, he'd turned into Jack's office and pulled the door shut behind him.

"So, we meet again, my old friend," Sergio began.

This riled Jack, though he'd known exactly what Sergio meant—the night Jack's parents were killed. "We never met, Sergio. Remember? I wasn't there."

"Ah, yes. It was your sister, wasn't it? Where is she now, Jack?" Sergio's thin smirk told Jack he knew exactly what, and why, he was asking.

"She's lost. Unable to be found," Jack replied. "Why are you here? What does Earth have for you?"

"The same things it has for you, Jack. Pleasures, adventures, company. Business opportunities. You should join me in this one, Jack. It will make us both wealthy beyond our wildest dreams."

"Wealthy? What would I do with wealth?" Jack demanded. "And I why would I join the—being—who killed my parents?"

"Now it is my turn to tell you, Jack. I didn't kill them. It was the others. I tried to stop them. I tried to prevent the whole tragedy. And I was punished for it, being sent away like the—the orphans."

Sergio's face looked as though he were trying to swallow a whole jar of pickle brine. "I'm like you, Jack. Just like you. Trying to make my way in this new world, trying to get by. That's why we should join forces, Jack. We are so much alike."

Jack's mind went fuzzy. Was Sergio right? Jack tried to remember his sister's story. She'd described shooting, lots of it, and then a boy, a boy with black eyes, stabbing his own father…she hadn't said the boy killed anyone else. Or had she? After all this time of trying to forget about her, Jack felt a kind of fog between himself now and himself then, the boy he was when his sister was with him.

"Alike? Hardly. I have at least ten kilos on you, Sergio. Seems I've learned a lot more about eating and drinking on this planet than you have," Jack heard himself say.

Sergio stared at him. "Ah, a joke. Very funny," although he did not smile. "Just remember, Jack, my friend, if you decide to join me, I can make your life very easy. Promotions, raises, you could actually buy a house to live in, or rent a fancy flat." Jack's ears burned. How did Sergio know so much about his living situation? "You could settle down, Jack. Find a wife. Stay here on this planet you love, without ever having to worry about anything. Or…"

Jack's inner battle was raging, and he struggled to hear Sergio's voice after that. His decision, when he'd made it, was clear and unambiguous, however, at least to himself. Jack knew what he had to do. For the first time since he'd followed Gil away from the concert hall in Seattle after losing his sister, he knew exactly what he had to do.

Thirty Three

Mac knew the worst thing about working at State was the weekly meeting in the Deputy Secretary's office. *Well, maybe that wasn't the absolute worst thing. Maybe the absolute worst thing was what usually happened after the weekly meeting in the Deputy Secretary's office, when the "boys" on the team jockeyed for position to see who could be the biggest prick.* But the meeting itself was pretty bad, because the boys used it primarily to posture, and to repeat whatever the Deputy Secretary said, as soon as they could figure out what the hell he meant. Even that wouldn't be so bad, except the Deputy Secretary was, to put it kindly, an idiot.

And I thought PPP3 was full of hot air. They got nuthin' on gummint.

It wasn't the Deputy Secretary who made an impression on Mac, though; it was the Secretary herself. The Secretary wasn't one of the boys, not at all. She was sharp, she was strong, she was devious, and she was committed to nothing so much as her own consolidation of power.

And this week Mac had something new to worry about. Either her friend Louie was going crazy, or there was some serious shit going down. Mac guiltily half-hoped it was the former. *If she's losing her mind, I know I can help. Best therapy money can buy, and it's hers. But if she's not? Then I have to pull a rabbit out of my hat, and somehow get her some help through someone who has access to the Secretary.*

Mac knew what she had to do, though it made her gag. "Dick, I need your help."

It about killed Mac just to practice saying it out loud. He was a prick, the kind of guy who always stroked his own, um, ego first, except when he was peeing all over himself in the presence of an alpha dog, like the Secretary. It galled Mac to have to ask him for help, knowing he would believe that saying yes to her meant she would owe him one. And the way believing that would make Dick smirk. But Dick Glenn was the Deputy Secretary's right hand man, and everyone knew the Secretary herself placed him there, as a kind of in-house spy.

For about the millionth time Mac also wondered at her own readiness to believe Louie's story. Aliens and cyborg armies—she should probably be calling the men in white coats to go get Louie, instead of walking into Dick's office to humiliate herself. *I guess working for the feds has prepared me to believe the completely absurd and nearly impossible.* At State, she'd seen things that would curl the hair of most civilians, and that didn't even touch the truly top-secret stuff.

If it was anyone but Louie in trouble, there was no way in hell she'd be doing this. Let the human race disappear into a vast cyborg army. Most of the time, they behaved like robots anyway. But ever since the incident with Idiot Boy, Mac and Louie always had each other's backs, and Mac would never be the weak link in the chain. And, to be perfectly honest, it was also the chance to get a bit of her own back by bringing Jones and Sergio down a peg or two. *I wonder if it's always selfish motives that get the world saved.* She chuckled. *Probably. We humans are like that.*

Here she was, right outside Dick's office. *It's now or never. Lou, you are going to owe me one, big time. Hell, if you're right, the whole human race is going to owe me one. The kicker is that if this works, I'll never be able to tell anyone what I did and collect from the human race, dammit. If this works, we humans will just keep on doing what we're doing now without noticing anything different. Great. Just great.*

"Dick?" Mac tapped on the door to get his attention. "Can I have a minute?"

"Sure, Mac, but I didn't think they allowed you into this part of the building, I never see you over here, heh heh! Or is it just me you're avoiding, heh!"

Oh god, Mac groaned inside. *What a prick.*

"Heh, heh, uh, good one, Dick!" The words tasted like paste in her mouth. *I can't believe I am sucking up to a guy named Dick. Ewwwww.* "How could I avoid you, even if I wanted to, heh?" *Ha, he won't notice but that last part is at least true.*

"What can I do you for, Mac?" Dick was the only person Mac knew who actually used that expression. Before she could answer he went on. "Hey, Mac, did I tell you that joke about the ghosts?"

"No, Dick, I don't think you did, and I don't really have time right now, maybe later."

"Oh, don't be such a party pooper, this won't take long!"

Liar, liar, liar, your jokes always take three times as long as when normal people tell them. But it was too late, he was off.

"See, there was this big convention of psychics, astrologers, palm-readers, and other new-age types. The last lecture was given by this professor who was a famous ghost expert, right?"

Mac realized Dick was looking at her expectantly. *Oh, crap he actually expects a response.* "Um, right, Dick." *Anything to hurry this up...*

"Okay, right. So he gets up to give this lecture in front of all these hundreds and hundreds of people. And he asks: How many of you believe in ghosts? And almost every hand goes up, right?"

"Right, right."

"Then he asks, how many of you have seen a ghost? Still lots of hands in the air, right?"

"Okay."

"Okay?"

"I mean right, Dick."

"Then he asks, how many of you have talked to a ghost? Now it's just a few hands. Then he says, I have one more question. The hall gets quiet. Has anyone here ever had sexual relations with a ghost? And one guy raises his hand, and there's this big gasp in the audience. The professor says, oh my god, sir, you must come up on the stage and tell us all about it! And so the guy comes up, right?"

"Right, right, right, right, right." *Get it over with, oh please finish it before I have to go find an ice pick to ram through my eye into my brain.*

"So the professor says, what is your name, sir? Sanjay, says the guy." Dick's fake East Indian accent was thicker than molasses. "Tell us, Sanjay, about your experience having sexual relations with a ghost! And you know what the guy says, right?"

"Right, Dick." *I'm very, very afraid that I do.*

"He says," and Dick slipped back into the thick fake accent, "oh my goodness, did you say ghost? I thought you said goat! Right?"

She couldn't stand it. "Right, Dick, you know, as funny as that joke might be to the right audience"—*morons, sexists, and racists,* Mac added silently to herself—"you should never, ever tell it at work again, Dick."

"What? Oh, heh, heh, heh, Mac, come on! You and I know each other well enough to have a little fun, right?"

Apparently not, or you would know that right now I want to rip your racist little heart right out through your moronic throat. "Okay, whatever, Dick. I really need to talk to you now, right?" Mac couldn't resist.

"Oh, right, Mac. What can I do you for?"

Even if I were straight, I wouldn't let you do me for a million bucks. Cyborg army is looking pretty good right about now, for people like you. But she asked Dick the question she came for.

"Dick, can you get the Secretary to make a call to the Navy for me?"

"Well, Mac, that is highly irregular. State does not, as a rule, interfere in Defense—"

"Don't give me that bullshit, Dick, I know the Secretary does it all the time." Mac stared at Dick while he squirmed, just a little.

"Well, in the most casual and informal way, maybe. What's the message?"

"The message is…Dick, this is completely hush-hush, Secretary's ears only. Can you keep a secret?"

"Would I have this job if I couldn't, Mac, heh heh?"

"All right, Dick." Mac leaned in toward him and lowered her voice. The more she made it sound top-secret, the sooner Dick would spill it all over this branch of State, and she needed the rumor mill to churn as quickly as it could for this to work. "The message is, *threat sixty-four alpha in process. Strongly suggest counter-offense bravo charlie forty-four.* Got that? It has to be exact."

Dick's face went white. "Shit, Mac, really? Where'd you get this? This should come through the Company Director's office." The Company—that's what they called the CIA over here. Mac knew Dick had bitten her bait, and bitten it hard.

"Where do you think I got it, Dick? He couldn't be seen to be coming here himself, could he?" Mac replied.

"No, no, no, I see, I see. Okay, Mac, I'll get it to the Secretary right away." Dick's face turned a pale shade of puke green.

Yeah, right, after you call your family and send them out of Washington, and call about ten of your closest friends in State, you little weasel. "Thanks, Dick, I knew I could count on you." He still looked so scared, she decided to throw him a little bone. "And hey…I owe you one, right?"

"Okay, right, sure, Mac," he replied with a weak grin.

That went better than I thought. Mac headed back to her own office. *He's so scared he didn't even grok he's doing me a favor. And when he repeats that message to the Secretary, she won't know whether to fire him on the spot, or….* Mac grinned to herself. *Heh, heh, indeed!*

If Mac knew the Secretary as well as she imagined, she was pretty sure of the Secretary's next move. *She'll call the Navy, all right, but not the Admiral on the Joint Chiefs. She'll call her old pal, Admiral Winston, to see if the message is legit.* Mac knew all about Admiral Winston from her mother. Her mother kept all the secrets entrusted to her in her Naval Intelligence job, of course, but Winston's drinking problem had nothing to do with national security, and Mac's mother never hesitated to use him as an example for Mac in one of their weekly phone chats. "He's an ass," her mother had said, "even when he's sober. Never forget, Mac, that drinking only makes you more of who you were before you took the first swallow."

Together the Secretary and the Admiral would consider the dilemma Dick's message put them in. If it was real, if a "sixty-four alpha"—an "alien threat"—was really surfacing, and they didn't act, the potential loss of Naval assets, and human lives, of course, would be laid at their feet. If it wasn't real, and they did act, the press would rake them over the coals so badly, they'd both have to resign and move someplace even media satellites wouldn't reach, if such places existed anymore. Soon they'd hear that everyone in this section of State was on the move—sending families on sudden "vacations" to the mid West, well away from both vulnerable coasts. *That should tip the scales.* Each action would reinforce the other, and the Secretary and her Navy pal would move two carriers into position, just in case. Mac could step in then and "help" the Secretary find the source of the threat, way over in Seattle.

And here was the best part. If everything worked out, and Mac's plans usually did, not only would Jones be contained, but Dick would be fired. Because the code phrase she gave him placed the threat not in Seattle, but in Phoenix, where he had a vacation home. The Secretary would immediately assume Dick mucked up the code, probably on purpose to save his own place.

Who was in line to take Dick's job, at a substantial raise in both money and prestige from his current position?

Sanjay Darwan, one of the nicest, smartest, most dedicated guys Mac knew at State.

Thirty-Four

Josef Tiso, the Vice President for Manufacturing and Positioning in Europe, had been a Paster pick up, or so most people in the company believed. They couldn't understand why Paster chose the little town near Prague as a place for a factory, or why the company even invested in its own factory when labor was so cheap in other parts of the world and the recession meant idled factories were available to use as needed for a song. But what really baffled them was the need for a Vice President to run it. Unless of course Paster owed Josef a favor or Josef owed him one. Debate raged, never being settled one way or another. Josef never engaged in the discussion; he kept away from PPP3's suburban Seattle headquarters as much as he could, and when he was forced to visit, spoke only with Jones and Sergio, and once in a great while with Mac, if he had to.

A couple months after Louie met Jack, Josef made one of his trips to PPP3's headquarters. Louie wound up sitting next to him at some dreadfully long meeting or other, one where she was supposed to be on the agenda, presenting the findings from her latest market research study. She'd snuck in one of those recommendations that "customers care about the working conditions of the people who make the products they buy," and that time she'd been determined to be ready, to say it out loud and not just in her head, because Josef was there and Jack, she felt, was counting on her, even though he was far away in Europe. She hadn't said anything to Jack about the study or the recommendation she snuck into it or her intentions to speak up, keeping silent to hedge her bets against his disappointment if she chickened out.

As the meeting rambled on, with Sergio talking and talking

about the company's latest gadget, one that turned hard-boiled eggs into cubes for "easier, more efficient storage and serving," Louie felt rather than observed Josef's growing impatience. Finally, uncharacteristically, Josef raised his hand to interrupt Sergio.

"Yes. Josef. You have a question?" Sergio couldn't ignore Josef any longer.

"Yes, I do." Josef waited. After a long moment of uncomfortable silence, Sergio prompted him.

"Please, Josef, ask your question. Others may be wondering the same thing."

Josef cleared his throat. "If I understand correctly," he used his most careful English, "the proposal you are outlining would require purchase of another factory in—where did you say?"

"Ecuador, most probably, Josef, although the true intention is to gain a foothold that would allow the company to build a South American hub, if you will," Sergio said.

"Ecuador," Josef repeated, "or a hub. Yes. And this purchase depends on bringing another partner into the deal, one who takes a share of the total revenues."

"Yes," Sergio replied. "The partner brings installed capacity in—"

"I understand that," Josef cut in. "And as a result, the company increases sales of its hard-boiled egg gadget by—how much?"

"At least, conservatively estimated, you understand, based on the partner's analysis, at least fifty percent," Sergio replied.

"Well, that sounds amazing. Miraculous, even, given that since I've been with the company we've never seen an increase in sales in any product line of more than three percent a year," Josef said.

"Yes, but—" Sergio started to reply, but Josef continued. "Now what I did not hear, or did not understand, is what the baseline sales figures for the egg-cubing machine are now?"

"Admittedly, it has not been a top seller, yet, but—"

"Forty-two," Louie heard herself say out loud.

Josef turned to her, his expression implacable, though she'd imagined a slight turn up at one corner of his mouth. "Excuse me?"

"Forty-two. Last quarter. We sold forty-two of those. At fifteen dollars and ninety-nine cents each, before shipping and handling. And local sales tax, if applicable."

Josef let her comment hang in the air, not bothering to add that the Ecuadorian factory deal would gross the company an additional three hundred and thirty five dollars and seventy-nine cents every three months, since shipping and handling was a wash, and sales tax went to the taxing authority. If, that is, it would meet Sergio's fantastic projections to grow by fifty percent. "Thank you," was all he'd said, and turned back to his laptop, and Louie probably only imagined the slight glint of humor in his eye. That exchange, however, ignited a furious debate among Jones, Sergio, and the other executives, one that lasted the rest of the meeting and beyond, creating more animosity toward Sergio, and pushing Louie's market analysis into oblivion.

Later that night, when Louie was awake again, trying to catch up on some work, she'd seen Jack's email pop up in her inbox, and read the subject line. "How's our travelling VP doing?" She pretended she was sleeping the night straight through, for once, snapping her laptop closed and crawling under the covers. She spent the next two hours lying awake explaining to Jack, in her mind, why she had let him down again.

Thirty Five

It was a good thing Louie thought better of staying with Jack, because he lived in his office. She discovered this by accident when they went there the morning after they visited the factory, after the goon attack at Louie's hotel. PPP3 shared an office suite with Josef's other enterprises. It wasn't much of a surprise that Josef had a few side businesses going, despite being on the payroll full time as a Vice President for PPP3; he seemed the type to always hedge his bets. The office suite was in a refurbished Soviet-era block, a building so utilitarian in design that the bright paint colors splotched on its hallway walls to bring it into the capitalist era seemed uncomfortable enough to jump back into the paint cans. Josef inhabited a large office with windows, not that the view itself was much, but windows mean status everywhere. His office was like him, inscrutably generic at first glance, until your eyes picked up a few tell-tale details, like the small but expensive, industrial-strength safe tucked in a corner under his large wooden desk, or the unrealistically small filing cabinet of black steel that said *I don't keep anything here, if it is valuable it is in the safe, or it is somewhere else, somewhere you can't find it.*

Jack's office was at the other end of the long hall, a small, interior space that seemed incongruously cozy. Jack's desk was too small to hold the piles of paper on it; they'd spilled over into stacks on the floor. The walls were full of framed photos and articles clipped from newspapers and magazines, it seemed—one showed a dam in rubble, several were reviews of concerts, artists like B.B. King, Chris Rea, and the Maldives; and there were some obituaries, too, of people Louie didn't recognize. All from his days in the States, she guessed, because the articles and captions were mostly English, except for a few of the Rea concert reviews, in Czech and one in Cyrillic—Russian? Bulgarian? In one corner a freestanding closet or armoire of some kind took up far too much room, crowding everything else.

Josef was away on one of his famous vacations, which meant no one knew where he was or when he would return. His private secretary kept a mobile phone number where he could be reached, and that was all anyone knew. These "vacations" were one main source of fuel for the rumors of Josef's eastern European mafia connections; every so often, the stories went, he had to disappear, go dark, until the coast was clear. Clear of what, no one knew for sure— police on his trail? death threats from rival mobs?—and then as suddenly as he'd left, he'd return, always in a bad mood, always ready to fire someone. The staff in the offices had a love-hate relationship with his vacations because of this; there was always a sense of respite, a chance to avoid work while he was gone, but there was always a victim upon his return.

Jack explained some of this to Louie over email, and some she'd put together herself. When they got to the building and rode the elevator up to the third floor, Jack grew quiet. His mobile phone buzzed a few times but he ignored it. He whisked Louie from the open elevator doors to his office, in order, it seemed, to avoid running into anyone else along the way. He immediately left again, to get coffee for them, he said, but he was gone quite a while, so Louie began poking around a little.

That big closet in the small office made her curious, but she wouldn't have opened it if she didn't need a key to the washroom. She'd noticed as they sped down the hall that the door had a lock with a little sign over it. She couldn't read the sign but could guess what it meant; and Jack had been gone long enough, and the thought of coffee had been in her mind long enough, she needed to visit there and wasn't content to wait. She figured there would be a key attached to something cumbersome, not a hubcap, probably, but a ruler or stapler, something you couldn't accidentally slip into your pocket and forget, walking away with it, leaving your office mates to worry about unauthorized restroom access for however long it would take to change the locks in a place like this.

Louie pulled on the handle to open the closet door. The piece was made of blond wood, unlike all the other furniture in the room, the dark steel desk and a filing cabinet plenty big enough to hold real stuff; maybe that should have tipped her off, because when she pulled the door it didn't open like most closet doors, like she expected it to. Her yank was forceful enough to bring the top down on her head, as it swung down to flatten out into a bed, which she would've seen if she wasn't standing under the door. The bonk on her head was sharp and surprising enough that she let out a yell of, "owouchwhatthehell," just as Jack came back into the room, snapping his phone shut but without any coffee.

He bent down to make eye contact with Louie crouched under his half-open Murphy bed. "Um, Lou? Can I help you find something?" Louie never handled embarrassment well, and this moment was no exception. The smarting spot on her head meant that for a moment she truly didn't remember why she'd pulled the door open in the first place. The first thought that came back to her was that Jack had promised to bring back coffee.

"Coffee, Jack, since you came back empty-handed, I was looking for coffee." Louie led with her offense.

"Sorry," he said, wondering how it turned out that he was the one apologizing. "I had to return a call and it took longer than I meant for it to. Can I help get that off your head, Lou?" He did, and as she moved to sit in his chair, she saw the bed that until recently was resting on her.

"You sleep here sometimes?" she blurted.

"Not exactly," Jack rubbed his chin, "not exactly on either count. I stay here at night, but I don't sleep much." Louie knew that from the late night emails and chats.

"But this is—I mean—you live here?"

"Yeah."

"Is that even legal?"

"Probably not, but it works," said Jack. "There's a gym on the first floor and the janitor lets me in there to shower most nights. I eat most of my meals at the coffee shop across the street; I don't eat much, and the woman who owns it lets me have my pick of the day-old pastries that she's about to throw out."

Louie flashed on her little house, in its constant state of repair, on Buddy, and the cats, Thing One and Thing Two. "Don't you get lonely?"

Jack's expression was far away. "Not these days, now you're here," he said finally, in a voice a bit too bright. "Now that you're here, the excitement is non-stop."

Louie grinned. "A thrill a minute, I know. Don't tell them back in Seattle, or I'll lose my reputation as the quiet one."

"They don't know you at all, do they." Jack intended it as a joke, most likely, but his expression as he looked at her told Louie she didn't have to answer him out loud.

Thirty Six

At that moment, Josef returned from his "vacation." His arrival was announced by Boris, the senior assistant at the property management company that took up the first office next to Josef's. Boris worked the hallway spreading the word from office to office, leaving a trail of caught breath and hastily swiped clean desktops and shut down online poker web sites. Jack pulled Louie's arm. "Oh boy. Watch this. Josef at his big-kid-bully best."

Louie raised an eyebrow. "You're not worried about yourself?"

"Me? Nah, I think Josef knows I'd be relieved if he fired me, so it wouldn't be any fun for him. Plus—" he dropped his voice. "My days here are numbered anyway. Either we beat Jones and Sergio, and there's no more PPP3, or we lose and—"

"No more us," Louie finished his sentence, but her voice was drowned out by the sound of yelling in the hallway. "Here we go." Jack moved to stand in the doorway. She watched him listen, then watched his face turn a little green. "Oh shit," he said to himself. "Tinka." When Louie joined him, she saw a tearful young woman with a box of what looked like personal things—a plant, a coffee mug, a picture frame—walking toward the elevator. She kept dropping things; the box was a little too full, or too hastily packed; but no one left their own doorways to help. Josef brushed past Tinka and into his office and slammed the door behind him. Louie brushed past Jack on her way to the young woman. "Don't," she heard Jack hiss at her, but chose to pretend she hadn't.

Louie met up with Tinka about halfway to the elevator, as she stooped to pick up the items she'd dropped—a little notebook, a brass bell, a framed silver and blue dragonfly brooch. "Here." Louie touched Tinka's arm. "Let me help you." The young woman looked at Louie with surprise, her eyes red, her brown hair plastered to her forehead with perspiration, her impromptu ponytail halfway undone. "I'm Louie, from Seattle," Louie went on, unsure if the woman could understand her English.

"Seattle?" Tinka blinked.

"Seattle, right, USA," Louie and Tinka made it to the elevator. "Let me." Louie pushed the button.

"Seattle, I know where it is," Tinka said. "You work for Josef?"

"No. I work for the same company, the same boss, though."

"Which?"

"Jones, at PPP3," Louie answered.

"Be careful." Tinka met Louie's gaze with serious eyes as the elevator doors opened. They stepped on.

"You mean the elevator door?" Louie was confused. "Careful about that?"

"No, no," said Tinka. "Josef. Jones. PPP3. Careful. Jack. Careful. Be careful."

"Jack? Why?" The elevator deposited them on the ground floor. Tinka didn't answer, but kept walking to the door of the building. Louie followed. "Where's your car?"

"No car. Bus." At the stop two blocks up the street, Tinka put her box down, and Louie helped her repack it so all her things were safely contained inside. "Thank you." Tinka gave Louie a quick, hard hug. "No one else tried to help...be careful, Louie. Watch him. He's not—" The bus roared up and Tinka hoisted her box.

"He's not what? Watch who? Josef? Jones?" Louie called. Tinka turned from the top step of the bus and said something Louie couldn't quite hear as the bus pulled into traffic. She couldn't quite hear it, but she could read Tinka's lips easily enough.

"Jack," Tinka had said.

Louie stood in the bus shelter for a few moments, collecting herself before turning and walking back toward the office building. When she got back to the third floor, the place was silent as a tomb. Every office door was closed tight. It looked like everyone had gone home. Louie walked slowly back to Jack's office door. She was almost there when she heard her name.

"Louie!" It was Josef, standing in his doorway at the top end of the hall. "Would you come here please." Louie thought for a minute about defying this demand, even though it was phrased as a question. Jack's office door stayed resolutely closed. She thought about what he'd said—either we win and there's no more PPP3, or we lose and there's no more us. *What the hell.* She turned toward Josef's open door.

He'd already returned to his desk, and was squinting at something on his computer screen. The monitor's back was to Louie so she couldn't tell what. Josef didn't look at her when he spoke. "It is nice of you to visit us here, and to take the trouble to say hello to me." His voice held no hint of sarcasm. "Would you mind telling me if there is any purpose to your visit other than social?"

Louie bit her lip. She decided to start with a bit of truth. "Jones sent me." She waited to see how Josef would respond to that.

"Of course he did." Josef kept his eyes focused on the screen. "He called me while I was in—he called to let me know you were on your way." Louie blinked. Did that explain the reception at the airport? The goons in the square? *Not Josef's goons, they're too good to be his,* Gil had said. Whose then? And the one waiting for her in the hotel? "He told me you were coming to—check on us," Josef went on. "But he failed to say what needed your checking." Louie had to smile a little at that. *Typical Jones, giving the easy half of the message and leaving the hard part to someone else.* She decided to stay vague herself a while longer. "That sounds like Tom. He sends me here on some ill-defined assignment, all I know is it's urgent, and he doesn't tell you what it's about, either—guess he thinks we'll figure it out. Tell me, Josef, what's your biggest problem? Because whatever it is, I'm probably supposed to be helping you with it."

That made him look up for a second. "Helping me?" Was that a smile again? Louie couldn't tell. "We have a saying here. *Uvidime.*" Josef made a spreading gesture with his hands. "It means—"

"We'll see," said Louie.

"Pardon me?"

"*Uvidime*—it means we'll see, a skeptical kind of we'll see, wait and see, or something like that, doesn't it?"

Josef nodded briefly. "It seems I may speak Czech with you."

"No, no, I just picked up a few words from—"she stopped, unsure why.

"Jack." Josef finished for her. "As it happens, that is also the answer to your question. He seems to be my biggest problem." His gaze was level.

"Jack is your problem? Of course, that's why you fired Tinka instead of him," Louie blurted.

But Josef was unruffled. "No, I fired Tinka because she used company time for non-company business. I don't tolerate that sort of thing here." Unlike you do in the States, the implication hung in the air. Something about his superior air made Louie a little pissed off, and a little reckless.

"What, did she call her poor sick mother from work?"

"Her mother died last year," Josef replied calmly. "Tinka made hotel arrangements for a non-company visitor." Josef's stare told Louie who the visitor was, and her heart sank. *Me. She made the reservation for me.* And then: *The goon waiting for me. If Josef knew Tinka made the reservations, for sure he knew which hotel.* Louie decided to play dumb with Josef a little longer.

"Me? But I work for PPP3 too."

"But Tinka does not. She works for my import-export company."

"Still, it must've taken her, what, all of five or ten minutes to make the reservations—"

"That is not the point. The point is, Jack is not in charge here. He cannot ask my staff from other businesses to do work for him just because I am not around to stop him."

"Then fire him," Louie said. "Not that nice young woman, who was just doing a friend a favor."

"I thought Jack was your friend?" Josef replied. "But you think I should fire him?"

"There's friendship and there's fairness. If Jack screwed up, he's the one who should be fired."

"Normally I would agree with you. But Jack has other friends. In high places. He works for them more than he works for me, it seems." Josef went back to his computer screen. "I can keep tabs on him," he went on, "but not much else. If you want to help me, tell him—" Josef's voice trailed off. Louie waited. He hit a few keys. "Tell him that. Tell him my best is only to watch. I can't promise to be there when—tell him to be careful."

"Tell Jack to be careful?" *Careful, careful, everyone over here needs to be careful.*

"He's hard to predict these days. He doesn't seem to care much anymore. He's either afraid or, worse, has gone beyond fear. A little fear is healthy." It was almost as if Josef was talking to himself now. "And with you here, it's going to be worse. You might be in the way of what—he wants, and if that is true, well—" Josef caught himself, and looked at her again. "*Uvidime.*" He stood, and so did Louie. "You should leave."

"I was on my way to Jack's office when you stopped me."

"No, I mean leave the country," Josef said. "Take him with you, if you can convince him to go. If not, go yourself." He paused. "In my country it is not polite for a man to initiate a handshake with a woman." It took Louie a moment, then she reached out her right hand. Josef shook it firmly, then sat back down and swiveled his chair so he was no longer facing her directly. Louie knew it was her cue to exit, and she did, wondering if Josef had sent that goon to her hotel after all, or if he was in his own way trying to help them.

Thirty Seven

Louie went back down the hallway toward Jack's office. She stopped a few feet from the now half-open door as she heard Jack's voice, sounding unusually tense.

"Hello? Oh, hello Sergio. I'm calling to report as we agreed."

Louie couldn't believe it. *Jack was on the phone with Sergio?*

"Yes, she's here. What? Yes, I met her at the airport. No, she didn't see them—she was looking for a little charm she'd lost from a key chain, a house or something, so I surprised her. Well, I'm sure you already know what happened in the square and we've been to the factory, too. No, I don't know for sure how long she's staying. I think she said about a week." Jack listened for a long time. "Yes, okay. I'll leave the document in the usual drop spot...Yes, I'll take her there tomorrow. We'll be there by noon." Jack hung up the phone, turned, and saw an empty doorway.

Louie ran down the hall, punching the elevator button, not waiting to see if it would arrive, running for the stairs, half running and half falling down them to the street level, running out the front door, and down the broken and uneven sidewalk, hoping beyond hope that she would trip and fall and break her neck and die before her mind could finish understanding what just happened, what she'd just heard.

Jack was not her chosen brother after all. He was one of them.

Thirty Eight

Five thousand or so miles away, Aunt Emma washed her dishes and talked to Buddy, the blind mini-Schnauzer from Mars.

"So Mars, huh? I always wondered what it was like there."

Buddy raised a Schnauzer eyebrow.

"I know, I know, you're not telling. At least not yet."

Buddy cocked his head.

"But one of these days we'll swap stories, right, little one?"

Buddy wagged his tail. Emma tossed him a scrap of turkey from her dinner. He pounced on it just as a loud thunk sounded from the roof.

"What was that, Buddy?"

Buddy barked.

"Now, I've never heard you bark before."

Thunk. Thunk. Thunk.

Buddy howled.

"Oh my, that doesn't sound good at all, does it, Buddy?"

Thunk. Thunk. Thunk. Howl. Howl. Howl.

"I think it is time. She must be getting very close."

Buddy started a low, deep growl. He took two slow steps toward the front door. Emma caught him by the collar. "Hang on there, now," she whispered.

The door banged open. Two men in black trench coats and mirrored sunglasses strode in. Behind them was a third man, smaller, skinnier, with black eyes. The two large men took positions by the front and back doors. The skinny man walked up to Emma and Buddy.

"I remember you," said Emma.

"Good evening, madam. It is so pleasant to see you again."

"The feeling is not at all mutual, you asshole." Buddy's eyebrows shot up as if he was shocked to hear such a word coming out of Emma's mouth. Then he went back to growling in the direction of the man's voice.

"I am so sorry to hear you say so, when we have finally converged again after so much time has passed."

"I suppose you want to know where she is. Well, I'm not going to tell you."

"On the contrary, I know exactly where she is." He paused to see the effect this would have on Emma. She blinked hard, twice, three times, but kept any other expression from her face.

"Then why are you here?"

"I want to know why she was sent there. And I want to know if she has it with her."

Emma laughed out loud. "Is that what you want to know? Then why come to me? She hasn't lived with me for years. She doesn't tell me anything about her life if she doesn't have to."

"Yet her animals are here with you, and she cherishes them more than anything in this world. You are still very close."

"You never had children, did you? They do not have to be close to you to ask you for favors."

"She is not your child. She is not even your real niece."

"Go fuck yourself," Emma replied. Buddy did not react this time. His sentiments, had he been able to express them in English, would have been much the same.

"Ah, I see that is still a sore point. I apologize if I offended in any way. Yet I must know the answers to my questions. It will be easier and quicker if you simply tell me now."

Buddy lunged, but Emma held onto his collar. "He's not worth it, Buddy. Besides, I have a feeling he would taste terrible."

Sergio sighed. "Still you waste time insulting me. I can see that I may have to resort to more direct pressure." He pulled a small tool about the size of a fountain pen out of his pocket. He pressed the end and it emitted a high-pitched squeal that made Buddy tremble. "I do not think you need to hold his collar now. He will not come near me."

Emma let go of Buddy's collar, and he shrunk into the corner of the kitchen, but he stayed focused on the man. She sent him her thoughts. *You'll know what to do and when to do it, Buddy. It will be okay.*

"Now, please be so kind as to tell me why she is there."

"I told you, I don't know anything. She only said it was a last-minute business trip."

"Who sent her?"

"How would I know?"

"It must have been Jones. Why did he send her?"

Emma laughed again. "You're an idiot. All this time I thought—but no, you're an idiot. He didn't tell you? He's keeping things from you? Then it has begun already. And you didn't even notice it."

"What are you talking about, old woman?"

"You believed you were manipulating him, but now you realize he's manipulating you. He's keeping you out. He's not telling you everything anymore. You are on your way out, just like always."

The black eyes flashed. "We are not talking about me. Now answer my questions. Does she have it with her?"

"Oh no, I took care of that. It is safe."

"Where is it?"

"I told you, it is safe. Even she doesn't know where it is. She can't tell you, and I won't tell you. So you are out of luck."

He hit the button on the tool again and the squeal stopped. Buddy shook his head, as if to get the last of the annoying noise out of his ears.

"I think, with a chance for further reflection, you will tell me." He flipped the tool in his hand and pointed it at Emma. He pushed the button again and a beam of copper colored light shot out. Emma screamed. A pin dot-sized hole in her arm was smoking. She slid down the cupboard to the floor. *Not yet, Buddy. Soon.* The dog stayed in his corner.

"Where is it? Tell me now or the next one will be worse." Sergio aimed the tool at Emma's forehead.

Now, Buddy. Now.

The little dog lunged at the man, teeth bared in a snarl. The dog landed slightly off-center, just above his left knee, and his momentum knocked the man to the floor. Both of the goons came running, drawing guns from their armpits. Buddy went for the man's throat but missed slightly again, and his teeth fastened on the left ear. The goons stopped. Any shot at the dog could just as easily go right through the head of their boss.

"Get this fucking dog off of me! What are you standing there for?" Sergio shouted.

"Boss, he's standing on your head. We can't shoot him, we'll kill you," the biggest goon explained.

"Well, pull him off me, then!"

"But—" the goon hesitated.

"But what? He's chewing my fucking ear off!"

"Right, Boss, that's the thing. If I reach in there, he'll bite me."

"What the fuck do I pay you for? Can't you solve the simplest problem? Grab his collar, for fuck's sake!"

"He doesn't have a collar, boss," the smaller goon said. Emma chuckled, and twiddled the collar between her fingers.

"Grab his legs then and pull him off!" Sergio yelled.

"Buddy, leave it!" Emma's voice rang out. Buddy turned his head toward her. "Come!" He trotted to her. She laughed. "What have you got there, dog? That looks tasty." Buddy dropped the ear in her lap. "Good boy!"

Sergio sat up. One goon turned and vomited onto the floor. The other laughed nervously. "Sorry, boss," they mumbled.

"You are worthless, and I will deal with you later. Now where—?"

"Over here, asshole." Emma held the tool up. "Looking for this?"

He stood and took a step toward where she sat on the floor. Buddy growled. "You will return that to me. It is mine."

"Hey boys," Emma waved. "Notice something funny about your boss?"

"Please do not make direct contact with my employees. I will deal with them later. Now, please give that back to me." Sergio took another step.

"He's not bleeding," Emma said. "My dog bit his ear off,

and he's not bleeding."

"Hey boss, she's right—you're not bleeding." The goon who hadn't vomited walked over closer to his boss.

"In fact, if you look closely, you'll see he's oozing a little green where that ear was," Emma went on.

"Holy shit boss, she's right again. Like a bad lime Jell-O—"

Sergio whirled and grabbed the gun from the bigger goon's hand and shot him in the head. His large body stood for a moment as it registered the fact that its head was no longer intact, in fact, it was spread all over Emma's upper cabinets. Then it toppled over and bounced off the counter on its way to the floor.

"Jesus, boss, what the fuck—" whined goon number two, just in time to take his own bullet in the heart. He crumpled immediately, almost as if it was a relief to leave the scene.

Buddy whined, barked, and trembled. Emma stared at the gun now pointed at her face.

"Now, ma'am. I am sure you regret that you forced me to remove my two employees. You will understand that I could not allow them the opportunity to disclose to anyone else the—greenness you so eloquently pointed out to them. You may also, now, appreciate precisely how serious I am in this matter. You have my weapon and I want it back, but in the meantime this crude weapon will do. It may not hurt you, but it will kill your dog." He swung the gun so it was pointed at Buddy. He stepped on Emma's leg and leaned his weight on his foot until he felt her bone snap. Then he did the same on her other leg.

"You know you cannot escape me. I will ask you again and I fully expect to ask only this one last time. I appreciate your cooperation in advance. Where is it?"

Emma stared at him, her face calm despite the two broken legs and the hole in her arm. "It is... up yours, asshole. Buddy, run!" As the dog headed for the still-open front door, she took the tool, placed its end at her temple, and pushed the button.

"You bitch," Sergio hissed as he watched her evaporate. He heard the faint sound of sirens. His face darkened. "Well, there are other ways to get what I need." He slipped out the back door.

Thirty Nine

Louie ran blindly, until she couldn't see the office building anymore. She was lost, of course, lost in a way that had nothing to do with not knowing the name of the street she was on or what town she was in or even what part of the world this was. Now that Jack betrayed her, she was alone, really and truly and finally and absurdly alone, over here so far from home. Her vision blurred, whether with fatigue or tears she couldn't tell.

A thought occurred to her. If Jack was on Sergio's side, if he helped Jones and the rest of them with the migration project…he was an enemy. Josef already implied he couldn't, or wouldn't, do anything to stop Jack. *He has friends in high places,* Josef had said.

Louie's cell phone buzzed. She looked at the caller ID—it was Mac's number.

"Hey Mac, thank goodness. Are you and the Secretary in Seattle already?"

"I am, but, Louie, I have some terrible news. Sit down. Is Jack with you?"

"No. Don't ask why. What is it, Mac? What's happened?

"It's your Aunt Emma. She's gone."

"What do you mean, gone? She's dead?" Louie's stomach tightened.

"No, she's gone. The police were called to her house, a neighbor heard shots or something, and when they got there, they found two dead guys and the front door wide open, and your aunt's clothes in a pile on the floor. But no Aunt Emma."

"What about Buddy and the cats?"

"They found all the cats, yours and hers, hiding in her basement. But no sign of Buddy, I'm afraid."

"They found her. Oh no, they found her. Why did I leave Buddy there?"

"No, listen to me Louie, she's lost, not found. So is Buddy. They're both just gone."

"Mac, Buddy is okay. He's probably just hiding somewhere near the house. Call Stuart at the doggy day care, ask him to come out and look. Buddy knows him—have him bring his dog Arthur. Buddy will come to them."

"Louie, are you hearing me? How do you know Buddy is okay?"

Louie wondered about that herself, but her heart felt certain. "Because if he wasn't, I'd know. Call me when he's found. Stuart will keep him until I get back."

"Are you in shock or something? Should I be worried? You don't sound worried."

"I'm horrified and incredibly pissed off and very sad about my Aunt Emma. She's gone, Mac."

"That's what I'm trying to tell you! She's missing."

"No, Mac, I think...she's gone. She won't come back. But Buddy will. Promise me you'll call Stuart. And will you watch the cats?"

"Of course, Louie. How the hell do you know that your aunt is gone and Buddy is okay?"

"I know it sounds completely absurd—but I just know. Take care of the cats for me, and call Stuart. He'll get Buddy."

"Jesus Christ Louie, okay, but—"

"I know, I know, add it to the long list of things I owe you that I'll never really be able to pay back. I've got to go."

"Okay—"

"Bye Mac. Good luck with the Secretary and Jones. And...thanks." Louie hung up. She took a deep breath. How the hell did she know these things? It was as if something clicked in her mind as Mac talked, and she saw the scene: her aunt's house, the dead goons, the open door. Buddy hiding in the shrubs next door. The smoke that was her aunt. And the black eyes. He'd been there. She was sure of it. She was equally sure that he hadn't got what he wanted.

But what did he want? Only one person could tell her. *Jack.* Now that she knew Jack was working with Sergio, it all became clear. She'd heard Jack say something about her house charm, coming from her Aunt Emma. So that's why Sergio would've gone there. To confront her aunt, to get whatever he was after. This was different from the migration project, Louie could feel it. This was personal.

As she looked around, Louie realized she'd run too far to see the office building from here. She took in her surroundings, trying to get a sense of where she was, and which way to go to get back. The area seemed bathed in a strange kind of light; the trees cast crooked shadows. She'd become closer to Jack in the last few months than to anyone else she knew. She remembered their first meeting, colliding in the hunt for coffee...the strange experience at Book Bargain Basement, when the books were flying at her, how she'd trusted him then and gotten on that absurd bus ride to Tukwila...how she told him right away once she found out about Jones and Sergio, how she'd told him when and why she was coming, and where she was leaving her critters...with her Aunt Emma. She remembered the battle in the square, the goon who knew Jack's name, Gil's crazy distraction...Gil, crumpling to the ground after the shot rang out.

It started to rain. The cold stinging drops washed the sentiment away from Louie's thoughts. She knew she had to go back, for Emma's sake, and do what she had to do to stop Jack, though it would kill her to face him again. She began walking in the direction she imagined the office building waited. The street she was on narrowed as it wound its way through the buildings; soon she couldn't see any landmarks at all. She began to believe she might have to turn and retrace her steps back to the spot where she'd been when she'd gotten Mac's call, and wondered how long she'd already been gone, and what Jack might have done in the meantime. He could've run, too, escaped; or sent some goons after her. She saw a dead end ahead, as she climbed a short but steep hill; she pushed on, reluctant to start over, and when she arrived at what looked like the end of the street, she could barely see over a hedge to another road— and a bus stop. She recognized it immediately as the bus stop where she'd helped Tinka repack her box. Soon she found herself back at the front door of the office building, pushing it open, dripping rain on the already slick tile floor in the lobby.

Forty

"You prick. No wait, you've gone right past prick to asshole." Louie stood, dripping wet and shaking with rage, in front of Jack's office door without remembering the last few steps down the long hall.

"Louie—" Jack pulled her inside, closed the door behind her.

"Emma's gone," she said.

"What? Emma's—your aunt is dead? How do you know? What happened?"

"Don't act like you don't know, Jack. I'm not an idiot. Emma's gone because he found her—Sergio found her—because you told him to. You told him all about her, didn't you? You told him where Buddy and my cats were, you told him they were at Emma's. You asshole." She grabbed her bag, which she'd left tucked in a corner, opened it, and glared. "The sales agreement, it's not here. That's the document you promised to Sergio, isn't it. What else have you told him? More to the point, what did Sergio tell you to do with me?"

"Louie, you don't understand."

"I do. I understand perfectly. All this time I thought you were helping me, and you've been telling him everything. You told him I'm here, you told him what I'm here to do, you gave him the only proof we have that he and Jones are aliens."

"Louie, believe me—"

"Why are you doing this? Why are you betraying me? Does he know you promised to be my brother? Did you have a big laugh over that one? Fuck, Jack, how much is he paying you to sell out the whole human race?"

Jack grabbed Louie by the shoulders. "Shut up." His voice

was almost a hiss.

"What? *You* are telling *me* to shut up? You've just been spilling everything to the Vice Chair of Darkness—oh, he probably knows I call him that now too, right?—and you are telling *me* not to talk?"

"Shut up!"

"Can't take the truth? Don't want me to remind you that you are selling out? Well fuck you, Jack." Before she knew what she was doing, Louie took a swing at him. Her right fist collided with his chin and she felt bones crack. *Probably mine, with my luck.* He grabbed his chin and stared at her. She wound up for another swing.

"Fuck you, Jack. I am sorry I ever believed we could be family."

"Shut up!" Jack grabbed her arm and pushed Louie into the wall, pinning her there. His face was white. His eyes bored into hers. Louie was shocked. She hadn't imagined Jack could ever get angry enough to get physical. All of a sudden she realized she should probably be afraid. Jack was working with Sergio, and here she was alone in his office with him, and even Josef was too intimidated to do anything.

"Okay, okay, Jack. Let me go. I'll just leave, I promise, and you won't see me again. Just let me go."

"Louie." Jack whispered now. "Louie."

"It's okay, I'll just go, and we'll never see each other again."

"Louie, I'm not working for Josef or Sergio or any of them. I mean, not in this."

"Sure, right, I believe you. Just let me go." Louie wouldn't give him the satisfaction of watching her cry. *First he betrays me then he lies to me about it? Does he think I'm a complete idiot?*

"Louie, you have to listen to me." Jack sounded like he was choking. *Would he choke me? Ten minutes ago I would have trusted him with my life. Now he's got me shoved up against the wall, and he's got my life in his hands.* Louie at least had to get out of his grip, so she could try to run. She looked him straight back in the eyes, eyes that somehow turned a strange, dark grey as they stared at her, only inches away. She flashed back to that first day they met, when she'd seen his eyes turn to the same grey color, when he'd heard about Sergio's promotion.

"All right Jack, I'll listen if you let go of me—I'm a little bit shoved up against the wall here, makes it hard to concentrate, you know?" She managed a thin smile.

Jack stared at her for what seemed like an eternity then his eyes softened back into their previous chocolate brown. Jack took his hands off Louie's shoulders and took a step back. "Oh, Louie..." he sighed.

"Do you have to kill me now?" she asked with a hollow laugh. "Or will you tell me about your plot to take over the world first, giving me a chance to plan my escape, like in the movies?"

"Louie—I had to tell Sergio you were coming. He would have known almost as soon as you landed here anyway. He has connections. If I hadn't told him, he would have been on us in minutes flat."

Louie was quiet. *Let him talk, and maybe I really will think of a way out of this, just like in the movies.* "Okay. Where does he want you to take me tomorrow?"

"To the migration center."

"To the...but that's where we were going anyway."

"Yes."

"That's where we need to go, to stop this whole thing. So he is going to have you take me there, and then kill me?" Something even more frightening occurred to Louie. "Or are you planning to migrate me? You are, aren't you? The two of you are going to turn me into a cyborg."

"Louie, you can't really believe that. You can't believe I would turn you over to them to migrate."

"Jack, an hour ago I wouldn't have believed that you would tell Sergio I was here. I wouldn't have believed that you would make a plan with him. And I sure as hell wouldn't have believed that you would shove me up against a wall and make me think—"

"Think what?"

"That you were about to choke me to death."

"Louie, sit down. Let me tell you the whole story." Louie moved away from the wall, and sat in Jack's desk chair, keeping it pointed toward the door, in case she got a chance to run. Jack paced between her and the door.

"Josef has been suspicious of Sergio for a long time. He's used his connections here to find out everything about him. And you know what he found? Nothing. Before Sergio came to PPP3, there's nothing. It's as if he didn't exist, at least…on Earth."

"Right, he's one of them, we know that. He signed the agreement for the UFO."

"I knew that before you told me about the agreement. That just proved the connection between Sergio and the Grythylwec."

"So Josef knows Sergio is an alien? You told him?"

"Not exactly. I kept that part more mysterious. He just knows that Sergio isn't who he says he is. So Josef's been hiding the money."

"Hiding PPP3's money?"

"Every euro they make here or send over here. So Sergio can't get his hands on it."

"You're telling me that Josef is a good guy? That he's on our side?"

"Sort of…he's on the side of his country. Anyone who wants to hurt this place or its people—other than its own leaders and businessmen, of course—any outsider who wants to use it for his own benefit, that is Josef's enemy."

"And you?"

"And I what?"

"Are you an outsider who wants to use this country for your own benefit? How do you benefit from the cyborg army? Why are you keeping information from Josef? How did you know about Sergio before I told you about the agreement? How did you know about the migration?"

"Oh Louie, you don't get it."

"Apparently not."

"Let's go for a walk."

Sure. I'll go for a walk, in this strange place, with this strange person who is about to tell me that he is not what he seems. This person who I thought was my chosen brother, who asked me to be his sister. This person who I let into my family. This person who might be getting ready to kill me, or might be getting ready to save the whole human race. Why not take what could be my last walk on Earth with him? She could only think of one question.

"Has the rain stopped?"

Jack almost laughed. "I think so."

"Okay then, let's go for a walk."

Forty One

Louie and Jack stood on the pathway through the park. The night was cold and clear. They could see the steam made by their breathing. After what they had already been through, neither wanted to do much more than watch that breath turn to steam—it was proof they were alive at least, although neither knew how long their luck would hold out.

Finally Jack turned to Louie. "It's time I told you the truth, Lou."

"That's what I was afraid of," said Louie.

Jack took her hand.

"Fuck, you're an alien too, aren't you?" asked Louie. "Are you going to unzip yourself? I don't think I could stand another vision of someone I thought I knew turning themselves into a giant blob of snot green goo."

Jack coughed. "Yes, I am an alien, as you would call us, but I'm not one of them."

"You're not?"

"No, I come from a very different planet than Jones."

"Called what?"

"You couldn't pronounce it."

"Fine. Is it hot or cold?"

"Huh?"

"Never mind. Where is it?"

Jack pointed up to the sky. "See those three stars in a row?"

Louie followed his hand to a spot in the night sky just above the southeast horizon. "Orion's belt, yes."

"You know Orion?"

"Orion the hunter, the warrior. It's the only constellation I could ever remember. The three stars in a row are so easy to spot, and they are Orion's belt. I could always find it, as a kid, when the sky was clear. And I always looked for it. It was reassuring, somehow, to see those three stars in a row, to find it every time."

"Well, if you look at the star in the middle of the row of three—"

"The middle of his belt—"

"Yeah, and then look straight down a little, there's a faint star—"

"That's yours?"

"Yes."

"Oh my god—you're from Orion's penis?"

"What? No, that star—"

"Hangs right down below the middle of Orion's waist!"

"It's his sword! The sword he uses to hunt—"

"No, his sword is over to the left, see?"

"What? No, wait—oh."

"You come from Orion's penis!"

"Well, okay, if you want to see it that way—"

"You come from a giant mythological hunter's pecker!"

"Okay, okay, it's funny. You've said it three times, now it's an old joke."

"I'm sorry, it's just—everything we've been through—" Louie was gasping with laughter, on the verge of hysterics. "It feels so good to laugh—"

Jack started to giggle. "Stop it, this is serious, I have to tell you—"

"About what life is like on a great big prick in the sky?"

They laughed until they had to stop to breathe again, creating wreaths of steam around their faces.

"Louie, really, I need to tell you. You have to understand why I'm here."

"Because that is why you are prepared to accept the completely absurd and nearly impossible as true?"

"That's right."

"Because it is completely absurd and nearly impossible that you are here at all."

"Yes." Jack's brown eyes held her green ones in a steady gaze as she considered for a moment.

"Well, you can explain it all to me if you want, but just so you know, it doesn't matter." As she spoke out loud, Louie realized it was true. Her mind argued she still shouldn't trust Jack—she had no real reason to believe anything he said about Josef, or Sergio, or any of it. But her heart had outmaneuvered her head again, and so she did trust him, anyway.

"What do you mean, it doesn't matter?" Jack asked.

"I know you're one of the good guys, I don't know how I know, but I do. And...you're still my chosen brother, even if you do come from another planet, one that I will remember forever as Orion's Penis. Hey, do you have a zipper?"

"A what?"

"A zipper—are you going to unzip your human skin and show me your alien form? Are you snot green?"

"Yes, I have a zipper, and no, I'm not snot green. I'm kind of....shimmery."

"Shimmery?"

"Yeah, you would see me as just a shimmery space, like a heat mirage or something."

"No body?"

"Not one you'd recognize."

"Oh. How do you..."

"What?"

"Do anything—eat, sleep...reproduce..."

Jack contemplated. "I'm in a human body, so I eat, sleep, and...reproduce, I assume, though I haven't, yet...just like any other human. And I find great joy in it all. That's one reason I wanted to stay here."

"One reason?"

"One, yes. I fell in love with the place, the people...the absurdity, the contradictions. On my planet, things were pretty simple. You're born, you shimmer, you die. Oh sure, it takes thousands of your Earth years, but there isn't all that much that happens during that time. Here...everything is always changing, always in flux. There's sunshine one minute and rain the next. The moon is never exactly the same two nights in a row. And the books, the movies…the color, the flesh. The food. The animals. The sounds and smells. The way your breath makes steam on a cold night. The coffee—"

"You left your family?"

"Not exactly left. I was sent. Most of my family was dead. The planet was running out of room, and the authorities were looking for expansion possibilities. They sent orphans and old people out to test possible locations."

"Test?"

"To see if we could survive."

"They didn't know before they sent you?" *That must be how he lost his sister.*

"No. In fact, they were pretty sure it was impossible." *It was impossible for my sister, after all.*

"Ohhh. You did survive …"

"And this prepared me to accept that the impossible can be true."

"Well, a week ago I would have thought that aliens in America and evil black crow bat monsters were impossible. Three days ago I would have thought having a chosen brother was impossible. An hour ago, I would have thought agreeing with Josef on anything was impossible, and twenty minutes ago I would have thought that trusting you again was impossible."

"No, it's absurd."

"Trusting you?"

"No, agreeing with Josef. It's only absurd, not impossible."

"Ahh. But of course, you are prepared to accept that, also."

"Indeed."

"Jack…" Louie knew she needed to ask something else.

"Yes?"

"Were you thinking about choking me?"

"What?"

"Back there, when you pinned me against the wall—your eyes got all funny, and I was almost sure you were thinking about choking me."

"No, not you."

"Not me? Then who?"

"Sergio. I wanted to choke the life out of him. And myself. I wanted to choke myself for…" Jack stopped.

"For what?"

"Scaring you, hurting you, making you think even for a minute that I would betray you."

Louie smiled. "Well, let's direct that rage back where it belongs. I've got a feeling we are going to the castle tomorrow."

"Yes, we have to."

"And, we are going to find the migration operation."

"I think so."

"And we are going to fight for our lives—again."

"I'm pretty sure we will."

"And we have nothing really to fight with."

"Now there, I have to disagree with you."

"Why? You have a weapon somewhere that destroys alien beings, cyborg armies, and migration centers?"

"Sort of—I have a friend who's willing to try to do all those things."

"Well for dog's sake, Jack, go get him and bring him along. We'll need all the friends we can get."

Jack smiled. "It's okay. She's here already. Now let's get going, my friend, shall we?"

Forty Two

Something red, dark, ruby red, caught Louie's eye as they walked down the street. She stopped to investigate. In the window of a little shop, she saw a pair of dark red shoes. Old-fashioned bowling shoes, with silver laces and rubber soles, they fascinated her. Jack came back. "What are you staring at?"

"Those shoes." Louie pointed them out to Jack.

"Why?"

"They caught my eye. I don't know, I think I should get them."

"Okay. Let's get them."

"Really?"

"Louie, this may be absurd—"

"But we're prepared to accept it."

Jack grinned. "By George, I think you're getting it!"

They went into the dark and dusty shop, full of old things. Candlesticks, oil paintings, chipped china cups. The shoes seemned oddly out of place, yet very much belonged.

"May I help you?"

Louie jumped. The old woman came up to her absolutely silently. Her hair curled silver around pink cheeks and a crinkly face. She wore a faded pink dress, once trimmed in frills, now just ringed with dingy strips of greyish pink cloth.

"You speak English?" Louie spoke slowly.

"Yes dear, don't you?" The old woman's voice chimed in a faint musical tremolo.

"Yes, well, I'm from America," Louie said.

"Of course you are." A patient tone, like she spoke to a young child. "Seven?"

"Seven, what?" Louie looked around.

"You're a size seven, aren't you?"

Louie stared at her, confused. *Hell, I haven't been a size seven since I was twelve. What is she talking about?*

"Not your dress size, dear, your shoe size." The woman seemed to answer her thoughts.

Louie sought Jack, but he was in the back of the shop, sifting through some old photos. He didn't seem to notice the old woman at all. "Yes, I'm a size seven in shoes."

"So are they. Try them on."

Absurd. This is absurd and nearly impossible. The shoes, already on her feet, fit perfectly.

"How much?" *Why fight it?* Louie reached for her wallet.

The old woman smiled. "I'll take this in trade." She opened her hand, revealing the little silver house charm from Louie's key chain.

"But I lost that at the airport. How did you…"

The woman took Louie's hand. "Their magic must be very strong to bring you all this way. Keep tight inside them."

"Louie?" Jack called from the back of the shop.

"Yes?"

"Do you want to get the shoes? Should we find whoever runs this place?" "I already—" Louie turned back, but the old woman disappeared. She glimpsed a faint pink shimmer but it vanished before she could be sure. *Probably a trick of the light.*

Jack made it back to her side. She pointed down at her feet. "I've got them."

"What? Who—?"

"Completely absurd and nearly impossible." Louie grinned.

"Well then, we'd better get going." Jack took her hand and they headed into the overcast daylight, almost blinding compared to the dim shop.

Louie turned back to the window. Lettering scrawled across the glass, *Žlutá Cihla Starožitnosti*. "What does that say?"

Jack scratched his chin. "That's odd. I didn't see any lettering when we went in."

"I didn't either, though it must've been there. What does it say?"

Jack squinted for a moment. "In English, it would be something like Yellow Brick Antiques."

Louie smiled. *Absurd and nearly impossible, indeed.* "Okay, let's get going."

Forty Three

The castle tower sat high above the little village. After an easy walk through the town center, the climb on foot up to the castle entry was steep, but manageable, and passing through the grassy field at its base, there might be a white billy goat or two, though the locals denied those billy goats existed. Upon entering the tower, people could walk at their own pace or follow one of the tour guides, who would claim their English to be very bad, though it was better than the English of most American high school students.

At the top of the tower, the height dazzled viewers. A walkway ran around its perimeter and the vista went on forever. The pattern of the ancient castle walls from that vantage recalled architectural versions of old spirograph pictures. On a beautiful early spring day, like the one Louie and Jack enjoyed, it was easy to forget this castle, like all its kind, was built with violence in mind. But Louie and Jack found themselves in another part of the castle, where legendary ghosts haunted the dark, dank hallways. A confrontation cannot happen in the spirit-lifting, pale blue glow of early spring sunlight. Confrontation happened in dark, dank hallways, near the old cells where men and women who threatened the powers that be were kept far away from any human comforts.

Instead of waiting for the nice young tour guide, they turned left, ducked under the heavy rope meant to keep them out, and plunged down toward the bowels of the place. In the oldest part of the castle, near a strange machine that could only be the migration equipment, Jack and Louie were cornered before they knew it. Sergio walked toward them. Behind him was a row of about two dozen monsters. They were covered in black hair and had horse's hooves. A strange sound issued from them, a kind of quiet wailing or moaning.

"The ghosts," whispered Jack.

"What?" Louie whispered back.

"The ghosts, the legendary ghosts of this castle. They all had black hair and horse's hooves. They wailed, or moaned," Jack replied.

Louie frowned. "This is no time for a 'History's Legends' episode. We're in deep shit here." She flinched unconsciously at repeating Gil's words to them—*you're in trouble, the deep shit kind.*

"Right," Jack said. "It's just so cool. The legends were real."

"Focus, Jack, focus."

Sergio took a step toward them. "Welcome, colleagues. I am so pleased to be reunited although I suspect we all wish it were in better, shall we say, circumstances."

"Cut to the chase, Sergio, and tell us what you want so we can give it to you and get out of this hell hole." Louie was surprised again to find her thoughts clear and focused, and to hear a calm in her voice she didn't feel.

"What I want? I believe you know exactly what I want. And I suspect, if you look behind me, you will get a strong indication of what will happen to you if you do not give it to me. My colleagues are, shall we say, quite hungry." The monsters' moaning, or wailing, rose a notch in volume.

"As usual, Sergio, you've fucked this up. We have no idea what you want which means we probably don't have it." This time it was Jack's turn to be surprised at his ability to be forceful in the face of such, well, seemingly absurd danger.

"Jack, I hoped I could count on your support. In fact, I was sure I had it. I am very disappointed to see that is not the case, in this case."

"I know who you are and I know what you are. I'm not going to let you do this."

"But I find myself having to regret telling you that it is impossible to stop me."

Jack's grin spread slowly. "Impossible? Thank you, you fucktard. That is exactly what I wanted to hear."

Sergio's black eyes flickered for an instant.

The doors to the room flew open. Large men, in tan trench coats and mirrored sunglasses streamed in. Each carried a Kalashnikov assault rifle. They ringed the room.

"Drop it, Sergio." Josef strode forward, hefting his own Kalashnikov.

"Drop what, Josef?" Sergio spread his hands in front of him. "As you can see, I carry nothing, no weapon."

"Oh. Well, in that case, we have you surrounded and we'll be taking you out of here," Josef said.

"I do not think so, Josef. Have your men looked behind them?"

Josef saw the monsters for the first time.

"It's the ghosts," Jack said, helpfully. "These are the legendary castle ghosts, Josef."

"Well," Josef replied, "let's see if a Kalashnikov can kill a ghost. Jack, Louie, I would advise hitting the dirt. Oh, and plug your ears. Men, open fire."

Louie and Jack did exactly as they were told, for once. They hit the dirt and plugged their ears as shots rang out. It seemed like the shooting went on forever. Finally, the roar reduced to a few last pops.

Josef broke the silence after the last echo of fired rounds dissipated. "Apparently not."

The monsters seemed confused by the noise and flying bullets, but were unhurt. Josef seemed more sad than afraid. "I never thought I'd see the day my Kalashnikov let me down. Parents, friends, wife, lovers, yes, I would expect it. Politicians, always, but never my Kalashnikov." Josef considered Sergio. "I guess we are in a—How do you say it?—a stand-off."

Sergio brushed some dust off his suit as he stood. "I do not think so. I think I will give the signal and these monsters will tear your goons limb from limb."

"Yes, Sergio, I have no doubt that you are right about that. I will be sorry to see them go, but there are always more where they came from," Josef said.

"Then I will win," Sergio replied.

"No, what you forget is that I always have Plan B. In this

case, Plan B involves some high-powered explosives that will, I'm sure, take all of us out, even if your monsters somehow survive. More importantly, the explosion will destroy what you are looking for. If I do not call a certain phone number within five minutes, the detonator will be set." Josef reached into his trench coat pocket. Before he could take anything out, Sergio pulled a gun from his belt, grabbed Josef, and shoved the gun into his temple.

"Call the number, Josef, my friend," Sergio hissed.

"No, Sergio, my friend, I do not think I will, after all." There were beads of sweat on Josef's forehead.

There was a moment of silence as they all stared at each other. Then Louie heard it again. The yell she'd heard when she was stuck under the car at the airport and the black bird-bat monster reached for her face with its talon.

"Ah ahahaah ahaahahah." *Just like Tarzan.*

Jack flew at Sergio, knocking his gun hand down, and putting his shoulder into Sergio's chest. The three men wrestled and grabbed for the gun, when a shot rang out.

"Jack!" Louie ran to them as they slumped to the ground. The goons stared through their mirrored shades and the monsters moaned, or wailed. *Typical, functionaries standing there, paralyzed if no one is telling them what to do.*

She grabbed Jack's arm. Blood covered his shirt. "Jack, no..."

"It's not mine," Jack said. "Louie, it's not mine."

"Oh my god, then..." she looked at Josef's face. White as a sheet, it contrasted with the blood seeping through his tan trench coat. "Oh no, Josef..."

"Guys!" Josef rasped out. "Grab him!" The goons descended on Sergio and pulled him away.

"They won't be able to hold him, Josef." Louie clutched Jack tightly.

"Not for long, no, but long enough, maybe. Jack, take my phone out of my pocket. Hit speed dial one when you get out of here."

"That will stop the explosion?" Jack took the phone.

"There is no explosion. I made it up to buy time. I really

believed the Kalashnikovs..." Blood dribbled from Josef's mouth. "Get out of here before he gets his monsters on my goons. Speed dial one will bring a car around for you. You can take it to the airport and get out of my country before you are responsible for its total destruction."

"Josef, I..." Louie choked on her tears. "I..."

"Jack, get her out of here." Josef's eyes closed. "Go!"

Jack reached out and touched Josef's face, ever so gently. "Goodbye, Josef," he whispered. He grabbed Louie's arm and pulled her up. "We're running, Lou. Let's go."

Forty Four

Sergio's father was his mother's second husband. Later, when Sergio was on Earth, he took to thinking of his mother as Flora. He learned the word referred collectively to all the plants in a region, beautiful flowers and weeds alike, and it struck him as fitting. Sergio's father was younger than Flora when they married, and from a social class two steps beneath hers. On their planet, she'd been a mid-level government bureaucrat—or so it seemed—but, in their byzantine system, it took a lot of connections with the right people to pull off the appearance of being a mid-level government bureaucrat. Those jobs came along rarely, once in a blue moon, and incumbents were essentially appointed for life. No one got fired for incompetence, though every once in a while, someone was fired for being too good at what he or she did. Flora used her mid-level bureaucratic position as a platform to influence those above her. The daughter of an immigrant, she'd enjoyed seeing herself as a power behind the throne and reveled in the intrigue and political machinations she could provoke. A leaked memo—real or fake—or an indiscreet word dropped. Sleeping with married men, photographs taken—she'd seen none of her meddling as betrayal, only as service to a higher cause.

Her higher cause was the elimination of the weakest, most useless members of their society in order to leave it stronger, more robust, and truly superior to any other. It always surprised Flora how easy it was to manipulate the populace into believing their planet was about to run out of resources and that they must find other worlds to colonize. It had been going on for centuries, and the vast majority of citizens never asked why such alternative worlds never seemed to be discovered.

It was quite likely her first husband didn't share his wife's views—even likelier he had not shared her tolerance for adultery. He was summarily eliminated before he could get in her way.

Flora's second husband, Sergio's father, was simply besotted with her. She was beautiful, in an angular and severe way, and he needed angularness and severity in his life. A drifter of sorts, he was a kind and gentle man with a tendency to fall in love easily and stay too long wherever he landed. When he'd come before Flora in her professional capacity, seeking some license or permit or other, he'd been immediately smitten. She found herself taken aback by his sincere infatuation and his initial absolute indifference to her work. She seduced him—it wasn't difficult—and they married quickly. He moved into her large flat, much larger than most bureaucrats of her level, decorated all in shades of white. "Moved in" might be an exaggeration. He brought almost nothing with him. She provided him with one small dresser and the left side of her huge, hard, all-white bed. At first it was enough because he could sleep next to her. His life finally had angles, definition, and a purpose—to do whatever Flora needed him to do.

She'd been shocked to find she was pregnant, having assumed she was barren. Her first marriage was rife with passion and she'd bedded many bureaucrats in the service of her purpose. She'd never even suffered a scare. Deep uncertainty about becoming a mother plagued Flora, but on their planet there was no such thing as family planning, so a mother she'd become. At birth, her son looked like a tiny version of herself. There was almost nothing of his father in his looks. Flora experienced a flash upon seeing the infant, an intuition or vision. This child was in fact nothing of his father, he was all hers, conceived without insemination. So she set about raising him that way, and the loss of his son to Flora broke her second husband's heart.

Sergio's father turned his broken heart to a new purpose. He strived to undo all his wife had done to strengthen their race, to weed out the weak and unworthy. Because she'd never seen him as a partner, it took her a very long time to see him as a threat. It made it easy for him to find out everything she'd done to advance herself and her cause, and only a little harder to find ways to set about undoing it. When Sergio neared ten years of age, his father stumbled on the group resisting the government's program of sending old people and orphans away to other planets. His father provided them with all the information they needed to realize the government lied about the need to colonize other worlds—in fact they tried to cleanse their world of those they found less than desirable. Sergio's father was ready to help the group to expose the practice and bring down the faction of the government behind it—the faction increasingly under the sway of his wife.

Sergio turned out to be his mother's son, just as she believed. Flora learned of her husband's treachery and she'd been patient in deciding when and how to respond. She knew Sergio would become her best ally. As she had been duped for so long about her husband's apparent harmlessness, he was also the last to expect any harm from his own son.

Sergio's father knew his wife intentionally kept his son from loving him but he loved the boy in his own way. Despite his broken heart, he clung to the naive belief his son would never actively seek to harm him.

But Sergio's mother worked on her son the same way she'd worked on so many upper level bureaucrats. She used similar seduction techniques of the intellectual and, eventually, of the sexual variety. Oh, she never actually touched her son in an indecent way. She simply knew how to create and pique his libidinous interest, to take advantage of that almost unwholesome love most sons feel toward their mothers at some point in their transition from boyhood to manhood. To manipulate, intensify, and use it to create a powerful and perverted love for her, and an even more powerful loyalty. It wasn't difficult to plant the idea in Sergio's mind that the death of his father would make his government stronger and, much more importantly, make his mother happy.

But of course, once he killed his own father, Sergio's mother needed to eliminate him as a risk, too. He knew too much and, more importantly, he'd mucked up his mother's carefully crafted plan. Flora constructed it precisely and planted it in Sergio's mind so patiently and so subtly he believed it was his own. One step at a time, over months and months, it took shape and form. The hardest part was not getting Sergio over some natural initial revulsion at killing his own father, or even the social prohibition against patricide—those things turned out to be surprisingly easy.

From Sergio's perspective, he woke up one morning with the glaringly simple and clear understanding that his father was a traitor. His treachery, if discovered, would bring shame on his mother and ruin her career. Therefore, the only solution was to eliminate him.

From Flora's perspective, it was only a matter of a few carefully chosen expressions of worry and fear, of pleading for her son to care for her if the worst happened, as he was now the only man in their world she could count on. She found it harder, so much harder, to overcome Sergio's natural tendency to veer off into a fantasy world of heroic deeds and focus on executing the plan carefully and systematically. Sergio's mother knew a heroic fantasy would never be enough to win the day and, in fact, it was just such a fantasy that proved to be Sergio's undoing. Of course, since no one knew him better than his mother, she anticipated this possibility and had her own careful, systematic back-up plan of betrayal ready.

Like most twelve-year-olds, Sergio felt an inflated sense of his own abilities and his own centrality to events. His world seemed to turn around him and the decision to protect his mother by killing his father only reinforced this belief. Fortunately, he'd picked up enough of his mother's hints and secret guidance to have at least half a solid plan. He knew he needed to infiltrate the resistance group his father joined. He realized he needed to find out when and where they met, and who usually attended. He also believed killing a single member of the group might bring too much attention to the identity of the victim. Better to make sure the whole group was wiped out. He informed someone who knew someone who knew the right someone and took pride in this secret chain of communication that would result in such a blow for the forces of order and superiority.

This overreaching was his mistake. If Sergio would have quietly removed his father, the authorities could have swept the whole thing under the rug as quickly and efficiently as they had the death of Flora's first husband. But Sergio hadn't paid attention to anything that happened before he came into the world, and something inside him refused to take his mother's hints in this regard. He wanted to do more than save her—he wanted to impress her. Truth be told, he'd wanted to join her, an ambition well above his ability. But aspiring above his ability was already a hallmark of Sergio's personality and soon it would be joined by an uncanny knack for surviving his self-made catastrophes. When his own mother betrayed and abandoned him to his fate, he had two options. He could give in to that fate or sneak around behind its back and trust the dregs of the universe to catch him. Sergio eventually chose the latter.

Sergio's mother immediately turned him in to the authorities, in a tidal wave of maternal tears and wifely grief. She had no idea what her husband was up to. She'd been proud that her son was willing to do whatever it took to stop such a traitor and heartbroken that he took it upon himself to commit patricide. She certainly could not continue to raise such a boy. He needed far more supervision than she could offer—needed protection from himself. Once a boy committed one such heinous act, what else might he do? The community needed protection from him, too. Within the equivalent of about a week on their planet, she signed the papers terminating all parental rights and responsibilities and gave Sergio over to the government's care—the government she claimed to love above all.

Sergio found himself fatherless, motherless, among the orphans and elderly he'd learned to despise so deeply. He decided to survive without affiliation to anyone, or anything, but himself. But fate still had plans for him, and fate would catch up to him via the green eyes of a girl his own age who saw everything, and then forgot it all.

Forty Five

A lifetime ago, Aunt and the girl found themselves blown across the river and the prairie and the mountains, to the west. They landed, finally, in small town in eastern Washington, Zillah, in the backyard of a small green clapboard house, on top of a pile of brush that waited for the owner of the house to burn it. But the owner of the house, a plump woman in her mid-sixties, lay inside on her kitchen floor, dead of a heart attack moments before, and not yet found by anyone.

The television set glowed like a beacon to Aunt and the girl that evening. They got up off the brush pile and walked to the sliding glass doors on the back of the house to get closer to it.

"And that's the way it was, June fifth, nineteen-seventy-six," the strangely reassuring voice of the man on the television screen said.

"Let's go inside there," the girl pointed. "It looks nice."

"All right, but be quiet," said Aunt. They shimmered their way into the house through a slightly open window. Aunt saw the body on the kitchen floor. The girl was right behind her.

"What is that?" asked the girl.

"I think it is one of them," Aunt whispered.

"Why isn't it moving?"

"I do not know. Perhaps it is sleeping." Aunt nudged the body. "It is very heavy. The things that live on this planet must get very tired of moving if they are all so heavy. No wonder it is sleeping."

"Should we wake it up?"

Aunt considered. "We should, so at least we can ask its permission to stay here a while. I will try to talk to it." She moved closer to the body and spoke to it. "Excuse me, thing, but we have come a very long way to your planet, and we were blown even further by a major disaster, which I am very afraid we caused. Now we are here and we would like to stay a while, to get our bearings and perhaps eat a little something, while we decide what to do next."

If the homeowner could hear Aunt, the little speech would have sounded very much like a summer breeze whooshing by her ear. Being dead, she did not even notice that.

Aunt waited a bit then nudged the body again. "No response, dear. I am beginning to think this particular thing has...expired."

"What does that mean, expired?" the girl asked.

"Its essence is gone from here, only its shell remains."

"Ah. Maybe that's why it is so heavy."

"Maybe. Let's take a look around the rest of the house." Aunt and the girl separated and moved through the small rooms—kitchen, dining room, one bedroom, bathroom. Stairs to an attic.

In the attic the girl came upon a small orange-colored furry creature curled up in a ball on top of a pile of clothing. She reached out to touch it and as she did it opened its green eyes.

"Hello, are you a baby thing?" The girl was proud of herself for knowing that the small versions of creatures were called "babies," and using the term correctly in a sentence. Maybe these creatures grew balder as they got older, she reflected, remembering that the big one downstairs seemed to have fur only on the top of its head. Then she made contact. The baby thing hissed and spit and swiped a paw with sharp claws at the girl. Fortunately, in her state, she couldn't really feel the blow, but she recognized the intention well enough.

"I'm so sorry. I did not mean to presume too much..." she searched for the right word in her head, "too much familiarity upon first introductions. My name is..."

The girl realized she didn't know her name on this planet, if she had one. "Aunt!" she called. "Aunt! Can you help me, please?"

Aunt came up the stairs quickly. "What is it, dear?"

"I met another one and it is a baby. It is not sleeping and it swiped at me because I forgot my manners and did not introduce myself. Then I went to introduce myself and I couldn't. I do not know my name on this planet."

Aunt looked at the little furry creature. "I don't think this is the exact same kind of thing as the big one downstairs," she said. "Look, it is put together very differently. And it has a long tail, which is flicking, it seems, to try to tell us something."

"Oh. Yes, I think you are right. It is a different sort of creature. I think it is much cuter than the big one downstairs. And more practical—a tail like that would come in very handy." Then the girl remembered why she called her aunt in the first place. "But Aunt, what is my name?"

"We will have to figure that out later, dear. Right now we need to get something to eat. Come back downstairs."

The furry creature—the girl would later learn the things on this planet called it a cat—stared at them with its green eyes as they left. Humans, it knew, would have seen nothing but a slight shimmer in the air, like heat rising from asphalt on a hot day. But the cat saw much more. She saw worlds colliding. And when worlds collided, someone was bound to spill something. She bounded downstairs after them. *I hope it is the cream that gets spilled.*

Aunt looked through the cupboards in the kitchen, trying to find something they could eat. The girl seated herself on a stool at the kitchen counter. "Aunt, will my brother and Uncle be joining us to eat?"

"No, I do not think so." Aunt didn't turn around.

"Why not? Aren't they hungry?"

"I think they are probably very hungry unless they've already found food."

"They why won't they come here?"

"I am afraid they are lost."

The girl felt cold. "Lost? What does that mean?"

"I think the wind that blew us here, blew them somewhere else. So we are no longer together and they are lost."

The girl saw this as a problem to be solved. "After we eat, will we go look for them?"

"No, dear, I don't think we will." Aunt tried to keep grief and fear out of her voice, busying herself in the search for something edible.

"Why not?"

"We have no way to travel and we have no way of knowing where they are."

"Could we build another pod?" The fear began to gnaw somewhere deep inside the girl.

"Even if we could, who would program it?"

"I read something about it in one of the books I found."

"We couldn't chance it, dear, if you made a mistake, we would wind up in outer space somewhere."

The girl couldn't give up yet and became angry at Aunt for seeming to do so. "Then they will look for us. My brother can do anything. He can build a pod and program it and he can find us and he will find us. Uncle will help him, won't he? He helped him before."

"Yes, if he can, he will help. But you should prepare yourself. It might take a very, very long time for your brother to find you."

"How long?" the girl demanded.

"Do you remember how quickly we were blown away from each other? How it seemed like a mere instant, between the time we were all together and the time we landed here, apart?"

"Yes, Aunt."

"Well, imagine a time that is as long and slow as that was short and fast. That's how long it might take for your brother to find you again."

"But, Aunt, that is impossible. I can't be lost from my brother for so long. I will die."

"No, it is only nearly impossible. And completely absurd."

The girl felt afraid and sad— even sadder, if it was possible, than when she saw her parents die. She started to tremble.

"I don't want to be lost again, Aunt. My brother and I just— oh Aunt, I can't be lost again." The trembling grew and the girl shook as hard as a dam with millions of gallons of water about to break through it.

The cat stared at the spot where the girl shimmered. It looked as though it was about to shake itself into a million little pieces.

For the girl, it seemed she was being pulled apart until she was no longer herself. She wanted to be pulled apart. She did not want to be herself. When she lost her parents, she still had her brother and that was her reason to hold on. Now she'd lost him, too. She might as well dissolve into thin air. She had no more family. She was alone. She did not need to exist.

The cat stared as the shimmers pulled themselves apart. Then the other shimmery spot moved across the room and gathered them up. *Yes.* The cat yawned. *Yes, gather up is the best way to describe what that looks like. Like when I gather all my toys in one spot, so that I can pick which one to play with next.*

The girl fought, not wanting to be pulled back together. "No, Aunt, no. Please do not make me. I want to disappear."

"I told you it would take a long time, dear. I did not say he would never find you. He will. Or you will find him."

"I cannot wait that long. I want to die."

"No, I cannot let you die. But I can help you wait."

"How?"

"I will give you two gifts, child. First, I will stay with you myself. We will belong to each other."

"Oh, Aunt."

"Second, I will bury your memory of your brother, of your past. I will bury it someplace special and safe and it will wait for you to be ready to find it again. Meanwhile, you will no longer remember anything before."

The girl let herself melt into her aunt's embrace. Aunt's voice continued. "You will go to sleep now and when you wake up, you won't remember anything. But it will all be there when you need it, when you are ready."

The little orange cat watched the shimmering places merge together, and there was a bright flash, and the cat blinked. Then the shimmers were gone, and the woman who had been lying on the floor sat up.

"I thought so," the woman said. "I thought I could get in here." She opened her clasped hands and there was a shimmer between them. She closed them again. "Let me find the right spot for her to wait until I find one for her." She looked at the cat. "Would you mind, dear, holding her, just for a day or so?"

The cat blinked again. The woman reached out and put her hands on the cat. The cat trembled for a minute and opened her eyes.

"Yes, she's in there, safe and sound. Thank you, little furry one. Hold her tight, now. She's exhausted, and will just sleep." The woman stood up. "Well, it isn't quite as heavy as I feared. I can move around all right—" she knocked the radio off the counter as she turned—"but it is clumsy."

When the radio hit the floor it turned on and music played. Later, the woman would learn the name of the song and the person singing it. At this moment, the sound captivated her, a sweet melody, sung in a haunting, raspy, knowing voice.

I see trees of green, red roses, too. I see them bloom for me and for you and I think to myself... what a wonderful world.

When she bent her new body and reached out to pick up the radio, she noticed a little charm bracelet on her arm, with two ivory cats, a jade dog, and a silver house dangling from it.

Perfect. The creatures will take care of her when she needs them. The house can hold her memories.

Forty Six

The Secretary waited for Jones in his office.

How unusual for so powerful a human to make such a long trip to see the CEO of a small company, Jones mused. The Secretary rose as he entered.

"Mr. Jones." She did not offer her hand, as was customary among her kind.

"Madame Secretary." He made a slight bow and noticed the second human, standing on the other side of his office. "And you? I'm sure you'll forgive me for asking why you're here, too?"

Mac stayed quiet.

"You are coming with us, Mr. Jones," the Secretary said.

"To where? And why?" He looked from Mac back to the Secretary. "Surely your laws—"

"There is no need to invoke the law," the Secretary replied. "This is a scientific operation. You will not be arrested, Mr. Jones. You will be," she cleared her throat, "*studied.*"

"Will I?" Jones spoke with some bravado, despite his inner blanching at the thought of joining his fellow aliens as he'd seen them on television shows—in secret government laboratories, with tabloid photographers constantly sneaking in to get their money shots. Then Mac pulled the sales agreement from her briefcase. "Where, who—?" Jones stuttered. *Not Louie.* She was too weak, too kind, to double-cross him so spectacularly.

"Not Louie," Mac echoed his thought. "Not Louie. Sergio."

Jones could only stare.

"How many times did we try to tell you he's a weasel?" Mac went on, her tone full of barely contained disgust. "As soon as Jack told him why you sent Louie to Europe—"

"Jack?" Jones couldn't stay quiet. "Betrayed Louie? And me? Absurd. Impossible, even."

"Jack only gave Sergio the information he needed to decide weaseling was the better part of valor," Mac answered. "Sergio got in touch with me, I brought the Secretary, and Sergio made a deal—"

Jones began to laugh hysterically. "This is a Sergio deal?" he choked out. "Take me wherever you please. Suddenly, I'm a lot less worried about my future."

Forty Seven

After escaping the castle, somehow Jack and Louie made it back to the Prague airport. The big black SUV they assumed held Sergio and his goons wasn't able to keep up on the narrow city streets. That kind of vehicle was great for creating the impression of wealth and power, but the Skoda Josef sent for them took corners at eighty kilometers per hour while the SUV slowed down to almost twenty kilometers per hour. At one point, they found themselves in a dead end and Louie thought they were done for. But a kind teenage boy at a bus stop pointed them toward a back alley and, before the SUV could catch up, they were on their way back to the highway.

On the highway, yes, but not at all sure they were going in the right direction. Louie hunted madly for the airport in the GPS system on Jack's phone.

"What's the Czech word for airport? I'm putting in the English word and it's got nothing."

"Try *letiště*."

Louie pushed the buttons. "Nothing. Do you see any signs to the airport?"

"No...but I don't see a giant black SUV, either," Jack checked the rear view mirror.

"That's a blessing anyway. Wait...I think I have it."

"*Letiště?*"

"No, points of interest, *Prague Ruzyne*. That's the name of the airport, isn't it?"

"By George, I think you've got it."

"Here's Philippa." Phillipa was the nickname they'd given the GPS system's clipped and proper British female voice.

"Prepare to turn right in five hundred meters," Phillipa

instructed.

"Thank dog," Jack and Louie said together. With Philippa's help, they arrived at the airport in about twenty more minutes. Jack pulled the Skoda up to the loading area in front of the terminal.

"Jump out and find a flight. I'll park and come find you." Jack put the car in park.

"What? Why? Leave the car here and come with me. A towed car would be the least of our problems."

"I just can't, Lou. Besides, something might happen and we'll need it. It won't take me but five minutes, you'll see. Get in there."

Louie grabbed her bags and ran into the terminal. On the first screen she saw a flight to London in an hour. *Perfect, we can get a connecting flight to anywhere from there.* She rummaged in her backpack for her wallet and passport. The passport was there, the wallet wasn't. *Shit, it's probably just buried under all my crap at the bottom of the bag.* She sat down in a seat and started unloading stuff into the empty chair next to her. As she did, Jack appeared.

"What's up?"

"Found us a flight to London in an hour, but now I can't find my wallet to pay for the tickets." Louie frowned.

"It's okay, I'll get them." Jack reached into his back pocket. "Um..." He turned pale. "I don't...."

"You don't what?" Louie's stomach lurched.

"Mine's gone, too. My wallet's not here." Jack's smile vanished.

"Did you leave it in the car?"

"No, I had it in my back pocket, like always. Found yours yet?"

"It's not in here. Dammit. We're stuck." Louie thought a moment. "Sergio took our wallets, during all the confusion in the castle. Then he let us go. We didn't outrun him. He let us go because he knew we couldn't go anywhere, not really." She wanted to cry.

"Let's think. I have some loose cash in my pockets." Jack rummaged through his jacket.

"How much?"

"Um, hang on." He counted the crumpled bills and coins.

"About a thousand crowns."

"That's about seventy dollars, Jack."

"Yup."

"That's not gonna get us to London."

"Nope. It might get us a cab ride back to the castle," Jack offered.

"We don't want to go back to the castle and, if we did, we'd take the car you so thoughtfully took an extra five minutes to park."

"Just trying to look on the bright side."

"There is no bright side, Jack. We are stuck in Prague, with Sergio and a big black SUV full of goons looking for us, and it's only a matter of time before they decide to look here. Our ability to get the hell out is severely hampered by the fact that both our wallets are gone, which I don't think is a coincidence at all."

"No, but you have to admit it is absurd." Jack tried a weak grin.

"Do I? Do I have to admit it?" Louie snapped.

"Sorry, Lou, just trying to make you smile. And remember, you did touch the dog. Back on the Charles Bridge? You touched the dog for good luck."

"That seems like a hundred years ago already. I think I used up that luck."

"Maybe not. Maybe there's a little bit more just waiting for us."

Louie stood. "I'm going to the restroom."

"You need a break from me, don't you?"

"I need to pee...and I need a break from you, yeah," Louie answered.

"Okay. Take your time. I'll watch your bag." He gave her a smile as Louie stalked off. She was frustrated, but not really with Jack. Something inside her knew they would get out of here, but she couldn't see the path yet. She could feel a solution was nearby, and Jack's silliness seemed to distract her from it. *If I could just have a couple minutes to think.*

On her way back from the restroom, Louie saw the little girl out of the corner of her eye. She was about six years old, wearing a blue and white checked coat, and twirling in random patterns like six-year-old girls will do. Louie knew she and the girl were on a collision course but didn't have time to move out of the way.

Smack! The little girl slammed into Louie at an oblique angle and they both fell down. Louie turned her ankle as she tried to catch herself, and the little girl went straight down on her butt. They stared at each other from their positions on the floor for a moment that seemed to last for a long, long time. Louie could see the girl was okay, but waited to see if her mother would look her way. *Don't look, don't make eye contact, Mom. If she doesn't see you checking on her, she'll just get up and all will be well...*

Just then the mother caught the little girl's eye, gave her a worried look, and the little girl began to wail as loudly as only little girls who aren't really hurt can wail.

The mother ran over and scooped her up, speaking to her in a language that was probably Czech.

"I'm sorry," said Louie. "I think she's okay."

Jack was there, too. "What the hell, Lou? Are you taking your frustration with me out on little girls, now?"

"She twirled into me. It wasn't my fault. You know how randomly little girls can move." Louie's face reddened.

"Well, get up off the floor, anyway." Jack tried not to laugh and annoy Louie even more. Louie tried to lift herself up, and realized her left ankle wouldn't hold her weight. She almost went down again, landing heavily against Jack.

"Shit, my ankle."

"Here, come back to the chairs." Jack helped her limp back and plopped her in a seat. "Take off that shoe, let me see the damage."

Louie reached down and winced as she pulled the shoe off her foot. She could see the ankle already started to swell. As she pulled the shoe, she saw her heel was twisted.

"Oh, great, I've broken the shoe, too. Being shot at by goons, losing my wallet, knocking over little girls, and now a busted shoe—this day just keeps getting better and better, doesn't it."

"Wait, give me that." Jack put his hand out for the shoe.

"Why? You have a shoe repair kit hidden about your person somewhere?"

"No, it's…" Jack took the shoe and turned it upside down. "I thought so. These are the shoes you got in the antique shop, right?"

"Yes," Louie nodded.

"Well, look at the bargain you got." Jack grinned. He held up a wad of cash.

"Where did you…?" Louie gasped.

"It was in the heel of the shoe. Quick, take the other one off."

Louie obeyed and handed it to Jack. He ripped the heel off in one quick motion then looked back at her with an even bigger grin.

"More?"

"Nope, nothing here. But at least the shoes match again." Jack handed them back to her.

"Funny. So how much is there?"

Jack counted. "Enough."

"Great. Give it to me and I'll go buy the tickets." Louie tried to stand up and felt the stab in her ankle. She plopped back down on the chair.

"On the other hand," Jack said, "why don't I go? You wait here."

"Okay, but hurry. That plane to London leaves in forty-five minutes."

Jack was back in about five minutes. "Okay, let me help you to the check in line. Put the shoes back on. Even without heels they're better than socks."

Louie did as she was told and her heart beat fast. The puzzle pieces were coming together again. *We're going to do it. We're going to get out of here, safe, together.* The line wasn't too long, and within a few minutes they were at the head of it.

"Here," Jack held out a piece of paper. "Here's your ticket, go up to the window."

"Come with me. We're travelling together, they'll check us both in." Louie started forward.

Jack shook his head. "Louie, I'm not coming."

"What? What are you talking about? We're in this together, we're going together! Don't tell me you are weaseling out on me now!"

"I can't go with you, Lou." The passengers in line behind them were getting impatient. "Louie, go check in. You are running out of time."

"Not until you explain, Jack. Is it Sergio? Did he get to you after all?" She didn't believe it, even as she said it, but her head swam. How was she supposed to go without him?

"No, you idiot. But thanks for the vote of confidence," Jack answered.

"Then what? Tell me fast or all these nice people behind us are going to get pretty mad."

"The money only bought one ticket, Lou."

"What? Jack, you said there was enough!"

"There was. Enough to get you home. I bought you a ticket all the way through to Seattle."

"Why? We could have gone to London together. We could have been safe, together." Louie trembled.

"No, we wouldn't be safe in London. We won't be safe anywhere until this is over. No one is. Mac's already in Seattle, isn't she?"

Louie jerked in surprise. She didn't recall telling him.

Jack went on. "Something else is waiting for you, too, I can feel it. You have to go home, Lou."

"Jack..." Louie wanted to protest. *But the bat-crow monsters attacked me in Seattle. Sergio found Aunt Emma there, and she had to disappear. How can I go back there now, alone?*

Somehow she knew Jack was right. She needed to go home—or the nearest thing to home she'd ever known—to finish what she'd started when she found the agreement and decided to confront Jones, when he split open in front of her—*How many days ago? A lifetime?*—when she made the bargain to try to save her own life and the human race, and now her time was almost up. Mac probably neutralized Jones by now, but Sergio was still out there and he was proving to be more dangerous than she'd imagined. None of the people, or critters, she loved would be safe until she finished this battle.

Jack held her hand. "Go check in, Lou. They're waiting for you. Don't worry, all will be well. You touched the dog, remember?"

An Alien's Guide To World Domination

"That's right, I touched it. You didn't."

"I can handle myself. In fact, something tells me I can help better from here. Go, Louie. Call me when you're home, okay?" Jack turned and walked away.

"Jack!" Louie cried.

He stopped and looked back.

"Idiot!" Louie hobbled up to him and gave him a quick, hard hug. "Idiot, you'd better take care of yourself."

"I will," Jack whispered into her ear.

"See you later, Jack."

"Good—"

"Don't you dare say goodbye or I'll tear this ticket up right now."

"It wouldn't matter, they have your booking. You just have to show your passport—"

"Jack! Don't say goodbye or I'll flush my passport down the toilet! Just don't say goodbye, it's too—"

"Okay, okay—see ya. Go get on that plane!" And he left and Louie didn't call his name again. She limped to the counter and handed over her passport. She didn't look behind her because, if she did, she knew the sobs would come and she would never make it to the gate. And she had to make it, because someone had to.

Forty Eight

After a quick and uneventful flight to London, Louie walked through Heathrow following the signs to her connecting flight's gate as if hypnotized. As soon as she got on the plane to Seattle, fatigue hit her. She was amazed to find, instead of fighting back tears, she fought to keep her eyes open.

Images paraded by when she let her eyes close.

Black crow-bats attacking Buddy, monsters with cloven hooves in the castle, goons in trench coats and mirrored sunglasses, Josef, bleeding from the mouth, books flying off the shelves at her and Jack, Gil, falling down in the middle of the square, her imagined vision of what Aunt Emma's last few moments on Earth must have been like...

And those beady, black eyes. Always those eyes. Now she had a new fear to add, but no image to go with it.

What was happening to Jack? While she was safe, at least for the time being, on this plane, what was he going through?

Oh hell, knowing him, he's somewhere reading a damn book. Louie drifted into a sleep not disturbed by the noise or movement of the plane, or by the murmured conversations of other passengers, or even the offers of complimentary beverages from the flight attendants. No, all the things that usually made it nearly impossible for her to sleep on planes faded into the background as the dreams took over.

At first it was just black...then the black focused itself into two shrinking ebony spheres, which slowly became two black eyes.

Then perspective shifted, as it does in dreams, and she was the eyes, or at least looked through them. Some almost-conscious part of her squirmed—*no, rebelled*—at being behind those eyes. But there she was, and the view was compelling. She could not, dared not look away.

She looked over Jack's shoulder. *He is reading, damn him. Figures.* He sat in a café, at a small sidewalk table, reading and sipping what looked like a caffe latte. As her—*its?*—vision took in more of the scene, she could see it was a clear late afternoon, heading toward dusk.

Where was he? Had he stayed in Prague for some reason, maybe waiting to meet someone? Or trying to avoid someone? Or was he already somewhere else? She couldn't see enough to tell for sure. At least he seemed safe...

Then she felt a cold wind blow across her face and, at the same moment, saw Jack start and look up from his book. She noticed, with a jolt, the title of the book—*The Joke,* by Kundera. The same book she'd pulled out of her bag for reading on the plane.

A dark cloud drifted across the lowering sun. Something moved between her and Jack so she could no longer see him.

But she could hear. She could hear him say, "You. It's you— what the hell?"

The sounds of a struggle and then a scream, an unearthly scream, choked off at its climax—

"Miss? Are you all right, miss?"

A kind face looked down at her as she opened her eyes. A young male face under spiky hair. *Oh god. Did I scream out loud?*

"Your pillow, miss," the kind young face spoke, with a gentle voice. "You seem to have knocked it into the aisle, and we really need to keep the aisle clear, don't we? Here it is." He handed it to her and she mumbled her thanks. "Would you like a cup of hot tea, miss?"

She answered yes before she thought about it, because she really didn't want to go back to sleep. *But it was just a dream, right?* She hadn't really slipped into Sergio's mind, seen through his eyes, seen Jack being attacked—in fact, she hadn't seen what happened to Jack at all, she now recalled. Something blocked her vision. Who had she seen? And who screamed? *Maybe Jack ripped out Sergio's throat, maybe that's what happened.*

The tea wasn't exactly hot, but it tasted good anyway. *It was*

just a dream. The in-flight tracking screen showed there was still four hours to go before landing in Seattle.

Forty Nine

In his natural form, Gil would remind a human of nothing so much as a hunk of desert sandstone. They'd have to watch a long time to see him move, but move he did. Slowly, steadily, purposefully—always purposefully—which contrasted with his behavior in human form. It was at first the liberation he felt being in a body that could move so much faster, the way its soft but strong muscles responded to his thoughts so immediately, so gracefully, he sought out all kinds of physical experiences. Even pain was a joy in some ways, he learned quickly, having moved into the body of a football player who'd been knocked out on the field in a "friendly" game, only it hadn't been so friendly. Apparently, the guy was kind of a prick, made a few enemies—one or two or three on the other team—and when they tackled him a bit on the rough side, he'd not expected it. One caught his head at a bad angle and triggered the hematoma that been waited there since the guy was a little kid. It could've been any blow, but it happened in the "friendly" game, and if Gil hadn't been there, watching and waiting, those guys would've experienced what it is like to be responsible for the death of their "friend." Even though he was a prick, they wouldn't have felt he deserved that, so it was lucky they were spared.

Gil arrived on Earth years before, from a planet where time moved slowly, as slowly as it does when you are on a glassy blue-green lake in the early morning with your line in the water waiting for a little tell-tale tug of a fish biting. It made him very patient and he'd waited for the right time to make his move. Someone in the small town where he'd landed—by the town's one and only playfield, on the south end of its small lake—must've noticed that one day there was a hunk of desert sandstone there that hadn't been there before. In this case, that would've been Lowell, the town drunk, and his dog, Tater Tot, named for his favorite drinking-binge snack. When Lowell tried to tell the boys in the Del Mar Tavern about it, they'd humored him but knew better than to believe him. Since Tater wasn't able to speak English yet, her barking confirmation of Lowell's report went unheeded. When the boys saw the sandstone for themselves the next day, they convinced themselves it'd been there for years, if only to prove Lowell wrong. Lowell was always wrong, that's how it was, and him being right about something like that while being the town drunk was far more threatening to the social order than the sudden and unexplained appearance of what looked like an innocent hunk of rock.

While he'd waited, Gil had all the time he needed to observe and learn. There was time, too, to reflect on what brought him here, launched him into exile so far from home. It was his boss's idea, and Gil found it hard to say no to his boss. He'd worked for an interplanetary security agency, one that was staffed mainly by the sort of people who'd tried to get into the official governmental security corps, but were rejected for some small thing. In Gil's case, it was a genetic deformity with the intriguing but inconvenient side effect of making him a little too attractive to women. The corps worried that its female officers would lose focus on their security assignments and spend their energy trying to fight off the attraction to Gil, or—worse—give into it. They were very strict about inter-agent fraternization, having seen the havoc it could wreak when a highly placed officer was discovered allowing an intern to, ahem, polish him in his office. It wasn't just the shitstorm of accusations of preferential treatment in return for the office polishing that prompted the rule-tightening, it was, the corps leadership noticed, how stupid this particular sort of polishing made the highly-placed officer for hours, sometimes days, afterward. They couldn't risk it spreading and when Gil showed up in the applicant pool and the selection officer, a highly-decorated female, found herself imagining what it would be like to polish him, she'd shaken herself twice—something that took about two Earth weeks for her stony form to accomplish—thought of baseball and selflessly rejected Gil, sending him to try the private agency. She hadn't, however, told him why, so he'd believed she'd pegged him as a coward and ever since then some part of him was always ready to prove her right.

His boss at the private agency sent him to Earth because he had no female agents there, the selection officer at the corps having tipped him off to Gil's particular challenge. Earth needed watching, the spot Gil landed especially, the boss claimed, because of rumors that it was about to become ground zero in a contractual dispute between the Grythylwec and the Kleptofargh. "About to," in this case, meant sometime in the next one hundred Earth years or so. In year one hundred and one, Gil watched the collision on the football field and took his chance to slip into that momentarily lifeless human body. The only ones who noticed the disappearance of the hunk of sandstone were Lowell III, following his grandfather's and then his father's footsteps as town drunk, and his dog Tater Tot XII. Their story fell on much the same kind of deaf ears as their predecessors' did, and Gil was finally free to wander around Earth. And wander he did—choosing his name after being inspired by reruns of a television show that featured three beautiful Earth women solving crimes and generally kicking ass—and he'd found it very easy to get human women to help him obtain all the identification papers and passports he needed to move about without impediment.

There was one other interesting thing about Gil, in human form. He knew other non-Earthlings immediately, no matter where they were from or what form they took. He'd paid very close attention in agency training, learning most of the planets and beings who wanted to cause trouble in the galaxy. Being able to recognize them all was a huge plus, one he was determined would pay off, sooner or later. When he saw Jack outside that concert hall, he'd decided to recruit him along, without giving away that he knew the truth of his identity. When he saw Jack and Louie in the square that much more recent day, he knew payoff was just around the corner. And with it, maybe a trip back home.

Fifty

After he saw Louie safely on the plane, Jack knew he needed to keep moving, do something, or the feelings of loss and worry would overwhelm him. He couldn't go back home—as if there was a home for him anymore—and he couldn't stay around here. Sergio was too close.

That's it, a voice said to him. *Sergio is close, here. Keep him here as long as possible, so she can get home.* Suddenly peace filled Jack's heart. He knew that's exactly what he had to do. He had to stay put, engage Sergio one more time, long enough, he hoped, for Louie to get home safe and—

He wasn't sure what would come next, but he was sure it didn't matter. Knowing it wouldn't change what he had to do. She was meant to do or find something in Seattle and he was meant to give her the chance to do or find it, even if it meant he perished in the process. That thought created a pang in his heart but it didn't change his mind. *I can lead Sergio on a merry little chase, only to find that we've ended right where we began.* He got back in the car.

Like many old European cities, Prague blocked its inner core to auto traffic, creating a pedestrian zone for its old town that allowed residents and tourists alike to walk the lumpy cobblestone streets, to encounter at one moment an old synagogue or church and at the next a Starbucks or Kentucky Fried Chicken, free from competition with automobiles. That meant the roads in the rest of the central part of the city wrapped around the pedestrian zone, and combined with the river Vltava cutting through the city, forcing traffic across one of several bridges, it made for perfect cat and mouse driving. Before long Jack was having fun, circling around, taking turns that would loop his route back on itself, counting how many times he could pass the building everyone called "Fred and Ginger" because of the way it swooped, like a couple dancing in alternating directions. Always in his rear view mirror, weaving in and out of the cars behind him, was the black SUV he'd seen when he parked the car at the airport. Knowing Sergio the way he did, Jack wasn't surprised that it kept a patient distance. *Always putting off conflict until the last minute, you old pantywaist. Well, in this case, I'm grateful for it.*

Finally, Jack decided it was time to stop and invite the conflict Sergio seemed inclined to avoid. Louie's plane would have landed in London a while ago, and she would be aboard the connecting flight to Seattle. He took a right turn at the last moment, watched the SUV go straight past his turnoff in his mirror, and then quickly found a spot to park the car. Somehow it seemed more honest to walk to this last meeting. He picked his way through the streets and alleys, knowing the direction he wanted to go. He entered the old town square from the west along Platnéřská Street. And there it was, standing out against the clear blue late afternoon sky. The Tyn cathedral, its twin spires beckoning and intimidating at the same time.

"Oh, shit," he said, out loud, as he always did when this view confronted him. Night or day, its beauty stole his breath, leaving him only able to swear. *If this is the last thing I see, life on this planet's been pretty damn good to me.*

It was warm enough for the cafe owners to push their tables and chairs as far out in the square as they could, all the better to tempt tourists to enjoy an overpriced coffee or beer. Jack chose the former, wanting to savor the experience of caffeine coursing through his system one more time. *And I can always have a beer after this if Sergio's as late as I hope he is.* He pulled out his book—Kundera's *The Joke*, aptly titled—and settled in to wait.

He'd read a few pages—the writing was dense, and he took his time reading it—when he felt eyes behind him and knew Sergio was there. Strangely calm, Jack kept reading, or at least scanning the page with his eyes, maybe not really taking in every word. He felt something else, too, or someone else. A twinge behind his left ear, and then warmth pouring down into his chest. She was here, too, his sister. Now he knew for sure she wasn't dead. He knew for sure she'd survived, just as he had, and made her way in this world, always seeking him, in her own way, although she didn't know it.

And then in a flash he knew he'd just put her on a plane back to Seattle, and might never see her again. He knew all this, and he couldn't be sad. He could only be ready. He took a deep breath and marked his place in the book with his napkin.

Someone else was there, standing in front of Jack's table. "You. It's you. What the hell—?" Jack stuttered.

Gil didn't take the time to answer him. He just nodded and grabbed Jack's hand, pulling him up from his seat, swinging him into position so the two of them faced Sergio as he emerged from the shadowy alley behind the cafe. As Gil pulled him, Jack's chair clattered to the cobblestones. Sergio looked to see the cause of the noise, and Gil seized his chance, took two long strides toward him, and swung a roundhouse right into Sergio's chin. The crack was sickening and Sergio's eyes went wide as he stumbled backwards. Jack got in three left jabs before he felt his arms pinned behind him. They were all in the alley, Sergio with his back to the wall of the old building on the north. Jack and Gil faced him, each held by a large goon in black trench coats, far better goons than Josef's boys. Sergio's goons. Gil's face broke into a huge grin as he caught Jack's gaze.

The fingers of Jack's right hand closed more tightly around what Gil put there when he pulled him up from the cafe chair. Somewhere low in his chest a scream started, long and unearthly, like Tarzan, and the goon holding him was freaked out enough to loosen his grip just a little, enough for Jack to shove the point of Gil's weapon into the goon's thigh. The goon crumpled like an old paper bag, and Jack kept screaming. Sergio tried to block his ears with his fingers, and Jack jammed the weapon into the goon holding Gil, and that goon went down, too, faster than the first, just as Sergio put his hands around Jack's throat, and then finally, finally, the screaming stopped.

Sergio and Jack were between Gil and the alley's only exit. "That paralysis gun won't work on me, as I am sure your reckless friend here knows," Sergio said quietly to Jack. "But I have something that will work on him."

Sergio pulled out a small tool the size of a fountain pen from his pocket, keeping his other hand around Jack's throat in a surprisingly powerful grip. Sergio pointed the weapon at Gil, who stood helplessly at the end of the alley, just as he'd pointed it at Emma, when she was trapped in her kitchen. "And I will use it on him if you do not tell me where she has gone."

"Who?" Jack gurgled.

"Do not be pointlessly stupid," Sergio snapped. "You know precisely about whom I ask. Tell me where she has gone or this person here will be evaporated."

"Why should I care about him?" Jack cringed, hoping Gil would understand.

"You shouldn't," Sergio responded, "but being weak as you are, you do. You care about these other people you have met here on this planet more than you care about yourself. It is completely absurd, but true, and it gives me an enormous advantage, as you are discovering in this very moment."

"I know where she's gone," Gil said. "I'm happy to share, provided the compensation is adequate." Jack stared at him. Which side was Gil on, anyway? He showed up at the most critical moments, but was he really helping them? Or just keeping them alive long enough to get the payoff he wanted?

"Why should I give you any compensation, when I could simply vaporize you if you do not give me the information?" Sergio shifted the tool in his hand.

"Vaporize me and you won't get the information," Gil answered. "Jack can't tell you what he doesn't know." They both stared at him. "I intercepted Louie at the gate," Gil shrugged. "Convinced her it was safer to change plans. I was glad you left the airport when you did, Jack, or you would've heard them paging the stupid American who didn't show for the flight to London."

Jack's head spun, from the unsatisfactory amount of oxygen making its way to his brain through Sergio's chokehold and from trying to follow what Gil said. "But…" he sputtered. "I saw…"

"You saw what you wanted to see. Right, Sergio? You and I know that one of our best weapons is the tendency of these kindhearted ones to see what they want to see. So, what do you say? Are you willing to compensate me for the information you need?"

"What compensation do you think you can demand?" Sergio asked. Gil smiled. *Pricks and assholes, they're all the same, no matter what planet they're from. They don't ask if they haven't already decided to give you something.*

"A plane ticket and guaranteed safe passage to Florida," he answered.

Jack gaped. "You...you'd sell us out for a ticket to Florida?"

"Man, you ever been there? It's beautiful, always warm and sunny, and the women...I'm going to the Keys, you know, and spend the rest of my life drinking beer and margaritas and enjoying myself. Like that guy who wrote those books...."

"Hemingway?"

"That's the guy."

"He wound up killing himself, Gil."

"He did? In the Keys?" Gil looked shocked.

"No, in Idaho."

"Well, that explains it. I won't make that mistake, I promise." Gil looked back at Sergio. "Well?"

"Your price is unsurprisingly cheap," Sergio sneered. "You will have a ticket in your name at the Delta counter at Ruzyne within the hour." He tightened his grip on Jack's throat. "Now, tell me where she is."

"Oh, one more thing." Gil tensed. "I nearly forgot. You have to get your fucking hand off Jack's throat, you motherfucking son of a bitch." From Sergio's perspective the swing came out of nowhere, and caught him squarely on his missing left ear. Thankfully, Jack saw Gil pull his arm back, and threw all his weight down toward the ground, breaking Sergio's hold. He heard rather than saw the hiss of Sergio's weapon, and felt a sting in his arm as whatever it was glanced off him on its way to hitting Gil.

"Run!" he heard Gil yell.

"No!" Jack insisted. "I won't leave you here with him."

"Run, you idiot. Haven't you noticed I come back from the dead? Like Superman?"

"Yes, Jack, run." It was Sergio's voice. "That is what you do best, is it not? You run. That is how you got here, to Europe, so many years ago. That is why you lost your sister, not once, not twice, but three times, now. You are losing her again, because you will run, again. Your friend here knows you well."

He knows? Jack's mind raced. *Sergio knows Louie is my sister? Damn. Oh, damn.*

And he ran, out of the alley as fast as he could, stumbling on the cobblestones, and away, away, away, without looking back, remembering how he wound up in this dog-forsaken part of the world in the first place.

Sitting in the coffee shop, across from the concert hall, losing track of time. Missing the B.B. King concert.

Yes, time was slippery for him on this planet.

But not that slippery.

He remembered the barista who'd made his dry cappuccino. Remembered her cute blonde bob haircut and sweet face, how the guy at the next table flirted with her when she brought him his mocha. He remembered that guy—tall, lanky, sandy blond hair, sitting at that table, reading a book. Reading *The Old Man and the Sea.* Hemingway.

He remembered the two black, beady eyes in the corner. Remembered passing them on his way to use the restroom. Remembered leaving his cappuccino on his table for those few moments, long enough for anyone to slip a few drops of something in it, something that would make time slip by faster than usual.

Damn, oh damn.

She had been at the concert. Sergio followed Jack to get to her. And Gil. He was there, too. Did he help her escape? Interfere with Sergio long enough to let her go? Jack would never know exactly what happened.

He remembered when he'd realized he'd missed the show, the feeling of despondence that overcame him, knowing he'd fucked up so badly. He remembered standing in front of the now-empty theatre. Remembered the tall, sandy blond guy from the coffee shop walking up to him.

"Hey. You look like you just lost your best friend."

He remembered how they'd got to talking, how the guy

introduced himself as Gil Munroe—how that name rang a bell he couldn't quite place, but made him want to trust Gil. How they went out for a beer, which quickly became three or four or six, and decided to try an adventure—going to Europe. Gil telling him about his job offer to write for a small ex-patriot newspaper in a place Jack only read about in books—Check-o-something. Gil telling him there was an American company there looking to hire someone to teach a little English to its factory workers. Jack, after the sixth or seventh beer, deciding to go and not look back.

Damn. Oh. Damn.

Jack unwrapped the little piece of paper from around the paralysis gun Gil gave him; he still clutched it in his hand, not having been able to let it go in the mad running away. He saw one word written there, only one word but it seemed to take forever for his eyes to focus enough again to read it.

"Seattle."

Thank you thank you thank you thank you thank you, Jack sent his gratitude to Gil, as intensely as he could, and hailed a cab to the airport.

Fifty One

Seattle's weather often made the city look like it shimmered. Not a heat mirage, but a drizzle mirage. Louie arrived in the middle of a typical mist storm—a soft steady rain that never seemed to hit the ground. After she picked Buddy up from Stuart, Louie knew the next place to go was her Aunt Emma's house. When she got there, she saw the remnants of the police tape that had blocked off the house while the crime scene was processed. Two dead goons, no Aunt Em. When Louie put her key in the lock of the front door, she felt dizzy and sick to her stomach. Her mind filled with images from their past in that house. Aunt Emma's cats trying to sneak out the door as soon as it opened. The television always on. The old tiny kitchen that never saw so much as a new coat of paint. The mismatched furniture, most of it found in thrift shops or even on the sidewalk. Emma's mediocre cooking that relied far too much on canned food. The daffodils that burst into bloom earlier every spring. The way they would both jump if the phone rang, and then compete with each other not to answer it.

Louie remembered all the times she'd been frustrated with her aunt, wishing she had a "real" family with two parents, siblings, blaming Emma for not being those things. Crying at night about not having the right clothes, the right friends, the right dreams that would help her get along with the other kids at school. Blaming Emma for that, too. Who else did she ever have to blame? All those years it was just the two of them. All of Louie's love, all of her anger, all of her grief, and all of her longing could only find Emma as a target.

Now Emma was gone. Louie turned the key in the lock and opened the door. Sure enough, as Buddy scampered inside, all four cats were right there trying to outflank her to escape. "Oh, you wouldn't know what to do if you made it," Louie mumbled as she herded them away from the door. To Thing One and Thing Two, she added, "I guess you're picking up their bad habits."

The house was as she remembered it, with the exception of the mess in the kitchen. Emma would never let her dishes go unwashed even for a couple of hours, but Louie saw dirty plates and silverware that sat for days. That was it—she dropped to the kitchen floor and sobbed.

Buddy and the cats gathered around her, not too close, except for Thing One, who walked onto Louie's lap and curled up there to give herself a wash. They stayed close while Louie cried until she could barely breathe, cried for Emma, cried for her parents, cried for Josef, cried for everything and everyone she'd lost. Then she cried some more, for Jack, and for Mac, and Gil, and Pete and for Buddy, and everything and everyone she'd found.

Thing One stopped washing herself and looked into Louie's eyes as her sobs finally subsided. It was as if she tried to communicate something to Louie. Louie felt the message enter her heart.

"I get it, little one. I get it. You're my family, and Jack's my family, and Mac and Gil, and Buddy. All of you. The truth is as much as I've convinced myself otherwise. I've never really been alone at all." Thing One blinked once, twice, the slow squeezing blink cats do when they want to express deep emotion. Then she cocked her head as if she'd caught some sort of motion on the floor behind Louie. She stood and stalked to a spot in the dark and dusty corner under the cabinets.

"What is it, sweety? Is it a spider?" Louie caught a glimpse of something silver. *It couldn't be.* She experienced another moment of feeling the world tilt and change around her. The little silver house from her key chain, the one she lost in the airport, the one the old woman in pink took in payment for her red shoes.

"How in the hell did that get here?" Then she heard Emma's voice whispering to her. *It's all in there, dear. Everything you need.* Louie reached to pick up the little silver house and—

"Woof! Woof! Woof!" Buddy's serious bark was accompanied by a low growl. He headed toward the back of the house, hackles raised. Louie looked.

And there he was. She saw his black eyes just as her fingers closed around the house charm and then it wasn't now, it was then, and she saw those eyes staring at her in her hiding place at the meeting her parents attended the night they died. She saw the men come and the gun fire and she saw the boy with black eyes shoot his father. She saw the orphanage, she saw the other boy—*boy? No, her brother!* She saw the old man and the old woman. The treasure trove of books where she spent all her time. She saw the pod, and she knew, in that moment, who Sergio was and what he wanted. He was the boy who killed his father, he was the one who orphaned himself and made himself an outcast, an exile. And he was the one who hunted her since that night. He wanted her memory, and her memory had been in the little silver house charm. Her aunt hid it there that first night on this planet—hidden it even from Louie—to keep her safe. Because Sergio was desperate to keep his secret, from whom she didn't know and didn't care. Sergio knew she was there that night. He'd recognized her and watched her since his first day at PPP3. Or before that, from the time she arrived on Earth.

This wasn't about dominating the world or the galaxy anymore. This was about Sergio saving himself. And he was there, right outside her aunt's back door, and now he was inside the house. And finally, finally, it was just the two of them.

Louie spoke first. "They were your goons, right? The two men murdered here. You murdered them."

No expression showed on his face as he spread his hands. "Josef's, actually, but they came in handy."

"And you tried to kill…her." Louie couldn't say her Aunt's name to Sergio.

"I regret to say she made it necessary to take extraordinary action."

"But she's not dead. She just moved on."

Sergio blinked, unsettled, but quickly brought himself back under control. "It does not matter significantly. She is no longer relevant, in any case."

"She will always be more relevant than you can ever hope to be."

"Now you are simply being sentimental. We have no time for that. I think you know exactly what I want."

"Yes, I do. And it is right here." Louie reached out and opened her hand, showing him the little silver house.

Sergio's eyes grew wide. "She put it all in that insignificant little—trinket?" He shook his head. "She was stupider than I imagined."

"Stupid? She hid it from you for nearly thirty years."

"Stupid. It could have been lost or stolen at any time."

"It was lost, and found again."

"You aren't making sense, Louise Armstrong Holliday."

"How do you know my full name?"

"What?"

"No one knows that. I never tell anyone. How do you know that?"

"I think you are trying to distract me with irrelevant questions. You should not waste time. Simply give me what I have come for and I will leave and we never have to cross paths again."

"Why should I?"

In the blink of an eye Sergio grabbed Buddy and picked him up, holding him with one arm while with the other he pulled out his gun. "I think you love this creature. I do not understand why, but I think you do. I do not think you will let me blow its brains out all over your aunt's house."

"You are beyond asshole. You are pure evil."

"No one is pure, Louise. Remember that. Not your dog, not you, not your friend Jack. No one is pure."

Louie felt something. "What do you mean, not my friend Jack?"

"How do you think I knew you were here?" Sergio's smile chilled her.

"You are lying. Jack wouldn't tell you where I am." *He's bluffing,* Louie tried to comfort herself but her dream on the plane came back to her, and she was afraid.

"You overestimate your, ahem, 'friend,' Louise." Sergio smirked. "I should tell you that it took remarkably little to get him to talk. He is far weaker than I imagined, after he attacked me in the castle."

"Where is he?" Louie sensed that Sergio was lying, but she didn't know exactly what he lied about.

"He, also, is no longer relevant. And this conversation is growing unbearably tedious. Please give me what I came for now, or this—dog—of yours will die."

"Fine. It's yours. I don't want it anyway. As you said, no one is pure, not even me." And Louie threw the little silver house right at Sergio's face. He dropped Buddy to catch it.

As soon as the silver touched his palm, it began to smoke. Sergio screamed in pain. His hand withered and shrunk into itself. The house dropped to the floor. His arm remained a twisted, black, smoking mess.

"You wicked, wicked girl," he hissed. "What spell did you put on it?"

Louie stared. "Nothing. I didn't do anything to it except take my memories back." She met his black eyes. "That's right. I remember everything about that night. It must have been something, all right, to fire a gun at your own father. Tell me Sergio, how did that feel? Did it feel powerful? You had to betray and kill your father to finally feel like a man?"

"Shut up."

"That was your first deal, wasn't it? Your first deal, the set up to murder your father and break up the group. You actually pulled it off, didn't you? And then it backfired. Instead of being a hero, you were an orphan. And you were in the orphanage with the rest of us, the ones you despised. That must have really stung, yes? Knowing that any time you could be sent into space, made to disappear?"

"Shut up!"

"Somehow you followed me, here, so you could erase the last evidence of that first deal, the only one you ever closed. Oh, that's why you've never been successful again, isn't it? Classic self-sabotage. Your unconscious always scotches things, forces you into stupid mistakes, prevents you from consummating. After the trauma of your father's murder and your exile, it won't ever let you finish a deal again. You always fail."

"Not this time." Sergio focused on her. "Despite your

attempt to delay the inevitable with your pathetic amateur psychoanalysis, Louise, your time is up. If your memories are now in you, then it is you I must destroy." He pointed the gun at her face.

What happened next happened so fast that it didn't have time to register completely in Louie's memory. Buddy leapt up and grabbed Sergio's arm in his teeth. The gun went off. Louie felt a sharp sting over her left ear. Sergio went down, the dog at his throat. The gun went off again. Louie heard her dog yelp in pain. Then the world went black.

Fifty Two

If Louie only knew the truth. Buddy really was from Mars.

Many billions of years ago, Mars supported life in forms recognizable as similar to those on Earth. Contemporary scientists were only beginning to figure all this out, of course, with their Mars Rovers. Buddy was one of the many dogs who knew just how ironic that name was—Mars "Rover." Because most of the life forms on Mars so many years ago looked a lot like Earth dogs. Not all Earth dogs—Labradors, Poodles, and Pekingese were among those unique to the third planet from the Sun, thank goodness. But Wolfhounds, Spaniels—except the Cockers—and Schnauzers were all really born and bred on Mars.

Back then, the atmosphere on Mars created dense pockets of certain gases. These gases were not toxic, but they were opaque, and made relying on one's vision nearly impossible. Blind Martians actually had the advantage, because they already learned to rely entirely on hearing and scent to find their way around. The social atmosphere also favored extremes—tough, feisty personalities or extremely laid-back ones. The larger Martians tended to be laid-back, easy-going types who let their large size intimidate anyone who got in their way. The smaller ones, such as the Schnauzer-types, they developed persistence—in other contexts it might be called stubbornness—and that's how they survived.

Martians were wise and good, most of them. The ones who weren't wise —who were kind of goofballs, truth be told—were still good. And they were excellent communicators. They could read subtle changes in body language, in the odors that were exuded by their fellow creatures when emotions were raised, and in the sound of one another's voices. A slight change in pitch or in timber communicated more than most Earth humans could understand in a lifetime.

When a few of the wisest Martians realized the planet's atmosphere was changing radically, due to the upset of the natural balance caused by some newcomers from a far-off planet who brought diseases and some strange things they called pfhooootahns with them, and would become uninhabitable for their kind, the Martians didn't dither or debate whether it was really true or only the ravings of a few especially goofy among them. They made a quick scan of the nearby planets, saw that Earth was readily colonizable, that it came with a species the Martians could train to feed them, give them warm places to sleep, and even dispose of their own bodily waste for them, and they immediately began to take it over.

Unfortunately, what the Martians didn't realize, what they had no way of knowing because the concept of "ownership" was completely foreign to their society, was that humans would decide the Martians "belonged" to them. It didn't happen right away. Early humans and Martians created a wonderful bond of equals with one another. But given long interplanetary travel times, Martians continued to arrive long after later, more "civilized," humans betrayed that early relationship and started breeding and abandoning the Martians. Buddy was in the last group of arrivals. He showed up in a town near Seattle, and his blindness made him less than desirable to these "civilized" humans. His first Earth year was far too unpleasant to recount. Finally, a human who had not forgotten the old relationship between Martians and his own species found Buddy and brought him to his small house, already filled with half a dozen other Martians of various types and sizes. They quickly socialized Buddy to his new environment, and when the human who rescued him invited a few friends over for dinner who might be interested in adopting a Martian—now called "dogs"—one of those friends was Mac, and Mac brought Louie. Louie didn't want a dog, or so she'd said. She'd only gone along because Mac was giving her such a hard time about never socializing or doing anything just for fun. So to quiet Mac's nagging for a bit, Louie agreed to go to the dinner.

Buddy spotted her in an instant, and when he'd put his paws on her lap and pointed his nose to the sky in an ancient Martian gesture of bonding, she belonged to him, from then on.

Fifty Three

"Louie."

The word came to her ears faintly, as if it were coming from miles away.

"Louie."

A little closer but still so faint.

"Louise Armstrong Holliday."

That opened her eyes. Her full name. The world swam in her dimmed vision.

"Louie, it's me. It's okay. You're safe now."

She tried to focus. She put her hand up to wipe her eyes and when she pulled it down, it was red. *Blood. Lots of blood. Mine?*

"No, Louie, it's not yours. You have a nasty bruise on your temple where a bullet grazed you but it's not your blood." Who was speaking to her, and how did the voice know what she was thinking?

Whose blood? Then she remembered the last thing she'd heard.

Buddy.

No.

Not Buddy. Oh please. Not my dog. He saved my life. Please. She turned her head to the right, searching for the sight of a scruffy little grey dog through her blurry vision. *Buddy. Buddy. Where are you?*

"He's right here. He'll be okay."

She turned toward the voice, and there he was. Her dog, lying next to her.

"He's going to lose that leg, Louie, but he'll be okay."

She felt a warm rough tongue on her face. Tears streamed down her cheeks. She reached her hand over and put it on Buddy's leg. Someone had wrapped it in a bandage but she could feel that the bone was at the wrong angle.

Where am I? She still could not make sound come out.

"You're in your aunt's house."

But Buddy has to go to the vet—

"He's okay right now, but we'll get him there. He wouldn't leave you."

Who are you?

"It's me. I'm here."

Now she could see the face behind the voice.

"Jack." It was the first word she'd spoken out loud, but it didn't seem to matter. He could hear her thoughts.

"Got it first try." He grinned. "You scared the hell out of me, you know."

"You? I was just a touch terrified there myself." And the barely-there memory rushed back. Sergio, the gun, Buddy....

"Jack! Sergio said you—"

"He lied, Lou, as usual."

"You're okay?"

"I'm fine. With Gil's help. But Gil..." Jack broke off. Louie couldn't ask what happened, not yet.

"What about Mac, and Jones?"

"The Secretary took Jones into 'protective custody.' Mac says he took it surprisingly well. No more migration project, Lou. No cyborg army, except for the staff of Human Resources, and most people think it's kind of an improvement. Humanity is safe. You did it, Lou."

"We did it." She tried to smile but her face hurt too much. And there was one more thing she needed to know. "Where is...he?"

"Sergio? He's gone."

"Gone where?"

"I don't know. But he's not on this planet anymore."

"How do you know?" Louie searched his face.

"I just know, Lou, like you knew about your Aunt Emma. Sergio's gone."

"He's gone, and you're okay, Mac's okay, and Buddy's going to be okay?"

"And I think, although for a while there it seemed nearly

impossible, you're going to be okay, too." Jack smiled again.

"Let's get Buddy to the vet. Then I have to tell you something."

"Okay, but don't you think you might want to try sitting up first?"

"Right. Good idea." Louie pushed into a sitting position.

"How is it?" Jack put his hand on her shoulder to steady her.

"Kind of spinny. But give me a minute and I'll be okay." She swallowed, hard. "Jack, I really think I'll be okay."

Fifty Four

Louie was propped up on the sofa in her own little house, surrounded by pillows, cats, and Buddy—dear, blind, three-legged Buddy. Jack finished his story.

"When we landed, we knew we had about five minutes to get far enough away from the pod so we wouldn't be hurt when it poofed. We grabbed as many provisions as we could and ran, Uncle with my hand, Aunt with my sister's. We'd landed in a canyon of some kind, on a hot day, in a landscape covered with sagebrush. All of a sudden we heard a noise, like a roar, and then a huge crash and cloud of dirt."

Jack paused and looked at Louie. She seemed to be gazing at something far away. "Are you okay?" She didn't move her head. "Louie? Are you there?"

"I was just remembering my dream."

"Your dream?"

"All my life I've had this recurring dream. I am with my Aunt Emma and two other people—a boy and an old man. We are running as fast as we can. Away from something that makes a loud poof noise behind us. We turn. There's nothing there." Now she turned and focused her green eyes on Jack's face. "Then there is something there. Something big and terrible, like a giant dirty cloud. I can't make out what it is, exactly, but I know it is bad. There is also a deep roar, like to shake your bones. My Aunt Emma grabs my hand and yanks me away, and we are blown into the dark."

"And?"

"That's it, that's when I always wake up."

Jack was quiet for a long time. Finally he spoke again. "Right after we landed, after the pod poofed, there was a huge crash and rush of water. It was a huge cosmic joke, really, bringing us safely and together all the way to Earth, on the fifth of June, nineteen-seventy-six, to Madison County, Idaho, on the Snake River, just to have the pod poof a hole in the Teton Dam as it was filling for the first time. The dam collapsed and water poured down the dry riverbed. Uncle grabbed me and we were blown away in the wind. All I could hang onto was my half of my book." Tears were streaming down Jack's face. "After all we'd been through, and after I'd only just discovered she could talk, and she knew things, she could tell me things, I lost her. In the first goddamn five minutes on Earth, I lost her."

He shuddered. "I haven't thought about that moment in so long. Uncle and I were blown to the west, and we landed in a little town in eastern Washington. Both of us were like sleepwalkers those first few months. We barely spoke to each other. Neither wanted to remind the other of what we'd lost. One day, Uncle just wandered off. I never saw him again."

"Oh, Jack. You must've been so lonely." Louie took a deep breath and went on. "That's all I've ever really wanted, you know—is just to belong. To belong to someone, to be a member of the pack. I never felt completely a part of the human race, and then it was up to me to save it, and these are the same people who always made me feel like I didn't belong to them." Louie's eyes were moist, too. "Jack, what did you mean about the book?"

"The book?"

"You said 'my half of the book.' What did you mean by that?"

"Oh, didn't I say? When we were getting ready for landing, I was showing my sister the little book-like device the scientists gave us, the one that would download information about the planet we landed on, the one that later turned into my first book, *House on Pooh Corner*. My sister was so upset about not having one of her own. She was really getting on everyone's nerves with her whining, so I took my book and tore it in half. I shoved one half into her hands, and said, there, now we each have a book. I didn't think it would matter at all, I thought we'd always be together. I thought we were safe."

Now Louie was crying. "I have it."

"Have what?"

"The other half of the book. I have it. On the shelf, over there, see? It's the only thing I still have from that year. I never knew why I had it, or why I kept it."

"Oh, Louie. Louise. Louise Armstrong Holliday." He touched her hair, smoothed it back. "Feel back here, behind your left ear."

"What?"

"This."

"Oh, that?" Her mind still fought. "That's just a little bump I've had as long as I can remember—Aunt Emma told me I got it as a little kid, when someone at school accidentally dropped a book on my head—"

"It's not a bump, Louie. Feel it."

Louie's fingers found the bump and felt it—suddenly she felt dizzy. Its shape was one her fingers recognized, one her mind couldn't process. "Oh, Jack. It's…. it's a zipper pull, isn't it?"

"Yes, it is." Jack's smile beamed through the wet tracks on his face.

"What happens if I pull it?"

"Let's find out."

Louie began to cry quietly. "But what if I…"

"Can't get back in?"

"Yes, what if I turn out to be a giant blob of snot green goo, and I can't get back in my body?"

"You won't be a giant blob of snot green goo. You're not one of them."

"Who am I one of?"

"You know. Go ahead—pull it."

"I'm afraid to."

"Louie, over the last week I have watched you fight monsters that would scare the shit out of normal people. I've seen you stand up to stupid, brutal evil. You decided to risk your own life to save someone you love, and to save humankind, a species you don't even like all that much most of the time."

Louie shook her head. "I was scared the whole time."

"But you did it, that's the point. You didn't let the fear stop you."

"I had help, Jack. Gil, Mac, Buddy, even Josef, as it turned out—and you, always you."

"You have help now. I'm here, and I'm not going anywhere."

"Promise?"

"I promise."

"Okay." Louie took a deep breath. She pulled Buddy to her. "Buddy, my dearest, stay with me, okay?" She turned to Jack. "Hold my hand, Jack." He grabbed her hand. "Can I come back?"

"I'm pretty sure you can—but you have to pull that zipper, anyway."

"Then just in case—" she put her arms around Jack, and held him tight. "In case this is the last time I get to do this. I love you, you idiot." They clung to each other for what seemed like hours, but it was only seconds later she pulled away.

"Here goes…" Louie pulled the zipper. Jack stood back. He held his breath. *We really are, aren't we. We're brother and sister. We're twins. We are completely absurd and nearly impossible. We're family.*

In the place where Louie's face had been, was a shimmer.

Epilogue

Jones

The being known on Earth as Thomas Lee Jones was taken to a top-secret installation near Edwards Air Force Base, to be "studied" by the finest military scientists. When Jones' wife heard about his incarceration, she immediately flew there to extricate him, having no trouble with relatively pitiful Earth security. She found him in a small, Spartan room with a single high window, barred on the outside, a sink, and one piece of furniture—a low wooden frame with a heavy stuffed cushion that could be converted from a bed to a sofa and back. It was covered in fabric printed with cowboys and horses.

Jones refused to leave.

Josef

After Josef's death, Tinka returned to the building that housed his office and his other businesses. It was late at night. She'd kept her key, no one asked her for it the day Josef fired her. No one knew that it was a master key—except Boris, who'd given it to her in exchange for real American peanut butter Tinka got from her cousin in the U.S. Boris made the mistake of letting his three-year-old daughter taste some when Tinka came back from a visit, and now the little girl refused to eat anything else, with the deathly stubbornness only three-year-olds can muster. Even a finicky old female cat will eventually eat food she doesn't like in order to stay alive. Three-year-old humans will allow themselves to expire, fully and completely, before giving in.

Tinka used the master key Boris gave her to unlock Josef's office. It hadn't been entered since news reached his staff of Josef's death. She saw the small filing cabinet and the substantial safe. Then, on the desk, she saw what she'd come for.

A picture in a black metal frame—Josef and Jack on the golf course—a pretty place on a pretty day. The angle of the photo showed quite clearly a knob or bulge just beneath Josef's left ear.

A bulge shaped just like a zipper-pull.

Tinka put the picture in her bag and dialed her cell phone, a Seattle number.

"Cousin Peter?" She locked everything up carefully behind her and hurried to the bus stop. "You were right, Peter. I'll scan the photo and send it to you as soon as I get home."

Sergio

Sergio Leone Eastwood found himself in front of the lord of Kleptofargh again. He had three new reasons to hate Louise Armstrong Holliday—he was missing an ear, an arm, and a cyborg army. But after her damn dog interfered—*again!*—and prevented him from killing her, he decided discretion was the better part of valor. He got in his mint-condition Lincoln Town Car/space ship and took off for planets unknown.

Tracked down and hauled in quickly by the Kleptofargh, he was left with only one bargaining chip—the sales agreement between the Grythylwecs and Paster for PPP3. Sergio gave Mac and the Secretary a copy of the agreement, of course, and was long gone by the time they realized he'd kept the original. The Kleptofargh would be very interested in the technology it used to change language depending on the reader and though Sergio knew nothing about how such technology worked, the Kleptofargh might believe he did, at least long enough for him to figure out what to do next.

Knowing it was likely the Kleptofargh would find him, Sergio took one other handy device with him as he escaped Earth, one that would help him when it came time to face that horrible lord again. Just thinking about being in the lord's presence was nearly enough to make him pee his pants. And the name of the device itself was so reassuring. *Depends.*

Emma

Being released so violently from her physical human body blew Emma farther than the dam collapse. Evil intent can do that—blow us much farther off course than mere accident, no matter how big that accident might be. Emma sailed into the Earth's atmosphere, her shimmer hurtling across the sky too fast and too furiously for her to wonder how she was surviving it. Before she knew it, she was scooped up by a tractor beam, and deposited unceremoniously in a holding cell on a large space ship sent to troll near Earth for another fugitive.

Yes, evil intent can impel us far off course, but it also has a way of biting itself in the ass. When Aunt Emma was brought before the lord of the Kleptofargh, and she found out his ship snared her while searching for the weasel who promised him the largest cyborg army in the galaxy, some skinny, black-eyed peon going by the name of Sergio, Emma's laughter rang through the ship.

"Oh, let me help," she beamed, when she finally pulled her shimmer back together. "I've got some unfinished business with that asshole."

Mac

After Mac saved the Secretary from the disaster of going public with an alien invasion alert, and being wrong about where the aliens were, no less, her rise at State was meteoric. It was complicated briefly by one thing—Mac and the Secretary fell in love with each other. To everyone's shock, the Secretary resigned her post so Mac's career could soar. They were married in upstate New York, where the Secretary's family farm hosted the festivities on a warm summer day, the air full of lovely heat shimmers. Two of those shimmers seemed to stand close to Mac as she said her vows.

After the ceremony, Mac told a friend that she hadn't felt that safe since she was twelve years old.

Jack and PPP3

With Paster long gone, Jones taken away, Sergio disappeared, Josef dead, Mac in DC, and Louie off on new adventures, the now ninety-four employees of PPP3 were at a loss. They kept going to work every day, driving or taking the bus to the suburban office park, battling traffic and allergies, watching the blackberry vines tangle, and sitting in one another's child-sized guest chairs to discuss their options. The first decision they made was to get the Pepsi machine back in the staff kitchen—and to install a Coke machine right next to it. The freedom represented by that first decision went to their heads. Color copies ran amok again. Mr. Sack was invited back because, truth be told, the employees loved him. The Human Resources staff, being cyborgs, were surprisingly easy to control—they only did what they were told, no more, no less. Most employees didn't know the HR staff were cyborgs, they simply gave thanks for the sudden end to the flood of new and ever more complicated policies that had marked the Jones and Sergio days.

The employees enjoyed themselves, but they were directionless. No one knew what gadget to invent next. Even the long-timers started to talk about leaving.

Jack moved into Louie's little house, cared for Thing One and Thing Two, and picked up where she left off in the renovations. The first room he finished was the spare bedroom—for himself. Louie would be able to sleep in her own room during what Jack hoped would be her frequent visits home. One day, Jack walked in to Jones' old office—no one took it over, though the best of his furniture, supplies, and equipment had been pilfered within days of his removal from the premises —"a real perp walk!" the employees said gleefully, not knowing that the jacket Jones held in front of his face wasn't there to foil paparazzi. It was to make sure no one saw the lime green goo seeping through his zipper.

That day in Jones' old office, Jack called a meeting with the Human Resources Director, the IT Director, and Alice, Jones' and Paster's assistant.

"Guys," Jack started, "we all know who, or in your case, Paul, *what* we are. Now let's see if we can do some good." The other two men looked at Jack, then at Alice.

"Oh, please, I know everything," she said. "You think I didn't listen in on all of Jones' calls?"

The IT Director nodded at Jack. Paul, the cyborg, chimed in. "You know I'll do what I'm told, Jack. My whole staff will."

"Great." Jack put a set of mechanical drawings on the large conference table—it was a nice table, and was too heavy for the PPP3 pilferers to move. "Here's my idea. What the creatures of this world need to survive, more than anything, is water. To get enough water, some places need dams. But dams, as you know, are notoriously fragile—they can burst at the slightest poof." The others knew nothing of the kind, but would rather let Jack lead than come up with their own ideas. "What you see before you," he went on, "is a bolt system for concrete dam panels that I believe—based on all the reading I've done—would be burst proof. Paul, I need your cyborg crew to run the calculations in the computer sides of their brains, to find out if I'm right. And you—what is your name?" Jack asked the IT Director.

"Just call me Bosley," he answered, a little sheepishly.

Jack grinned. "Okay, Bosley, I need you to program Paul and his cyborg team to do these calculations, and then to help program a machine I know about so it can make the bolts. It's in a sweet little factory in Eastern Europe. I know the manager personally. The people there will do the job right." *And get their raises, finally, and what the hell, new floor mats.* Jack smiled a ridiculously big smile.

Buddy

Buddy adapted well to being a three-legged, blind dog, playing it for sympathy and treats, faking helplessness to lure squirrels into coming far closer than they should before he would spring up to joyfully chase them away.

He also took Louie's transformation into a shimmer in stride. He'd never seen her anyway, and he liked how her shimmery-self tickled when it scratched him behind his floppy ears. Wherever they traveled, they took long walks and talked about everything under the sun and moon, for years and years, until Buddy's heart gave out, suddenly, so that he fell asleep one day under a pleasantly warm summer sun and did not wake up again.

Gil and Louie

Gil Munroe survived the blast from Sergio's vaporizing tool. His true nature akin to stone remained even in his human form, making him just plain hard to kill. After meeting Louie and Jack in the factory town square, he'd decided to finally prove that the governmental security agency selection officer who rejected him so long ago was wrong—he was not a coward, after all. It was a nice side benefit to also prove it to himself.

He caught up with Jack and Louie in Seattle. His intention was simply to check on them, to be sure they were both all right, before heading back to his home planet. He felt that his job on Earth was done, helping them take care of Jones and Sergio, averting the conflict that would have been the inevitable result of the successful conversion of all Earth humans into cyborgs. Done, time to call it a day. He was too young to retire, but a long rest seemed just the ticket.

When he encountered Louie in her shimmering natural form, all his plans disappeared from his mind. He remembered the charge when he met her in the town square and, though it was lovely, it was nothing compared to the pure excitement of this. *A hunk of sandstone and a shimmer—that's going to be interesting.* Louie agreed, and they fell into a dizzy kind of love.

Gil and Louie went on to have many other adventures together before the end. Because time moved so slowly for Gil, to him they shared only a fraction of it, only a moment, a blink. But on Earth, it was the equivalent of years and years, time enough for the differences between them to bring joy, sorrow, and a child.

Gil hadn't been joking when he told Jack about reading Hemingway. During his time as a journalist, Gil fell in love with storytelling, and the written word. He sent his first manuscript to Jack, dedicated, "For our daughter, so she will know her mother led quite a life before she came along."

The story began with a prologue.

"Have you brought me what I seek?" The continuous sonic boom of the alien lord's voice came from somewhere near the middle of his giant black bulk, poised on his throne in a shape that recalled a comma.

About The Author

Elizabeth Fountain lives in Ellensburg, Washington and teaches university courses in psychology and leadership. Her professional experiences as a counselor, instructor, university administrator, and failed barista contribute to her short and long fiction and creative non-fiction that finds the unintentional humor in everyday life. She loves books, movies, dogs, vegetarian food (yes, French fries are vegetarian), and aspires to live according to a line from singer/songwriter Chris Rea: *every day, good luck comes in the strangest of ways.*

Visit our website for our growing catalogue of quality books.
www.burstbooks.ca